Antiques Disposal

A Trash 'n' Treasures Mystery

Barbara Allan

KENSINGTON BOOKS

http://www.kensingtonbooks.com

KENSINGTON BOOKS are published by

Kensington Publishing Corp.
119 West 40th Street
New York, NY 10018

All Kensington titles, imprints, and distributed lines are available at special quantity discounts for bulk purchases for sales promotion, premiums, fund-raising, educational, or institutional use. Special book excerpts or customized printings can also be created to fit specific needs. For details, write or phone the office of the Kensington Special Sales Manager: Attn. Special Sales Department. Kensington Publishing Corp., 119 West 40th Street, New York, NY 10018. Phone: 1-800-221-2647.

Kensington and the K logo Reg. U.S. Pat. & TM Off.

ISBN-13: 978-0-7582-6361-2
ISBN-10: 0-7582-6361-9

First Hardcover Printing: May 2012
First Mass Market Printing: April 2013

10 9 8 7 6 5 4 3 2 1

Printed in the United States of America

for bj elsner

Brandy's quote:
*Americans are like a rich father
who wishes he knew how to give his son
the hardships that made him rich.*
—Robert Frost

Mother's quote:
None but a mule denies his family.
—Moroccan proverb

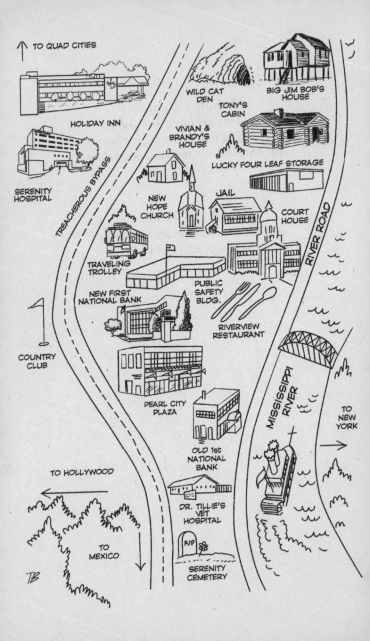

Chapter One

Mother Takes Auction!

My dearest ones! You are in luck, because I, Vivian Borne (aka Mother), am scripting this opening chapter. Normally this honor goes to my darling daughter Brandy, but due to the poor girl being down in the doldrums, I am taking necessary measures.

We simply *must* get this book off the ground to meet our publisher's deadline!

And I must thank those of you who have written in to say that you consider *me* the better writer. That, of course, is not mine to say, but I would admit—if pressed—that Brandy displays certain literary shortcomings. For one thing, she uses far too few exclamation points for emphasis! For another, she takes off on one pointless discursion after another.

And talk about malapropisms and foul paws—*Andy Griffin*, indeed! Despite the best efforts of our indefatigable editor and my humble self, we cannot seem to catch all her boo-boos and blunders. When I pointed out this embarrassing error in *Antiques Flee Market,* Brandy said, "So I confused Sheriff Taylor with a talk show host. No biggie." No biggie my patootie! That gaffe insulted both Andy Griffith *and* Merv Griffin aficionados.

(Didn't you just love it when Merv would show off the lovely lining of his sport coat? But I digress.)

Of late Brandy had taken to her bed, heartbroken over the departure of the (most recent) love of her life, Chief of Police Tony Cassato, whose current location remains (as of this writing) unknown.

My contact at the PD, Mona the Mole (my code name for the female dispatcher, whose name isn't Mona, though she *does* have a mole) has hinted that Anthony C. may have disappeared into the Witness Protection Program. Prior to moving to Serenity, the chief had given testimony against the New Jersey mob, resulting in a recent attempt upon his life.

But our M.I.A. chief is not *all* that is bothering Brandy. I believe some of her trouble is postpartum depression; even though she was a surrogate mother, her body doesn't know that. (And I certainly couldn't be the cause of any melancholia!) And so, dear reader, I do hope you will cut her some slack if she seems a trifle short-tempered.

In our previous nonfiction accounts, Brandy has taken great care to bring you, our fan base, up to date with each subsequent missive, and this has become quite the tedious chore, for author and reader alike. Besides, recapping an ever-growing plot might discourage new readers by bogging them down in data not needed to understand the new narrative, even while burdening them with "spoilers" that might damage their enjoyment of earlier episodes.

After all, who really cares how we got from A to F? Anyone can jump on board the F train without first having taken the A train (a little jest for the over-sixty crowd). I have faith that our readers can absorb and retain past and present information provided along the way—they *are* mystery aficionados, after all!

As I have told Brandy time and again, these narratives would be well served by getting right into the story. Enough of this shilly-shallying! Of course, some small background is, I suppose, necessary. . . .

Sixteen months have passed since Brandy (divorced; age thirtyish) came home to live with me (widowed; age available on a need-to-know-basis) (you don't need to) with scant more than the designer clothes on her back and her little shih tzu, Sushi (blind; age sevenish).

Since then, an abundance of murder and mayhem has delivered itself upon the small Mississippi River town we call Serenity, which has resulted in much sorrow, misery, and tragedy. It's been simply exhilarating!

This particular autumn morning, however, was rainy and dreary, and I knew such gloomy weather would only encourage Brandy to remain under the covers unless I sprang into action (with as much spring as two hip replacements will allow, at any rate). Wearing my favorite pantsuit (emerald-green velour), I sailed into her bedroom.

"Rise and shine!" I said, clapping my hands,

marching around the bed in full parade mode, wishing I had cymbals or perhaps a bass drum. "We have places to go, things to do, and people to see!"

Brandy, a tangle of blond hair protruding from beneath the leopard-print coverlet, muttered something. I couldn't be positive of what she said precisely, though it just *might* have been unkind. Since my ears were suffering a terrible wax build-up presently, I gave her the benefit of the doubt.

When Brandy failed to stir further, I grasped the edge of the cover and yanked it back, unveiling a snoozing Sushi, who lazily lifted her little head and aimed her white-clouded *Exorcist* orbs my way.

And growled.

"*You*," I scolded, "are aiding and abetting," waggling a finger at the small brown and white fur ball.

Sushi pouted, but at least she didn't relower her head.

To Brandy, I announced, "Dear, are you aware that we have not sold a single item in our booth at the antiques mall this month?"

She said nothing.

"I will take that as a 'no,' " I said. "Well, dear, we need to find more merchandise . . . otherwise, I don't know *why* we bother renting space."

She said nothing.

I said, "You know I rely on the extra money the booth brings, and now with your *sister* living with us, well, I'm starting to feel the pinch."

And I was. A financial pinch nearly as painful as my too-tight girdle. (No SPANX for me—I'm an old-fashioned lass, like my stomach.)

As our longtime readers know, Peggy Sue (attention, you readers taking the F train!) is my older daughter, now in her very attractive early fifties, recently widowed and forced to move in with us, after discovering that her husband had bequeathed her a mountain of unexpected debt.

With a deep sigh, I delivered the clincher: "But I suppose we could take in a *boarder,* just to make ends meet. Naturally, of course, that will necessitate your sharing the *bathroom*—"

"I'm *up!* I'm up. . . ."

"Very good, dear . . . breakfast in half an hour. Plenty of time for a nice, long hot shower." At the door, I glanced back. "And slap on a little lipstick—you'll feel better!"

I'd seen that little homily on a placard in a gift shop, and its truth reverberates within me still. Why, I wouldn't *consider* going anywhere without first putting on Estée Lauder's lipstick ("Pink Passion"). Did you know that Estée built her whole cosmetic empire on a single shade of red? Just goes to show what a smart gal can accomplish! With a tube of lipstick, that is.

Down in the kitchen, I began to prepare our breakfast—cinnamon coffee cake, crisp bacon, scrambled eggs. This may sound fattening, but I had an eventful morning planned, and neither Brandy nor I could afford to run out of gas. (NOTE TO EDITOR: Perhaps you would prefer "steam"—"gas" in reference to a meal has an unfortunate resonance.)

Anyway, Brandy had become too thin as of late. As a Dane myself, I feel she should *look* like a Dane—a Danish strudel, that is!

With coffee cake baking in the oven, and bacon sizzling on the stove, I whisked together eggs, cream, and butter. Now, Nero Wolfe may insist that scrambled eggs are only worth eating if cooked slowly for forty-five minutes, but Vivian Borne didn't have that much time on her hands. Besides, I'm surprised that stout know-it-all could wait forty-five minutes for *any* meal. . . .

Sushi, drawn by the aroma of bacon, slumber forgotten, was dancing at my feet.

"Oh, *now* you're friendly?" I chided. Forgiving the little doggie her earlier bad manners, I snapped off the end of a cooled bacon strip and handed it down to her. She might have been blind, but she had no trouble "seeing" food.

Outside, the dark sky growled, as if it, too, were a hungry dog, albeit a trifle bigger than Sushi. (NOTE TO BRANDY: Darling, notice the mood and wit provided by the occasional writerly metaphor.) (Or is that simile?)

While waiting for Brandy to appear—and to hasten our departure—I fed Sushi, making sure she had plenty of water (diabetic dogs drink a lot), then gave her a shot of the insulin needed to counteract her disease.

Finally Brandy materialized and sat herself down in the dining room at the Duncan Phyfe table that had been in my family since I'd been in diapers (and I don't mean Depends). Cheerful as Christmas, I served up our sumptuous breakfast on Royal Victoria china plates I'd snagged at a garage sale. (I'd gone extra early and had to rouse the residents out of bed; but I forgave them, first-time sellers who needed to learn that an 8 A.M. listing means 7 A.M. (Or 6 A.M., in my case.)

Brandy, freshly showered, her shoulder-length blonde hair sleek and squeaky-clean, was wearing a forest-green cardigan over a crisp white blouse, and tan slacks. (I couldn't see what was on her feet, as they were under the table, but most likely some designer shoes bought at a fraction of the retail price—that girl has a nose for a bargain . . . also, longer arms than the next gal.)

Brandy has such a lovely, heart-shaped face—big brown eyes, small nose, high cheekbones, wide mouth—typical features courtesy of my Danish side of the family. But I suspect her nature must harken back to the Vikings—impetuous, headstrong, obstinate, and sometimes reckless. She certainly didn't get those characteristics from *moi*.

In addition, Brandy can often be defiant, as evidenced by the red lipstick she had clown-smeared on her mouth.

"You look so much better, dear . . . almost human," I commented, ignoring her crimson lips.

"Thanks . . . almost."

I cocked my head. "Have you had your Prozac this morning?"

Oddly, Brandy had felt the need for the depression-easing pills ever since coming back to live with me.

"Yes, Mother—have you had your Prolixin?"

"Why, of course, dear."

Unlike Brandy, I didn't really need *my* medication, but I took the bipolar drug, just to keep the peace.

Once upon a time, in the early seventies, I admit I *might* have been better off taking Prolixin . . . such as when I mailed all our doorknobs to then-president Nixon. In my defense, Tricky Dick had expressed a fondness for Victorian hardware, and I was merely trying to support our leader in troubled times.

Then, after the Watergate fiasco, when I found out what a stinker Nixon had been, I wrote and asked for the doorknobs back; but the FBI insisted they'd never gotten to the president. So I asked, *Where were they?* And they said—

Oh, well, I suppose what they said isn't terribly pertinent to the tale at hand, which could go on for quite some time, and as I've told Brandy again and again, we need to get *right into* the narrative.

(Something wonderful, though, *did* come about from all of that tit-for-tat with the federal boys—they created an FBI file on me. Can *you* say as much?)

(I'll save the story about sending roller skates to Neil Armstrong for another time.) (I thought it might add zest to his next moon walk.)

I told Brandy, "You'll be glad to know that I have already fed Sushi and given the little darling her insulin."

Her eyes flared. "The correct *dosage,* I hope!"

"Yes, yes. I checked it twice."

Would the child *ever* let me live down the time the little doggie had that teensy-weensy seizure because I hadn't been wearing my glasses?

"So," I said cheerfully, "we are *all* of us, women and canine, well and truly medicated . . . and ready for the new day."

Brandy looked pointedly at the empty chair opposite. "I notice you didn't blow your bugle and get Peggy Sue up."

"No, dear. She's utterly depressed . . . whereas you're only mildly in the dumps. Besides, I don't need her this morning." I gave her the Uncle Sam pointing finger. "I need *you.*"

"That sounds ominous. . . ."

"Not at all, dear. We're just going off to—"

"See the wizard?" Brandy raised a palm like a traffic cop. "Please. I don't want to hear your plans for me—not on an empty stomach."

"Perhaps that's wise."

She took a big bite of scrambled eggs, chewed, then muttered, "*These* sure weren't cooked for forty-five minutes."

The child was clearly testing my patience.

And I was just about to launch into a lecture about feeling sorry for oneself—using the story about the man with no shoes who met a man with no feet (or was it a man with no gloves who met a man with no fingers?)—when I noticed (despite the smeary lipstick) Brandy's tiny upturned smile.

This signaled the end of her funk.

Brandy stabbed a hunk of coffee cake with her fork. "Okay—I'm ready for action. What's our mission? Where do we attack?"

"An auction, dear, at a storage facility. We'll be bidding for the contents of units in arrears of rental payment."

Brandy put down her fork and gave me a long unblinking stare, waiting for me to explain myself further.

So I said nothing. I know well, from my years of

the theater, of the power of silence. That less is more. That running things into the ground gets you nowhere. At all.

Finally, Brandy said, "I don't want to go."

"Why ever not, dear?"

"Because that's *despicable*—taking advantage of people who couldn't pay their rent! The last thing people like us should be doing, with the kind of financial hassles *we've* had—that Peggy Sue has right *now*—is going out preying upon . . ."

But she ran out of steam. Or maybe gas.

So I said, "*I* don't think it's at *all* despicable, dear. Why, we'll be giving someone's possessions a new lease on life! Possessions that would otherwise languish forgotten, left to rot and mold and face the fate of an evitable landfill. Think of Planet Earth! Besides, who's to say these folks couldn't pay the rent? Maybe they *wished* to abandon the contents."

"Why would they?"

I shrugged. "Some people simply don't want the items anymore, or they can't bring themselves to throw them away. Or perhaps moving to another locale, the expense of a rental truck or trailer is beyond their means. In any case, we are doing them a favor."

"A favor? I don't think so. This doesn't feel . . . right."

Wherever did the child suddenly get such a conscience? Not from me. And certainly not the Vikings.

"My darling girl," I said, "most of the contents of these units are junk."

"Then—why bid on one?"

"*Because*," I said patiently, as if talking to a small child, "sometimes in all that trash? There's treasure to be found!"

A pause, and then a clap of thunder punctuated my point. If I'd known that thunderclap was coming, I might have added a nice Long John Silver "*Matey!*"

Brandy, looking at the rain beating against the window panes, whined, "But it's *lousy* outside."

"All the better! You know what they say—inclement weather today keeps bidders away!"

"Yeah, the smart ones."

Tiring of the child's negative attitude, I pushed back from the table. "You know, you need to consider, as you grow older, that those frown lines will become permanent."

She grinned broadly with her clowny lipstick emphasizing her sarcasm. "Better?"

"Ugggh! You look like Cesar Romero playing the Joker."

"I was going for Heath Ledger," Brandy sighed, then used her napkin to wipe the crimson color off her lips. "Okay. You win . . . like *that's* a surprise. Let's go hunt for treasure in the trash."

Thunder cracked again. *Matey.*

"Now there's a good girl!" I enthused, standing, pushing farther away from the table. I ticked off on my fingers: "We'll need raincoats, umbrellas, and Wellies."

"And a rowboat."

But she was smiling. Looking not at all like Cesar Romero.

*   *   *

Okay, Brandy taking over.

In previous books I usually have allowed Mother to write only one chapter, appearing around halfway through, when it's a little late for readers to bail. So I apologize for subjecting you to her so early. On the other hand, some people get a kick out of her. Trust me—it's more fun to read about than to live through.

Also, I do apologize for confusing Andy Griffin and Merv Griffith. Mother is right to give me a hard time on that account. But she was herself incorrect about Estée Lauder—the woman built her empire on *face cream,* before expanding into cosmetics.

So there.

Anyway, I still wasn't convinced that what we were about to do—bid on past-due storage units—was morally right, or at least that we weren't at real risk of earning some seriously bad karma.

Don't get me wrong, I'm no Miss Goody Two-Shoes—I was, after all, responsible for the bust-up of my marriage, losing custody of my twelve-year-old son, Jake, to my ex, Roger. Readers looking for perfection in their protagonists may have noticed, in Mother's preceding section, that they are in the wrong place.

But confiscating other people's possessions—legal or not—gave me a skin-crawly feeling. I wouldn't want a stranger pawing through my stuff, would you? (That is, *you* wouldn't want a stranger pawing through *your* stuff.)

And I couldn't very well ask Mother to go alone, because she can't drive. I don't mean she doesn't know *how* to drive, rather that she lost her license—and I don't mean misplaced it. Due to various vehicular infractions—little things, like carving through a cornfield and hitting a cow, by way of inventing a shortcut to make community-theater curtain time (Mother, not the cow), or running over a mailbox and scattering letters like oversized snowflakes.

That Mother wouldn't be allowed behind the wheel for another three years was good news for Serenity. But it meant bad news for her chauffeur. Me.

After gathering our rain gear, Mother and I headed out to my gently dented burgundy Buick. For once Sushi hadn't begged to go with us, having headed upstairs to get back under the covers to sleep off breakfast. Smart doggie.

"Where to?" I asked, raising my voice above the rat-a-tat-tat of the rain on the car roof.

"Take the River Road north about three miles. To Lucky Four Leaf Clover Storage."

I grunted. Not so lucky for certain renters today.

Traffic was light along the twisting, hilly two-lane highway, which really was lucky, because visibility was poor thanks to pounding rain (and worn-out windshield wipers). With the mighty Mississippi to our right, and limestone bluffs to our left, I had to concentrate on keeping the hydro-planing car on the road.

Mother, for a change, kept her chatter to a minimum, talking only now and then about the storage facility owner, one Big Jim Bob, who—according to the all-knowing, all-seeing Mother—

was raised in Serenity, moved away some years later, then came back to take up the storage unit business.

Amid the intermittent chatter, Mother was saying, "Big Jim Bob gave me a tip on one of the units up for auction."

"Why would he do that?"

And anyway, why would I believe a tip from anyone named Big Jim Bob? (Maybe Jim Bob, or Big Jim or even Big Bob . . . but *not* Big Jim Bob. That was one good-ole-boy name too many.)

"We're *old* friends," Mother said.

I had come to know that when Mother emphasized the word *old* in this fashion, it meant she and the man in question had once enjoyed an amorous relationship. Jonathan Borne had passed away nearly thirty years ago, shortly after I came along. And Mother, being a statuesque, attractive woman, was not content to become a wallflower. But she *was* content to remain a widow, and keep her independence.

Navigating a sharp curve, I asked, "So what's the tip?"

As if intoning the location of a pirate's map, she said, "I am informed that I should try to win the bid on unit number seven."

"So, then—your old friend's been inside and knows what's in it. That *can't* be legal."

"No, dear. Only the renter has a key to the padlock. But Big Jim Bob has reason to believe the unit may contain some nice antiques."

"Why?"

"Because Big Jim Bob talked to the woman when she took out the unit, and she mentioned her collecting had gotten to the point of overflow. She even asked if the unit was climate controlled."

"Well, that says antiques, all right—"

"Oh, I do hope we get it!"

Throwing a little water on Mother's fire, I asked, "What's to prevent Big Jim Bob from breaking the lock on the unit, helping himself to the good stuff, then putting on a *new* lock?"

Out of the corner of my eye I could see Mother frown. "Only the ruination of his reputation, and a charge of theft if caught," she responded, adding quickly, "but I *know* Big Jim Bob, and I assure you he's a gentleman."

Know was further code for . . . you know.

More water needed.

I risked a glance. "You mean, he *was* a gentleman, back when you 'knew' him. But where has he been since? And why did he come back?"

Mother gazed at me, eyes narrowed to near normal size behind her large buggy lenses. "You seem awfully suspicious today, dear . . ."

"Well, I—"

Then, to my surprise she chirped, "And I most *heartily* approve!"

A word about Mother and me, on the subject of renting a storage unit of our own. Four words, actually: *over my dead body!*

Currently, our (mostly Mother's) overflow flea-market/yard-sale finds were stored in a stand-alone garage next to our three-story, 1920s-style house. And I have made it clear to Mother that, should the overflow keep flowing over, under no circumstances would I *ever* consider renting a storage unit. Because I knew what the inevitable would be: she'd die peacefully in her sleep, smiling like an angel, and leave *me* with all that garbage!

Okay, so maybe Mother was right on one point: some folks *do* abandon their units because they don't want the stuff. Or, anyway, want to deal with it.

"Pull in here, dear," Mother said, pointing to a sign shaped like a shamrock, the words LUCKY FOUR LEAF CLOVER spaced cutely out on the four leafs. But what exactly was "lucky" or "cute" about having your possessions overwhelm you so much that you had to rent a sort of garage away from home to house the junk?

I drove into a gravel lot, dodging water-filled potholes, then pulled up to the white, boxy low-slung facility, home to several dozen units, each garage door shut and padlocked.

We exited the car—Mother holding a red umbrella with enormous wingspan, and me sporting a 1970s vintage clear plastic number shaped like a bell, that covered me down to my waist—and joined the handful of bidders that had braved the weather, huddling under their umbrellas.

I couldn't see too clearly through my plastic bell (maybe that's why this type of umbrella went out of style), but I did recognize a lanky guy as a fellow dealer at the antiques mall, although I couldn't recall his name.

Next to him were a man and woman, sharing an orange umbrella, both middle-aged and maybe a little too fond of food. He had eyebrows in need of a trim, and she wore an ill-fitting short brown wig.

The other bidder was a muscular young man in a black Harley T-shirt, his arms exposed, possibly to show off his biceps and formidable forearms.

Too manly to carry an umbrella, he just stood there letting his dark hair get matted by the rain.

Mother's mouth was moving, and when I didn't respond due to my Maxwell Smart "cone of silence," she kicked me. Kicked me!

"Owwww!" I said, rubbing my shin with my other, uninjured leg. "Whatcha do *that* for?"

She ducked down, stuck her head under the umbrella, and her eyes gleamed up at me, like those of a coyote who smelled blood.

"Get rid of that thing," she snarled. "I need you *sharp*—front and center!"

She did her Sgt. Bilko troop-summoning *hey-harr-uppp*.

Mother withdrew, and I came out from under the umbrella, snapped it closed, then saluted.

A shiny red pickup truck rolled up to where the six of us were gathered, then the truck's cab door opened, and a blue-jeaned leg with a brown pointy-toed cowboy boot swung out and down to the ground.

"There's Big Jim Bob himself!" Mother burbled, suddenly a giddy schoolgirl.

How I hated it when she ran into an "old" somebody she had "known."

While the man *was* big—over six feet, two hundred plus pounds—he was not the potbelly redneck his name had promised. He had thinning gray hair, tired eyes, bulbous nose, and a mouth that had become a mere slit between sagging jowls. He'd been handsome once. Once.

Still, when Big Jim Bob spotted Mother, the eyes suddenly twinkled, and his broad smile gave him an instant face-lift.

Beneath the umbrella of hers that we now shared, I leaned closer to Mother and whispered, "There'll be none of that."

"None of what, dear?"

"Making goo-goo eyes."

"I'm not making goo-goo eyes."

"I know goo-goo eyes when I see them, and you're making them, so stop."

"If you say so, dear."

Big Jim Bob was retrieving a wide-brimmed black cowboy hat and tan oil-cloth coat from his truck, which he put on. Then he greeted the group with a "Howdy, folks." Whether his drawl was an affectation or the result of living down south, I couldn't tell ya'll.

"Nice to see you, BJB," Mother gushed.

BJB. Gag me with an antique spoon.

"Nice to be seen, Vivian," he said to her. "Every day 'bove ground is a *good* day." Then to the small assemblage: "And thank ya'll for coming out in such fine weather for ducks."

Everybody managed a damp laugh.

Then he made a "gather around" gesture, and we crowded in, knocking umbrellas, bumper cars at the carnival.

" 'fore we get to the auction," he began, "ah'd like t'make a few announcements. Firstly, there's only one unit up for bids. Number seven. T'other one's rent got paid, last minute. As some of ya'll know, ah try hard t'contact past due renters 'fore goin' t'auction . . . and any money ah make goes toward their past due rent. Ah'm not here t'take advantage." He paused, then added, "That said, we'll proceed."

Big Jim Bob stepped back to his truck, and from the cab produced a wicked-looking steel cutter, which he used on the padlock of unit seven, only a few yards from where we stood.

As he rolled up the garage door, everyone moved closer, craning their necks to get a look into this magical cave of pirate treasure . . .

. . . but Big Jim Bob obstructed the view with his large frame.

"For you first-timers," he said, "here's the rules— each one of ya'll can come forward t'get a real good peek. But that's all. There's no goin' in. You have a minute to get your eyeful."

Since that didn't make sense to me, I asked, "How are we supposed to know what we're bidding on?"

Big Jim Bob turned his weary eyes toward me. "Well, that's the point, little lady. Ya don't. When everythin's boxed up—like in this here unit— you're takin' a chance. Kinda like a big ol' grab bag. Your proverbial pig-in-a-poke."

I never had any luck with grab bags, as a kid— best I ever did was wax lips twice and a paddleball once.

Mother, moving from beneath our umbrella, muscled her way to the front of the bidders.

"*Ladies first!*" she announced.

The ill-bewigged woman blurted, "Well, uh, *I'm* a lady. . . ."

"Ladies of a *certain age*," Mother said, already with her toes at the very edge of the threshold.

Nobody tried to stop her.

I was impressed—this had to be serious, if Mother was playing the age card.

Armed with a flashlight from home, she leaned in as far as she could, and started weaving back and forth, occasionally issuing a loud cough, from her toes up—she might have been drunk, or maybe sick. . . .

To me, her antics seemed predictable if pointless, unless she had suddenly acquired X-ray vision, and I was pretty sure she'd have mentioned that over breakfast.

Finally, after the longest minute in recorded history, Mother resumed her decorum, straightened, stepped back, then turned to her audience with a disappointed sigh that would have registered on the back row of the local Playhouse.

"Well!" she said, "*whoever* wins *this* bid will have quite the *mouse* infestation to clean up."

The small group of bidders surged forward, and Mother proved her point by directing her flashlight beam toward the evidence.

But I stayed put.

Having grown up in an old house, I didn't need to get any closer—I knew mouse droppings when I saw them. And there were plenty, resting on the tops of the boxes, littering the exposed concrete floor.

The woman in the ill-fitting brown wig said, "Oh, my! The damage *they* can do."

At her side, her bushy-browed mate shrugged. "I've seen worse. . . ."

Mother offered, "Might not be mice at that."

All eyes were on her, mine included.

"Could be rats."

Brown Wig snapped, "You're not bringing *those* filthy boxes into *my* clean house!"

The woman turned abruptly, taking their umbrella with her. Bushy Eyebrows dutifully followed.

Two down, two to go.

Not waiting for the starting gun (or auction gavel?), the lanky dealer from the antiques mall said, "I'll go fifty dollars."

The muscleman in the Harley T-shirt muttered, "Not worth it." And he, too, departed (but in a car, not on a Harley).

Three down, one to go.

Mother straightened herself, dug her Wellies in, and announced, "I'll bid *one hundred*—I am not going home empty-handed. I spent hours making room in the garage!"

"You did?" I asked, surprised.

Mother shot me her "*Will you just play along!*" look.

She could lie with such conviction that even *I* believed her, and after all these years. She kind of was a good actress.

Lanky scowled at Mother. "Oh, all right, it's all yours, mouse turds and all . . ."

"Most gracious," Mother said with a nod.

". . . but you'll let me know if there's anything good?"

"Of course," Mother said with her sweetest smile. Then she added, to soothe the burn, "But you *know* it's almost *certainly* just junk."

The lanky dealer grunted and strode off to his car.

(Can anyone tell me *why* antiques hunters want to be told when they miss out on something? I wouldn't want to know if I got beaten to a pair of half-off Louboutins.)

Big Jim Bob, who had stood by silently during the impromptu bidding, commented, "Hope ah was right about this here unit, Vivian . . . and that y'do find somethin' worthwhile. And ah apologize about the mice—never had nothin' like that here b'fore."

Mother waved a hand. "No apology necessary— I'm quite used to mouse doo-doo. Those little rascals can get in just about anywhere."

Including her sock drawer. One lived snuggled in a nest of support hose for months before Mother noticed it. (I couldn't kill the thing—too cute. Anyway, it wasn't *my* sock drawer.)

Big Jim Bob was saying, "Now, ladies, y'understand, ya have t'have the stuff outta there in twenty-four."

I blinked. "Days?"

"Hours."

"Could be a problem—we don't have a truck."

Mother said, "Not to worry, dear—we can make multiple trips."

Meaning *I* could make multiple trips.

Big Jim Bob was removing a new padlock with two keys from its plastic packaging, handing us one. "This here's t'secure the unit, and when ya'll're done, lock 'er up and toss the key. I'll keep this here second key to get back in, after. The new renter'll have a brand-new lock."

Mother touched his arm. "Thank you for calling me about the unit, BJB. I'm quite sure we'll make back our hundred dollars."

"Sure hope so, Vivian. That rain's a slice of luck for you gals. These units can go way higher. I don't usually go to all this trouble for just a hundred smackers."

She batted her eyelashes. "If you're ever in our neighborhood . . . why don't you stop by and see me sometime?"

I squirmed in my skin, but at least she hadn't said it in her Mae West voice.

He smiled a little. "Thank ya, Viv, just might take ya up on that. Well, gotta skedaddle—have t'call a fella about rentin' this here unit, when ya'll're done with it."

Big Jim Bob strode to his truck, then drove away.

We turned our attention to the unit, stepping inside as far as we could. Rain drummed hollowly, but the space was anything but hollow, filled with all sorts of "surprise package" boxes. We had a lot of work to do. . . .

I said, "We could probably get five or six boxes in the car at a time, and with a trip every hour, should be done in about—*Mother!* What are you *doing?*"

She was idly picking up a mouse dropping from the top of a box. She gave the tiny brown ball a smiling look . . . then proceeded to pop it into her mouth!

"What's the matter, dear?" she said, still smiling. "Haven't you ever seen anyone eat a chocolate cake sprinkle?"

"Mother, you *didn't!*"

"Oh, but I did, dear—indeedie diddie do."

And she reached into her coat pocket and withdrew a handful of the tiny mouse-turd-shaped candy.

No wonder she wanted to be the first bidder to view the unit . . . so she could toss the "droppings" around. What a cheat! What a crook! Still, you had to admire her ingenuity.

But I couldn't let her off scot-free. "Don't you think that was a little underhanded?"

Mother's eyebrows rose above her thick round glasses. "They were *all* underhanded tosses, dear, or else I might have been spotted. Anyway, all's fair in love and war, and bidding on storage units. Now chop chop! We've got work to do."

Meaning me, the worker bee, under the supervision of her, the queen.

I hefted a box from the nearest pile, carried it to the car, letting the rain mingle with the sweat already forming on my brow. Then, after loading the box, I backed the Buick up to the unit to make my work easier.

That's when I noticed a white utility van parked on the shoulder of the highway near the mouth of the storage facility's driveway. The van—free of any markings—was too far away for me to make out the driver.

Suddenly, its engine roared to life, and the van pulled onto the highway, then sped away.

Had the driver merely stopped for some innocuous reason, like to make a cell phone call? Or had he been watching us? If so, *why?*

Mother was right; I *had* become suspicious.

As we drove home with the first load of boxes, the rain letting up, I kept watching for the van in my rearview mirror, driving with one hand, popping chocolate sprinkles in my mouth with the other.

A Trash 'n' Treasures Tip

Wear old clothes when clearing out a storage unit; the contents can be dusty and dirty. Also, don't assume any little black specks are chocolate sprinkles—pop one into your mouth at your own risk.

Chapter Two

Going, Going . . . Gone

Noon was approaching when I pulled my burgundy Buick, loaded with storage boxes (and Mother), into our drive and up to the unattached garage, its old wooden door shut tight to hide the clutter inside. I felt sure someday it would simply burst, spewing garage-sale shrapnel.

With a curt captainlike "To the music room, dear," Mother hopped out, scurrying ahead to make way for the boxes of treasure that would surely bring wealth and happiness and change our lives forever. No, that was not sarcasm—I was truly caught up in the chase, ever the optimist on my Prozac.

I hefted a heavy box from the backseat and gave it a good, hard shake, hoping for the jingling of coins, but hearing only the tinkling of breaking china.

Oops.

I set that box aside—best leave the bad news for

last, *after* we had discovered an unknown Picasso—and selected another heavy one, which I definitely didn't shake. Then up the walk I trudged to our white two-story house with its old-fashioned wraparound porch, rebuilt not long ago from the original Depression-era plans after the original structure blew up (another story) (*Antiques Roadkill*). I found Mother waiting in the doorway, one arm holding the screen door open.

"Hurry up, dear," she said impatiently, eyes dancing crazily (more crazily than usual, anyway) behind her magnifying lenses.

"I am, I am," I grumbled. "You want me to be careful, don't you? I'm taking the heaviest ones to give you a break."

That word *break* summoned the image of broken china to my mind, but at least I was setting the stage for my later defense.

Passing through, I nearly stepped on Sushi, hopping underfoot, sensing the excitement.

The little fur ball trailed me into the music room, and when I placed the box *gently* down on the Persian rug, Sushi began barking at it, apparently not liking the box's foreign scent.

"Stop that!" I commanded.

The doggie did, retreating a few feet to sit, lower lip extended in a pout. I ignored this display of emotion, feeling quite smug knowing that at least one creature was beneath me on the Borne family food chain.

Mother popped her head in like a demented Jack-in-the-box. "Well, don't just *stand* there like a ninny . . . more boxes! *Mach schnell! Mach schnell!*"

She'd been watching *Hogan's Heroes* reruns again. She had a thing for Richard Dawson.

"I'm on it, *Mein Führer!* I'm on it!"

I could *not* wait for this day to end.

About our house: while Mother had insisted on rebuilding according to the old blueprints, to preserve the uniform look of the neighborhood's architecture, she *had* allowed a few tweaks at my suggestion. We had extended the porch, enlarged the kitchen, and—thanks to a tidy insurance check for exploded-to-smithereens contents—embarked on a unique refurnishing plan. The idea was for each room to reflect a different period, which made our ongoing collecting much more fun.

The living room contained Victorian pieces, including a Queen Anne needlepoint couch with matching chairs and a Victorian tea table with an old silver set (which of course I got stuck polishing), plus floor lamps with tasseled shades.

French doors led to the music room with its oaken missionary furniture, and Arts and Craft lamps; floor-to-ceiling shelves showcased Mother's recent obsession with old musical instruments—although none of us were remotely talented in that department, with the limited exception of my ability to knock out a mean "Chopsticks" on the old upright piano. As for Mother, notwithstanding claims of having once played with the Serenity Junior High band, her contributions appeared limited to going "Blat-blat" on an ancient horn.

The dining room's decor was Mediterranean (yes, there *are* a few such pieces worth collecting), while the kitchen was strictly 1950s, Mother insisting on using only authentic-era appliances. As funkily aesthetic as this approach might be, it did have its hazards—like when I tried to make a malt on the vintage malted-milk machine and got shocked silly. *(Bonus Trash 'n' Treasures Tip: Watch those frayed cords!)*

We'll go over the upstairs and its furnishings later, when I/we check in on Peggy Sue.

After four more trips to the car, with all of the boxes delivered to the music room, Mother arranged herself Indian-style on the Persian rug, a pen and paper at the ready.

"Now," she bossed, "you record each item as I—"

"No," I rebelled. "*You* record each item all by your lonesome as *I* go make lunch."

"How can you eat at a time like this?" Mother bellowed, hands on hips. "Anyway, this is a two-man job!"

I raised a finger skyward—*forefinger* . . . get your mind out of the gutter. "Mother, we *are* after all *women*, not men, and I can think of no job that two men can do that Vivian Borne couldn't manage single-handed."

Her eyes narrowed in consideration of that twaddle before she said, "You're absolutely right, my dear. Considering how you've been simply wasting away of late, lunch is a capital idea!"

In the kitchen, I set out an array of vintage 1950s items—green Fire King mixing bowl, red hand-turn can opener, and yellow strainer. To paraphrase Norma Desmond, *They had colors then.* From the cupboard I removed a large can of white albacore tuna—*not* 1950s vintage, one would hope— and proceeded to make sandwiches, one for me and another for Peggy Sue, which—along with slices of locally grown cantaloupe, and glasses of unsweetened ice tea—I placed on a tray. And yes, that tray was fifties vintage—a Sundblom Coca-Cola girl.

Sushi, having followed me into the kitchen (food easily trumping strange boxes), trailed me upstairs, making it time for your tour of our second floor.

My bedroom was streamlined Art Deco, Mother's room ornately Art Nouveau, while the guest room—where Peggy Sue had encamped—featured Early American. The latter is my least favorite period (Mother agrees), but we'd been running low on styles for our room-by-room plan. Mother had suggested the swinging sixties or possibly psychedelic seventies, but they both seemed to me a little too close for comfort.

Tray balanced in one palm (eat your hearts out, French waiters), I knocked on Sis's door, but didn't wait for an answer.

Peggy Sue was curled in a fetal position on the Jenny Lind bed, wearing a pink bathrobe (Peggy Sue, not the bed), her feet bare, dark shoulder-length hair stringy and lacking its normal luster, face puffy, devoid of her usual, dare-I-say trademark meticulous make-up.

The Jenny Lind seemed fitting, however, in that its history began as a sick bed for children. . . .

And Sis looked something like a child herself, or at least a young girl, a fairly good trick for a woman in her early fifties, yet somehow not a positive thing. Not in this case.

"Peggy Sue? You awake? Getting kind of late."

Her eyes fluttered open, as expressionless as a doll's glass orbs, albeit red from crying.

"I've brought you some lunch, honey."

A deep sigh. The eyes closed again. Again, the way a doll's eyelids close when you tip it just so.

I set the tray on a night table with spindly legs (table, not me) (sorry, I'll try to be more clear), then sat on the bed and stroked her arm.

"I have tuna salad sandwiches," I said, "made just the way you like 'em—with dill, celery, and hardly any mayonnaise. And fresh fruit on the side."

No response.

A decade ago, during my one-year stint at Serenity Community College, I took a course in creative writing (doesn't show, does it?) (don't answer that) instructed by a wonderful teacher, Keith Larson (not his fault). He said a good writer *shows*, not *tells*, the reader.

(He also said a good writer doesn't overuse parentheses.)

But I just don't have the time or maybe not the talent to show you what Peggy Sue is like, so I'll have to tell you. Besides, I don't think Peg would cooperate in the show department, not in her particular state of mind . . . so, forgive me, Mr. Larson.

In addition to being eighteen years older than me—not helpful in sibling bonding—we were polar opposites in every respect, from politics to religion, social standing to clothing styles, and all points in-between. With our age difference, having a prickly relationship over the years was understandable . . .

. . . made even *more* understandable when I recently learned Peggy Sue was my biological mother, Mother (as in Vivian Borne) having raised me as her own.

Still perched on the bed, working at being cheery, I said, "Well, I'm not going to wait for you . . . *I'm* starving!"

And I reached for one of the sandwiches, and began to eat noisily, making smacking, yummy sounds. I tore off a piece for Sushi, holding it over her head just out of reach, so she would jump repeatedly toward the smell, barking all the while.

"Oh, all right," Peggy Sue moaned, not smiling at this circus act but at least capitulating, "if you're going to make all that racket and get crumbs on the bed. . . ."

"Good," I said with a smile. "Come sit by the window."

I gave Soosh the treat for her performance, picked up the tray, and moved it to the old wooden storage trunk that doubled as a coffee table.

When Sis finally dragged herself out of bed, I was shocked by the weight she had lost—not that Peggy Sue had ever been heavy; but she had been zaftig, or "curvy," as the fashion magazines politely put it now that "pleasantly plump" has gone un-PC.

Sis tightened her pink robe, then put on pink slippers like a kid reluctantly tugging on overshoes for a snowy trudge to school; finally she shuffled over to a rocker.

I sat opposite her on a rickety yard-sale-purchase chair that threatened to collapse at any moment, and handed her a plate.

She took a bite of tuna, then chewed unenthusi-astically, eyes as lidded as a bored housewife's.

I said, "You know, meaning this as strictly con-structive criticism . . ."

Her eyes found my face.

". . . you could stand a new hairstyle."

She stopped chewing. "What's wrong with the one I have?"

"You mean, when it's washed? It makes you look old. Old*er*."

I was picking a tiny fight. Just enough to get her to come back to life.

And the dull eyes flashed. "It does not! It's still quite modern. Lots of women my age have shoulder-length hair. *You* for example."

"We aren't exactly the same age. If we were, that would be some trick. Anyway, *mine* doesn't empha-size sagging jowls."

Her checks flushed. "*I* have sagging jowls?"

"Let's just say you have jowls."

As Mr. Larson would have said, the "sagging" was understood.

Peggy Sue put her plate down on the trunk with a clunk, rose from the rocker, crossed to a vanity mirror, and leaned in at her reflection.

"I do *not* have jowls—sagging or otherwise." She whirled. "And if you want to talk about *appear-ances*—how about *your* hair? I don't think you could get a comb through it if you tried. Maybe if you used a *rake*. It's *always* a mess . . ."

True. And a rake *was* an idea. . . .

". . . and the clothes you wear? So *tacky*. So terri-bly *tacky*."

Not true. They just weren't Sis's Burberry or St. John preference.

Getting no rise out of me, Peggy Sue put her hands on her hips. "Did you come in here *just* to pick a fight with me?"

"Absolutely," I said. "And to put a spark in your pretty eyes and color in those pretty cheeks."

Then I smiled at her.

"Oh." Sis dropped her arms in defeat.

My turn to stand. "Now that you're feeling better . . . take a shower, why don't you? And get into some old clothes."

"I sense a hidden agenda."

"I'm not hiding it. I need your help."

"Doing what?"

"I'll tell you downstairs. Now, chop chop."

Suddenly I had become Mother. But at least I hadn't gone *Hogan's Heroes* on Peg.

She lifted an eyebrow. "What if I don't want to leave this room?"

"Then I'll just have to call Senator Clark."

Who is Senator Clark, you ask? Merely the man I had recently discovered to be my biological father.

You see, Peggy Sue—the summer after graduating from high school, with college waiting in the wings—had worked for the then-young politician on his first campaign, during which time he was elected . . . and I was conceived.

Sis had kept this little morsel of my ancestry to herself, until just lately, even from the senator himself (also, until just lately). Back in the day, she hadn't wanted to force this (you should pardon the expression) on-the-rise politician into a career-ruining marriage.

And as the years passed, and Senator Clark's career advanced, Peggy Sue had felt no desire to be at the center of a scandal that would destroy her own happy marriage, not to mention the reputation of one of the state's most admired men. And one of Serenity's most admired women of the country club set.

"Don't you *dare* call Edward!" she blurted. "You *know* he's in the middle of a *very* important campaign." She put her hand to her chest in a melodramatic gesture worthy of Mother. "The last thing I want to be is a burden!"

"Then stop being one," I said matter-of-factly, "and get dressed, why don't you?"

Peggy Sue's response was to call me an unprintable name, which was bad form for a sister (or a mother for that matter); but a good sign that she was returning to normal.

Before heading downstairs, I stopped by my room to get some old tennies, and check on the spider that had made its home inside one of the windows.

I peered at the little tan insect. "Nothing yet, huh?"

At what point does a spider realize it's built its web in a bad place? It'd been there for weeks without a nibble. I even tried to help by wiping out the web and opening the outer glass so it would leave . . . but *noooo*, the next night it was back, persistent and stubborn as ever, making the web even bigger.

Why do I get all the dumb spiders?

In the music room, Mother stood in the midst of open boxes and packing material, the rug littered with the cast-off belongings of a stranger.

When she saw me, Mother exclaimed, "Feast your eyes on this treasure trove, my dear. A myriad of merchandise for our booth!"

"Such as?"

"Such as *this*, for instance!" She bent, her knees cracking, and swept up a yellowed piece of paper. "That's Superman, isn't it? Signed by the original creators?"

I took a closer look. The drawing of Superman with his *S*-emblazoned chest expanded, hands on hips, smiling big, was a classic pose. It was a pencil drawing signed "Siegel and Shuster." Dated 1946.

"Give me a second," I said, and went upstairs to my bedroom and used my laptop. According to Wikipedia, Siegel and Shuster were the creators of the famous superhero, all right.

Back downstairs, I told Mother she was correct, and that the drawing might well be worth something. I would check later with our friend Joe Lange, who was something of a pop-culture authority. Which was to say, geek.

Feeling her oats now, Mother gestured grandly. "And just look at this wonderful old cornet, a perfect addition to my growing collection!"

Mother set the drawing carefully aside, and plucked up the instrument, her eyes gleaming as if reflecting solid gold, not tarnished, brass.

Great—another smelly old horn. . . .

"But you don't need another!"

Mother made a sour face. "You're clearly thinking of my trumpet. *This* is a cornet."

"What's the difference?"

"A cornet is smaller. It has a richer, more mellow tone."

I took a closer look. "Wait a minute—you already have one of *those,* too! This makes *three* trumpets!"

"One trumpet and two cornets, and since *when* do I limit myself to just *one* in a collection?"

"Judging by the half-dozen old chamber pots gathering dust on the back porch? I would say, *never.*"

"Besides," she was saying, ignoring my minirant, "*this* cornet is much nicer than the one I already have. *And* the trumpet."

"You mean it isn't a dented-up piece of junk."

" 'Junk' is a trifle judgmental, dear, and . . . well, I just have a good feeling about this new horn." Mother's eyes were gleaming again. "Maybe it even belonged to Louie Armstrong himself!"

"Oh, sure."

"Or Harry James!"

"Right. Maybe it's the horn Al Hirt was playing when somebody threw a brick at him."

Mother gave me a hard stare. "Dear, sarcasm makes wrinkles around your mouth, which are *far* worse than a frown. You are forgetting the first rule of antiquing . . ."

"Check for mold?"

"Anything is possible! One man's trash is another's treasure!"

That was two rules, but never mind.

"Okay," I sighed like a cop at a crime scene. "What else have we got?"

Mother turned back to the clutter. "Well, we have a wonderful set of Haviland dishes—which would have been *complete*, only *somehow* a few cups managed to get *broken*."

Her magnified eyes focused on me, shooting demented laser beams of suspicion.

"Oh, sure, assume it's *my* fault. *I* must have done it. Not the person who originally packed the darn things."

With Mother, the best defense is offense.

That, and changing the subject.

"What are those?" I asked, pointing to a stack of letters.

A hand fluttered. "Oh . . . just some old correspondence. Not important, I'm sure."

"Mind if I take them?"

Mother raised her eyebrows.

I cocked my head. "They could shed some light on who the owner was. Maybe we can trace that Superman drawing, or even your new trumpet."

"Cornet." She shrugged. "Help yourself."

Rather than hear Mother's knees crack again, I retrieved the letters off the rug, only to have *my* knees pop. Heredity is a harsh mistress.

Speaking of which, Peggy Sue appeared in the archway of the French doors, damp hair pulled back in a ponytail, face freshly scrubbed with just a hint of make-up. She was wearing a plaid shirt and jeans—clothes from *my closet.*

Noting my displeasure, Sis said, "You told me to put on old clothes."

My displeasure deepened. "They *aren't* old—I just bought them."

Sis looked down at herself in astonishment; whether this was a ploy to irritate or actual ignorance on her part, I couldn't say. "Really? The shirt is frayed, and the jeans are torn. . . . That spells old to me."

"They're supposed to be that way."

Peggy Sue laughed, then saw my serious expression, and her forehead frowned while her mouth smiled. "You *actually bought* torn clothes? On *purpose?*"

"It's the style," I said defensively.

"Then"—she shrugged—"why didn't you just rip up clothes you already had?"

"Because they can't be *person*-ripped . . . they have to be *factory*-ripped."

Long lashes batted at me. "There's a difference?"

"The *difference*," I exclaimed, "is that the former is trash, and the latter is fashion."

"In your case," Sis sniffed, "the former is the latter."

"And in *your* case," I snapped, referring to her taste in clothes, "the latter *is* the former."

Mother interceded, which was a good thing, because I was getting mixed up about which was which.

"Girls, girls, *please!* You're giving me one of my sick headaches!" She turned to Peggy Sue. "Dear, I understand that you are hurting after your recent, uh . . . setback . . . but being unkind to Brandy isn't going to make anything better." Then she turned to me and raised a teacherly forefinger. "And Brandy, *you* should know better than to bicker. It's up to you to set a good example!"

Me set a good example? My lot in life was to provide a terrible warning to others about what fate might await them, if they *did* follow my example. . . .

Mother clapped her hands, as if a performance had just ended; maybe it had.

"Girls, the afternoon is slipping away, and there are more treasures to be unearthed!"

Peggy Sue said, "Huh?"

"I refer, of course, to more boxes that need hauling home from our storage unit."

"What boxes?" Peggy Sue asked. "What storage unit?"

This was what happened around the Borne homestead; if you risked sleeping in, the world could pass you by.

Briefly I filled Sis in, taking the lead, knowing Mother *wouldn't* have been brief. . . .

When I'd concluded, Sis gestured to the clutter. "Is *that* what all this is? The contents of your mystery boxes?"

"Yes," I said.

"Treasure?" Her pert little nose turned up. "Looks like trash to me."

"That trash might be worth something," I said.

"That's right," Mother chimed in.

I told Peg about the Superman drawing by its creators, mentioning that it was dated 1946.

Arms folded over my bosom, *I Dream of Jeannie* style, I said, "I'm pretty sure *that* piece of 'trash' is valuable."

Suddenly Peggy Sue seemed interested. "How much?"

I let Mother reel her in. "A great deal, from what our preliminary research indicates. And that's just one item! Who knows what other treasures might be in store?"

"Well, what are we waiting for?" Sis said. "Let's go." Then: "Do I get a percentage? There's a new Burberry jacket I have my eye on."

Peggy Sue *was* getting back to normal.

Then I had an idea—not surprisingly, an idea that would make my work easier.

"If we take both cars," I suggested, "we can get done quicker."

Peggy Sue had a Cadillac Escalade, the only possession she'd managed to hold onto out of the financial debacle her late husband had bequeathed her. Well, she did hang on to her clothes and jewelry, too. The sheriff didn't exist who could pry those from my sister's clutching fingers.

"Capital idea, Brandy," Mother said, beaming. "And let's bring along the push broom from the garage. Peggy Sue and I can load boxes while you sweep out the unit."

After the broken Haviland cups, Mother didn't trust me with handling the boxes anymore.

"Fine by me," I said, then reached for the old horn that Mother was still holding as if it were an Oscar she'd won. "But this goes out to the garage until you promise to clean it."

With a sigh worthy of Camille on her deathbed, Mother handed over the trumpet. Cornet. Whatever.

Outside, with an early-evening fog settling in, I retrieved the broom from the garage, tossing the cornet on one of the many scrap heaps. Soon Mother and I were climbing into the Buick, with Peggy Sue set to follow us.

As I drove, Mother sat uncharacteristically silent—her mind most likely buzzing with thoughts of further valuable discoveries—which was fine with me, as the twisty river road took all my concentration, having become nearly obscured by fog.

Suddenly Mother wheeled toward me, her face clenched in anguish, and she pleaded, "Dear— *please* don't turn me into a paperweight."

Now even for Mother, that was a doozy of a non sequitur.

"Sure," I said. "I promise not to turn you into a paperweight. Might I ask one small question?"

"Certainly, dear."

"What are you *talking* about?"

"Eyes on the road, dear."

"I'm waiting."

"For what, dear?"

"An explanation!"

"Careful, dear, don't slow down too much or Peggy Sue might ram you."

Peggy Sue, impatient as always, was indeed tailgating me—particularly dangerous under these conditions—so I tapped my brakes to put a little scare into her. She honked at me, to put a scare into me.

Finally, Mother said, "It's my aunt Olive, dear. You remember her."

"Vaguely."

"Well, she's lost."

"I don't get it. Didn't she die a couple of years ago?"

At the ripe old age of ninety-five. At the time, Mother was having one of her "spells," and I was in the midst of a divorce, so neither of us attended Olive's funeral out in Ohio.

"So, what, then?" I asked. "Was she a sinner and you figure she's lost in the throes of hellfire damnation or something?"

"Don't sound ridiculous, dear."

"Yeah. I wouldn't want to sound ridiculous. So. Don't turn you into a paperweight?"

Mother's nod was barely perceptible, as if taking a cue from offstage. "After Aunt Olive was cremated, her daughter had the ashes turned into a paperweight." She sighed. "I suppose it was comforting, still having her mother around the house . . . but something tragic happened."

"It broke?"

"No. Much worse. The paperweight accidently got sold in a garage sale."

I might have laughed if Mother hadn't sounded so distressed.

"And now?" she said to the car's ceiling. "Now, poor Aunt Olive is in some stranger's house, gathering dust."

"Maybe she's being put to practical use. Sitting on top of a stack of bills or something. Wasn't she a math teacher? That would be kind of fitting."

Mother was ignoring my comments. "Or *worse*—thrown in the trash, to be buried in a landfill along with the rest of the disgusting garbage!"

"Don't worry," I said, too kind to point out that she had just classified Aunt Olive as garbage, and disgusting garbage at that. "You won't end up as a paperweight, Mother, or anything else. You'll have a proper burial, somewhere I can visit you, and weep."

Mother touched my arm. "Thank you, dear. That's reassuring."

"I was thinking of a storage unit."

And to her credit, Mother laughed rather heartily at that.

"Good one, dear," she said. "Good one."

By now, the fog was so thick I almost missed the entrance to the storage facility, and when I made a sharp left turn, Mother slid into me, as far as her seat belt would allow.

"Nice save, dear."

Peggy Sue, having wisely put some distance between us, had no trouble pulling into the graveled drive, and she trailed our car up to the unit, where soon we were all standing while Mother fished around in a jacket pocket for the padlock key.

Peggy Sue, having second thoughts, asked, "These boxes won't get my car dirty, will they? I try to keep the Escalade clean, you know."

"Should be fine," I lied. "Of course, there may be a chocolate sprinkle or two."

Sis frowned. "What?"

I gave her a quick summary of Mother's mouse dropping trick, and if I'd thought that would disgust her, I was wrong.

"Ingenious," Peggy Sue said admiringly. "The old girl's got a head on her shoulders. Have to give her that."

That head was wagging side to side, as Mother was having trouble with the lock; but finally she gave it a good jiggle, and it snapped open.

I grasped the door handle, pulling it up, revealing darkness; the ground fog swirled in as if seeking sanctuary from the night.

Mother, poised for action, switched on her flashlight (retrieved from her jacket), aiming its beam inside, light-sabering it around.

We stood and stared.

"Empty," Mother murmured.

Sis asked, "Are you sure this is the right unit?"

I stepped back, checked the metal number nailed to the outside. "Number seven. This is it."

Mother had gone on in. "I don't understand," she exclaimed in disbelief. "It was half full when we left this morning!"

Peggy Sue pointed. "Looks like a rolled-up rug in the corner. Maybe it's a valuable Oriental."

I took the flashlight from a befuddled Mother, and went deeper, for a closer look.

"It's not a rug," I said after a moment.

"What is it?" Mother asked.

"Uh . . . it's your friend Big Jim Bob."

"Whatever is he doing in there?"

"Not much."

A Trash 'n' Treasures Tip

Before an auction at a storage facility, rules and regulations will be provided to prospective bidders. Such conditions vary with each site, so be sure you understand them before bidding—if you are required to clean up the unit after you've removed its contents, and fail to do so, the cleaning bill you receive may be no bargain.

Chapter Three

Calling All Units!

I handed Mother my cell phone so she could be the one to notify the police, knowing how much making a call like that means to her. And she was very businesslike about it, though unfortunately that included using the fake British accent she sometimes affected to sound more important.

"Vivian Borne here," she said crisply, chin up. "There appears to have been a murder at the Lucky Four Leaf Clover Storage facility. River Road. Mind the fog."

I couldn't make out the dispatcher's response, but judging by Mother's reply—"My dear, I'm *always* 'for real' "—you can extrapolate it for yourself.

I was tending to Peggy Sue, who had actually passed out or fainted or anyway melted into a human puddle, after I'd announced Big Jim Bob's presence (and lack of a pulse).

I was doing my best to lift Sis up off the gravel

when the flutter of eyelids indicated she'd returned to consciousness. I helped her up, then walked her to the Caddie, and eased her into the front passenger's seat, reclining it for more comfort.

"Please," she murmured.

"Yes?"

"Please take me home."

It was fairly pitiful. Did all the older women in my family have to be so childlike? When *I* was the most mature one around, we definitely had problems.

"We can't leave," I told her. "Not until the police arrive. And then there'll be questions."

"But I don't want to get involved!"

"You *are* involved," I said. "You're a witness."

"I didn't see that man get killed!"

"No, but you were here when I discovered the body." Then I added, "I'll do my best to keep you out of it."

Sis moaned. "Just when I thought my life couldn't get any worse, I get dragged into another of your stupid murders."

My chin wrinkled in irritation. "First of all, it's not one of *my* murders, stupid or otherwise. Second of all, we don't even know if it's a murder. You think I *like* this?"

"No. But *Mother* is relishing it."

I couldn't deny that.

I patted her shoulder, cutting her some slack. The tragic way her husband had left this life really had been enough of a hardship for her. "You just try to rest. . . ."

Inside the unit, I found Mother standing near

the late Big Jim Bob, his prone form awash in the beam of her flashlight. The owner of the storage facility lay facedown, arms extended, the back of his head matted with blood.

Okay, so maybe it was *a murder. . . .*

"We have precious little time, dear," Mother said brusquely.

"For what?"

"Evidence gathering. Appraising the crime scene."

"We're not detectives. We're a couple of unlucky females who have had the misfortune of getting involved in a couple of . . . of—"

"Homicides," Mother snapped. "We have to complete our preliminary investigation before the boys in blue arrive and compromise the crime scene."

"Aren't *we* compromising the crime scene?"

"Not as long as we don't touch anything." She looked at me with her *Mrs. Bug Goes to Town* eyes huge behind the glasses. "Now, take notes!"

"I don't have a pad or pen."

Mother frowned. "You should always be prepared for this kind of contingency, dear."

"It's not like murder is an everyday occurrence in our lives!" Even if it was starting to feel that way. "Why weren't *you* prepared?"

"Preparation is *your* job."

"Why my job?"

"Because *I* am Holmes, and *you* are Watson."

"How do you figure that?"

"It occurred to me when we began watching that new modern-day Holmes series. The BBC one?"

She was standing over a corpse, the flashlight now dancing nervously against the wall of the unit as she extolled the virtues of a television show. How exactly did this become my life, anyway?

"Such a brilliant idea!" she told Big Jim Bob and me. "Bringing that Victorian duo into contemporary London, with all the gadgetry of the twenty-first century! Holmes with a cell phone! Who'd have thunk it?"

I wouldn't have thunk it. Apparently Big Jim Bob, either.

Mother is an actress who needs more than her share of prompting, so I said, "Precious time?"

"Quite right, dear. Now, without writing utensils, you'll just have to remember what I say."

"Okay . . . because I'm Watson."

"Precisely."

"*Which* Watson?"

"Not following you, dear. . . ."

"Which *Watson?* The buffoonish Nigel Bruce? The more intelligent Edward Hardwicke? Then there's David Burke—he was a likable chap." For just a moment I had fallen into Mother's British accent. "Personally, I like Jude Law."

And not necessarily as Watson.

"Whichever one you prefer," Mother said impatiently. "Can we get on with it?"

"Think of me as Nigel Bruce—less pressure."

"Brandy!"

"All right! I'm ready. Go."

Mother took a deep breath, then her words came rapid-fire. "Note that Big Jim Bob—while wearing the same clothes as this morning—has on different boots. They're dry, so he had to have come back here *after* the rain stopped."

She touched the corpse's head with her flashlight beam.

Ick.

"Death blow delivered by a heavy, blunt object."

The light moved to his jeans.

"No bulge in the back pocket, so his wallet would appear missing. Robbery? Possibly, *but . . .* his expensive gold nugget ring is still on one finger. What does that tell us?"

She turned for my answer, the flashlight coming along for the ride, its beam blinding me.

I shielded my eyes. "That you're getting pretty good at this?"

"Thank you, but no. What does it *tell* us?"

"The killer doesn't dig bling?"

Hey, I was Nigel Bruce—a bit of buffoonery came with the territory.

"Nooooo," Mother replied. "It tells us the crime scene was hastily *staged* to appear like a robbery."

"But it *is* a robbery," I protested. "Otherwise, where are the rest of our boxes? And another thing . . ."

"Yes?"

"Get that light out of my eyes!"

She did. "Dear, I'm talking about the murder *itself* being staged to seem part of the larger over-all—and very *real*—robbery. We can't, at this stage, know for certain that the killer was the same person who emptied the unit of our remaining boxes. We could have two different crimes here."

I said, "Well, at least we know the murder weapon."

"We do?"

"Big Jim Bob's steel cutter?" Wasn't *I* supposed to be Nigel Bruce? "It's lying over there. . . ."

Mother flashed the beam where I was pointing, the tiny spotlight suddenly showcasing the cutter, a few yards away, its steel jaws blackened with blood.

"Missed that," Mother said.

A rare admission from Holmes.

"But," I said, "you're right about the staging of a robbery as the motive. A thief would have taken the ring. And if he couldn't remove it, there was always the cutter to use to get it."

Mother was nodding. "Very astute, dear."

A rare compliment for Watson.

"Why," she said, "that finger would have snapped right off like a tiny twig."

A nauseated moan came from the entryway—apparently Peggy Sue had been standing there long enough to hear the last part of our conversation.

"I think I'm going to be sick," she said, clutching her stomach with one hand. Her other hand made a small fist that shook at the air. "Sometimes I think you two are crazy. Demented! There's a man murdered in there, and you banter back and forth like some silly comedy team. Don't you have any respect for the dead?"

Raising her voice, Mother said, "Go back to the car, dear. You'll soon feel better. Brandy and I are old hands at this kind of thing, and no disrespect is meant for—"

"Mother," Peggy said, "shut up."

Mother gave me a *whatever-did-I-do-to-deserve-that* expression, and I shrugged in agreement, though of course Peggy Sue was exactly right.

But I didn't think our conduct came out of being "old hands" at this—I think we were numb, even in shock, at finding ourselves caught up in a homicide yet again.

As Sis left, shaking her head, the distant wail of a siren brought an end to our preliminary sleuthing. We scurried out of the storage unit like frightened mice, leaving nary a dropping, to stand by the Buick and await the police.

Soon the wail became a scream that cut off abruptly as the squad car with lights flashing burst through the fog, seeming to leap toward us before coming to a gravel-grinding halt.

This nerve-jarring arrival was followed by that of another vehicle, which pulled up with considerably less melodrama: the unmarked car of the chief of police. Two officers hopped out of the squad car, male and female, both well-known to Mother and me (and vice versa).

The driver was lanky Scott Munson, mid-forties, his oblong Herman Munsterish face in a sorrowful cast, possibly because this was a homicide, or maybe he was just reacting to finding Mother and me at the scene.

His partner, Mia Cordona, was my age, a darkhaired beauty whose masculine uniform couldn't hide her hourglass shape. Mia had once been a good friend but we'd drifted apart.

Exiting the unmarked car was Brian Lawson, interim chief since Tony Cassato had entered the Witness Protection Program. Brian had a leanly muscular athlete's build and was (if it's not bad taste to say so in this context) drop-dead handsome, with sandy hair and the kind of brown eyes a girl could get lost in.

And, once upon a time, I had.

Which is to say I had history with these officers, even before Mother and I had begun making a bad habit of turning up at crime scenes.

Mother was the first to speak. "In there," she said to Munson and Mia, who had reached us first.

Munson hurried past us, but Mia paused long enough to give me a disparaging look, which I responded to with an elaborate shrug.

Then, with Maglites shining, the uniformed pair disappeared inside the unit.

Mother faded back, leaving me to deal with Brian.

"Are you all right?" he asked, concern tightening his boyish face.

"I'm fine." I cocked my head. "But I'm surprised to see you here. The chief himself?"

He lifted an eyebrow. "I was just leaving the station when the call came in. Wanted to make sure you were okay."

"I'm fine. But Peggy Sue isn't." I gestured toward the Caddie. "She actually fainted when we found the body. I don't think I ever saw anybody faint before, except in movies."

"Does she need medical assistance? The paramedics are on the way."

"She's all right—just shook up," I said. "Why paramedics? It's not like Big Jim Bob needs them."

"It's procedure." His concern, maybe because I was being so flip, switched over to curiosity. "How did you happen onto him, anyway? Guy owned the business here, right?"

I nodded, then filled him in on everything that had happened since this morning. Had it really only been eight hours? On the other hand, I was wiped out enough for it to have been eight days.

I was wrapping up my account when Mia's sharply raised voice interrupted, echoing within the unit.

"Get *out!*" she shouted.

"Why, Officer!" Mother retorted, and hopped out, landing a little unsteadily. "I was merely trying to be useful."

"You mean use*less*," Mia said. Like a teacher sending a very bad child to the principal's office, she pointed a finger at Mother, then away from the unit. "This kind of nonsense landed you in jail not so long ago, Vivian. If you don't want to go *back* there, stay *out!*"

As Mia withdrew into the crime scene, Mother came toward Brian and me, smoothing her jacket like a bed she was making.

"*They* don't seem to value my insights," she huffed, "but *you* do, don't you, Interim Chief Lawson?"

Brian's jaw muscles flexed, ever so slightly. "That's 'Chief Lawson,' Mrs. Borne."

"Oh, please feel free to call me 'Vivian.' Any friend of Brandy's is a friend of mine. So, you *have* been made permanent chief, then?"

"No, but I *am* acting chief."

Mother's eyebrows climbed her forehead. "Oh my *bad*, as the children say. *Not* Interim Chief Lawson."

"That's right."

"I won't make that mistake again, Acting Chief Lawson."

Brian's jaw muscles flexed again, *not* so slightly, so I said, "Chief? I'd like get to Peggy Sue out of here. Could you take our statements tomorrow, either at home or at the station? Whatever's convenient?"

I only dared to suggest that the Borne girls might all leave the crime scene, knowing Brian stood between Mother and me—otherwise she would have kicked me in the shin. Or shins.

"All right," he said. "Late morning? Station okay?"

"Fine," I said, and gave him as warm a smile as I could under the circumstances. "We'll see you then."

He smiled tightly. "Just you, Brandy. Your statement should cover it. I can always follow up with a phone call to Mrs. Borne."

"*Vivian,*" Mother insisted.

"Vivian," he said with a nod.

I'd expected a vehement protest from Mother, being excluded from the police station visit, but to my surprise Mother only added, "I'm quite content having Brandy speak for the two of us—after all, *she* was first to discover poor Big Jim Bob."

Munson, having stepped out of the unit, was motioning for Brian, who then left us to huddle with his officer.

Mother whispered in my ear, "Dear, you'll be able to get more information out of the acting chief without me along. He's still mad about you, you know. A perfect opportunity to deploy your feminine wiles."

Feminine wiles: beauty and charm used by a woman to get a man to do something.

You're right—I don't think it sounds like me, either.

Brian returned to us. "The coroner is on his way."

I nodded. "Then it's okay for us to leave?"

He nodded back. "We have a lot more work to do here and . . ." He flicked a glance at Mother, and I got the picture: we would just be underfoot.

So before Mother could make any more trouble, I took her by the arm and led her to the Buick; after telling her to stay (knowing she was no more liable to follow that command than Sushi), I went over to the Caddie to see if Peggy Sue was up to driving herself home.

She insisted she was, and in fact seemed just fine now. Soon our two-car caravan was moving slowly out of the drive, passing the paramedic truck as it rolled in with lights flashing but no siren.

As we passed, Mother powered down her window, stuck her head out, and shrilled, "Not needed! Not needed!"

I cringed. "Well, your *yelling* wasn't needed, all right!"

"It most certainly was." She powered the window back up and folded her arms like a nightclub bouncer. "Dear, it's a waste of taxpayer money to send a vehicle like that out burning fuel, and wasting electricity with those flashing lights. If I don't make my opinions known, how are improvements to be made around this town?"

We were in the country, but I didn't point that out. We just fell silent. Sis was back to her tailgating ways again, but this time I let her get away with it. The fog was still thick and we were just crawling, anyway.

"You know, Brian would make a suitable husband," Mother mused, shifting gears even if I was the one driving. "He may not be the brightest crayon in the box . . . but with my help he could make a decent chief of police—interim, acting, or otherwise."

And a great conduit for police information.

Mother went on: "I *do* understand that you're still pining away for Tony Cassato, and he *was* a handsome brooding brute of a man . . . but, dear, you can't be certain you'll ever even *see* him again. It's time to move on. Just step up to that counter and say, *'Next!'* "

I kept quiet.

"By the way, dear, were you ever intimate with Tony?"

Good thing I wasn't drinking anything, because that one rated a spit-take all over the dashboard.

I shot her a glare. "Mother, there's such a thing as privacy! How can you ask me that?"

She was staring into the fog, perhaps looking out for icebergs. "Because I'm your mother—*and* grandmother. That gives me *twice* the right."

Typical Mother reasoning.

I said, "I was seven months pregnant at the time Tony and I got serious, so what do *you* think?"

(Last year, I played a role that outperformed anything Mother had ever done at the local Playhouse—I was surrogate mother for my best friend and her husband, who couldn't have children. Are you newbies keeping up?)

Mother was saying, "A third-term pregnancy never stopped me. Why, it was some of the best—"

"Stop! La la la la la la! Don't want to hear it! Do *not* want to hear it!" Much less have any images form in my mind. . . .

"Very well, dear. I just wanted to show that I was willing to tear down the walls of my own privacy, in order to enlighten you."

"Well, I'm plenty enlightened already, thanks. Keep your walls up and untorn."

"Fine."

We fell silent again.

The fog began to clear; after a while, I risked a glance at Mother. "I *am* sorry about Big Jim Bob."

Staring out her side window now that looming icebergs were no longer a threat, she sighed. "I am, too. He was such a *dear* man. I'll cry about him later. In my own veil of privacy."

Mother did have a remarkable ability to compartmentalize, to handle a crisis first, then deal with emotions later. To some, her lack of empathy made her seem cold. I knew better.

But she had touched on what was bothering me about my relationship with Tony: our love, if that was what it was, had been frozen in the early stage of our courtship, when everything was exciting and heady and just on the brink of intimacy. *Swell of music here.* Had it been allowed to progress, we might well have discovered we weren't meant for each other, and our love could have withered and died. *Music down.*

But with Tony suddenly yanked from my life, I somehow couldn't seem to move on. . . .

I pulled into our driveway, Peggy Sue nosing in behind. The house was dark—which of course wouldn't bother blind little Sushi—but seemed unsettling in the aftermath of a murder discovery.

Inside, I switched on the entry light, then the ceiling lights in the living room, and there was Sushi, sitting patiently on the Oriental rug, waiting. And clutching by one corner with her sharp little teeth . . .

. . . *that valuable Superman drawing.*

Mother and I froze, Peggy Sue bumping into us. Still tailgating.

I whispered to Mother, "She's upset we've been gone so long."

"Yes," Mother whispered back. "How did the little devil know that particular item was the one we cared about most?"

"Must have our scent all over it . . . plus she heard us oohing and aahing. *Don't anybody move.*"

"What's going on?" Sis demanded.

"Shhhh . . ." I ordered.

I moved forward, slowly. "Sushi, honey, be a good girl. Let it go."

Soosh backed up with her prize.

"I know what will do the trick!" Mother said, then rushed into the kitchen.

In a moment came the sound of a potato chip bag rustling.

But Sushi remained still, spooky white eyes unblinking. If her little head had done a complete *Exorcist* turn on her little neck, I wouldn't have been a bit surprised.

"Try cookies," I hollered.

"We're out of cookies," Mother hollered back.

"How about that leftover meat loaf?" To Sushi I said, "I double-dog *dare* you to ignore that."

Our eyes were locked in a battle of wills. And I knew I was very likely outmatched. . . .

Mother returned with a container of yesterday's dinner, which she placed in front of Sushi.

The little dog's nose twitched, but the drawing remained clutched in her teeth.

I said, "Mother, *she* doesn't want the meat loaf, so why don't *we* have it?"

"Ah! Capital idea, dear!"

And I got down on my hands and knees in front of the bowl, pretending to eat.

Mother followed suit.

Two adult women, huddled around a Tupperware bowl like a couple of hounds at a doggie dish. Dignity be damned—a valuable collectible was at stake.

Peggy Sue, still in the entryway, muttered, "Oh, for pity's sake. You're worse than that silly animal. I'm going upstairs."

I could see Sushi weakening, jaw going slack, then, finally . . . the drawing fluttered to the floor.

Whereby, Mother snatched it up.

Soosh scurried over and began gobbling the meat loaf, as we examined the drawing.

Finally, Mother concluded, "Surprisingly unharmed . . . a few tooth marks on this one corner, but not a nibble on the artwork."

I pointed. "Little slobber, there."

Mother brushed it off. "Good as new."

We both sighed with relief.

To avoid any further act of canine retribution, I

spent the next hour playing with Sushi, until she and I were exhausted. Then I took her upstairs, depositing her on my bed.

But before turning in, I went to check on Peggy Sue. A light was shining beneath the closed door, so I knocked, then went in without waiting for permission.

She was in her pink robe, propped up in bed, reading Mother's tattered copy of *The Power of Positive Thinking*, itself darn near an antique.

"You okay?" I asked.

Sis set the book aside. I sat on the edge of the bed near her.

She opened her mouth, closed it, then opened it again. "I . . . I don't mean to be offensive."

"Go on."

"It's just that . . . I don't want to be like you and Mother."

"You won't be."

"I *will* if I stay here." She burst into tears, covering her face with her hands.

"Book not working, huh?"

She continued to sob.

"Look," I said softly, "I know you're in a bad place right now, but it won't last forever. Things will get better. Mother and I are a quirky couple of kooks. But it's not catching."

"It's in the blood."

"Seems to have skipped a generation."

She smiled weakly and sniffled mightily, looking up from her hands. "You don't know what I'm going through— what it's like to lose everything and come crawling home."

"Really? Kinda sounds like me not so long ago."

Peggy Sue stared. Then, looking a little sheepish, she said, "I suppose you're right. I was just thinking of myself. *Typical.*"

"Oh, that's not so." Sure it was.

Her eyes searched my face. "It's just that, well, you seem to *like* it here."

I grunted a little. "I wouldn't say that. Life around the Borne homestead's just a comfortable old shoe I can slip on—doesn't mean I wouldn't like a brand-new pair. Anyway, I'm only here because I don't know what I want to do next with my life."

"Me either."

I touched her arm. "Maybe we could . . . figure it out together?"

She granted me the tiniest smile. "Maybe."

I returned to my room, where Sushi had stretched out in the middle of the bed. I turned out the light and, not bothering to remove my clothes, flopped on the slice of bed she had left me.

I dreamed my teeth were falling out. First the front ones, then all the others. I was trying to shove them back in their sockets, when I forced myself to wake up.

Okay, so I *was* overdue for my yearly dental checkup . . . but did I *have* to do *that* to myself? What was wrong with just dreaming I needed to make an appointment? Or maybe having an angel appear to remind me?

Then I heard a terrified scream.

Was I still dreaming?

I felt for Sushi, but she was gone.

I jumped out of bed, ran into the hallway, where I met Mother, coming out of her room.

"What was that?" she asked, also alarmed.

I dashed into Peggy Sue's room, where I found her bed empty.

From below came a pitiful canine yelp.

"Sushi!" I yelled.

I raced past Mother, taking the stairs down, two steps at a time.

On the lower landing, despite the darkness, I could make out a prone form . . .

. . . Peggy Sue!

On her stomach by the entryway, arms stretched out, blood oozing from the back of her head.

Just like Big Jim Bob.

Mother had reached the phone in the alcove, and was calling for help.

I checked Peggy Sue for a pulse, found one, but she was unconscious. I tore off my shirt, used it as a bandage, applying pressure to the wound on her head.

I glanced over my shoulder. "Sushi?"

"She's by the front door." Mother knelt beside me. "You best check on her, dear. I'll take over here. . . ."

I went to Sushi, who was lying on her side, and put a hand on her chest, feeling for the rise and fall of her rib cage. Finding no sign of life, I lifted her chin to straighten out her neck, then, with one hand holding her mouth shut, I put my mouth over her nose, and blew gently. When her chest expanded, I waited until the air left her lungs, before going through the process again.

"Please God," I said. "Please God. . . ."

After the longest minute of my life, Sushi stirred, and began to whimper.

"She's hurting!" I called to Mother. "I've got to get her to the vet, right now."

"Go, dear. Take her."

"What about Peggy Sue?"

"The paramedics are on the way—there's nothing more either of us can do."

"Is she going to be all right?"

"She's breathing steadily. Now *go*."

I ran for a new blouse, then came back and picked up Sushi, grabbed the car keys off the entryway table, and my cell phone, and hurried out the door to the car.

I drove and phoned with one hand, having arranged Sushi on the rider's seat. The cell phone took me to an answering machine, but that wasn't going to stop me.

Once, Dr. Tillie had saved Sushi's life. Afterward, he told me that if she was ever at death's door again, to bring her to him, no matter what time of day or night.

I was taking him at his word.

He lived on the edge of town, by himself, in a small ranch home behind the clinic. I drove there at a reckless speed, Sushi lying still—but breathing—beside me. My hand would find her coat and gently stroke, and I'd speak words of encouragement, though I doubted she heard me.

As I pulled down the gravel lane to Dr. Tillie's house, the porch light came on—perhaps he'd heard my call on the machine—and before I could bring the Buick to a stop, he was out his front door, coming toward me, pulling a robe on over his pajamas.

As I hopped out of the car, Dr. Tillie—a stocky,

older man with a kind face and whose gentle demeanor often kept him from getting bitten— opened the passenger door, quickly picked up Sushi, then turned and headed into the clinic, while I followed, sobbing uncontrollably.

Inside, he carried Soosh back to an examining room, placing her on an aluminum table, immediately checking her eyes and gums.

"What happened?" he asked.

I told him about the intruder.

When his fingers probed her side, Sushi whimpered.

"Bastard," the gentle man muttered.

This startled me. "What?"

"She's been *kicked,*" he said. "I'll need X-rays."

I had stopped crying. "Do you think she'll be all right?"

"If there's no internal bleeding."

I swallowed. "I know I . . . know I should be with Peggy Sue right now, but I don't want to leave Sushi." I couldn't help crying again. "I'm a terrible person!"

"Sushi is part of your family, too, and your mother is taking care of your sister. As for Sushi, I'll do everything I can. Why don't you go join them now . . . at the people hospital?"

That phrase got an involuntary smile out of me. "Okay, Doc. I'll do that."

I gave him a kiss on the cheek, and raced out of there, my heart breaking at leaving the little thing behind.

At the people hospital, I expected to find Mother pacing the long corridor of the ER, but she was in the waiting room, sequestered with Mia in a corner, the officer making notes on a small pad.

Mother stood as I rushed forward.

"Peggy Sue?" I asked.

"She's having an MRI," Mother responded.

"Still unconscious?"

"Yes—and the doctor may keep her that way . . . *if* there's swelling in the brain."

"Oh my Lord. When will we know?"

"Soon, I hope. . . . How's the little doggie?"

Was Mother that concerned about Sushi? Or was she just trying to divert my thoughts from the possibility of Peggy Sue having brain damage?

I sighed, shaking my head. "We won't know about Soosh for a while, either."

Mia stood. "I think I've gotten everything I need for the time being. . . ."

I jumped her. "You're not leaving *now,* are you? Whoever hit Peggy Sue probably killed Big Jim Bob, too . . . and if Peg got a look at him, her life is still in danger."

Mia gave me a "calm down" gesture. "No, I'm not leaving—your sister will have police protection as long as she's here."

"What about us?" Mother asked. "That intruder could come back!"

Mia said, "Officer Munson is at your house right now investigating the break-in—he'll stay on, parked in his car out front." She patted my arm. We'd once been close friends, remember. "Try not to worry, Brandy. . . . Now, I've got to see hospital security. . . ."

Mother and I hung around the waiting room a while longer, hoping the doctor might come and give us an update on Peggy Sue; but when that didn't happen, I worried that Dr. Tillie might try to reach me at home.

So after making sure the receptionist had our contact information, Mother and I slipped out, just as an ambulance pulled up and the ER turned frantic.

Dawn was breaking as we arrived home, and I was relieved to see a squad car parked at the curb. I pulled into the drive, and up to the garage. We got out, me heading to the porch, Mother going back to speak to Officer Munson.

I had forgotten what awaited me inside: Peggy Sue's blood on the floor, now dark and crusty-dried and ominous, some smeared where we had walked through it.

I sidestepped the scene, then flopped onto the couch, closing my eyes.

Then Mother was nudging me awake.

I bolted upright. "What's happened?"

"No word yet, dear, about either Peggy Sue or Sushi . . . but come with me."

I rose unsteadily, then followed Mother into the music room, where the storage unit items were still spread out on the floor.

"What's missing?" Mother asked.

"Not the Superman!"

"No. What's missing, dear? Think!"

"I'm still Watson?"

She nodded.

I didn't feel like playing her game; but I looked anyway.

Then I shrugged. "I don't know what's missing. . . ."

"Nothing, dear. It's all here . . . and yet, the intruder *was* searching for something, because he—for purposes of discussion, we'll assume it's a he—went through the boxes I had repacked with the wrapping material."

She pointed to the scattered newspapers and bubble wrap.

"So," I said, "he didn't find what he was looking for. Then, on his way out, he encountered Peggy Sue."

"That's right. She probably heard something. And so did Sushi."

"Mother?"

"Yes?"

"Something *is* missing from this room."

Her eyes bugged out behind the glasses. "*What*, dear?"

"Your old horn—*not* the one from the sale. I took that one out to the garage."

Mother's eyes flitted around the room. "Good gravy Marie! You're right."

"Maybe because he thought it *was* the one from the sale."

We stared at each other. Then we both said, "What's so important about an old cornet?"

Well, she said "cornet."

I said "trumpet."

A Trash 'n' Treasures Tip

When viewing a storage unit, look for clues as to the value of the contents. Are the boxes store-bought, or scavenged? Contents listed, or left unmarked? Carefully stacked, or tossed in? The former indicates a higher value, the latter a bad risk. As Mother says, "Even a pig in a poke should have decent grooming."

Chapter Four

X Marks the Spot

The next day, I arose midmorning, after only a few hours of rest. I probably should have slept till at least early afternoon, but the moment I woke, thoughts of yesterday's troubles kicked in and I couldn't have gone back to sleep short of somebody conking me with a big cartoon hammer.

I had just gotten out of the shower—washing the long night away—when Dr. Tillie called with an update on Sushi.

"She's doing fine," he assured me. "Undoubtedly she's a tad sore, but there's been no internal bleeding."

I sighed with relief. "Oh, thank you, Doctor."

"I would like to keep her for another twenty-four hours, for observation. Better safe than sorry."

"Can I come out and see her?"

There was a slight pause. "I know you're anxious to visit the little angel, but right now I'd prefer you didn't. Best to keep her quiet—no undue excitement."

"I understand."

"Call at the end of the day, if you like." His tone was upbeat. "Otherwise, we'll see you tomorrow morning."

I began thanking him effusively, particularly for having let me interrupt him in the middle of last night, but when I could tell I was embarrassing him, signed off.

As I hung up the phone, I thought of Peggy Sue, hoping she was faring as well as Soosh.

Wondering if I was the worst daughter in the world, when my first concern seemed to be my dog. . . .

Half an hour later, Mother and I headed to the hospital. La Diva Borne, too, had managed precious little sleep, but it didn't seem to have done the old girl any harm. She was chipper in her favorite Breckenridge emerald green slacks and top, while I wore a black cashmere sweater and DKNY jeans.

Jeaggings—really? Skinny jeans weren't skinny enough? How much more torture must the female sex endure at the hands of the fashion *fascista*? And while I'm at it, here's my take on the correct jean cotton-to-spandex ratio:

100% cotton: girl, you rule! Unless those jeans get unbuttoned after every meal.

99% cotton, 1% spandex: the best; that touch of

stretch will keep you from strangling the next passerby, or yourself at the waist.

98% cotton, 2% spandex: a deal with your inner devil to gain five pounds.

97% cotton, 3% spandex: admit it, honey—you just don't care.

The intensive care unit was located on the hospital's top floor, and when Mother and I arrived at the nurses' station, we were given the good news that Sis had regained consciousness. Seemed her vital signs were strong enough that she'd been moved to the floor below. Apparently, with each improvement a patient was transferred downward, until, *woosh*, out the door. Then came the bill, which was enough to *woosh* you back in again.

Peggy Sue had a private room at the end of the hall, and, as Mother and I stepped off the elevator, we could see a uniformed police officer seated just outside her door.

As we walked closer, the identity of that officer was another pleasant surprise.

"Mr. Grady," I said, approaching. "I thought you had retired some years ago."

The former sergeant—neat as a pin in his uniform, albeit the shirt buttons straining at his midsection—stood to greet us, beaming. Pushing seventy, medium-height, Sergeant Grady had a silver crew cut and light blue eyes that had a twinkle. Over the years, whenever Mother hit one of her "rough patches," he'd been helpful and kind.

"Yes, Leonard," Mother asked, "have you gone back on the job?"

"On the job" was police jargon Mother had

picked up from TV. I had no idea whether real officers used the term in Serenity or anywhere.

"Only occasionally, Vivian," he said. "When the PD's overstretched, I'm back in harness." He winked at me. "Or anyway, I *try* to squeeze into it."

Uniformed officer or not, Sergeant Grady was good enough a detective to have caught me glancing at his midsection. I blushed at that. Yes, I can feel shame.

Mother tossed her head, girlishly. "Nonsense, Leonard! You look fit as a fiddle."

What's so fit about a fiddle, anyway? And where would we all be without the likes of Mother to keep these mysterious old homilies in play?

Mother was saying, "We're delighted *you* are guarding our precious Peggy Sue. Aren't we, Brandy?"

"Uh-huh."

I was pretty sure that just because he was retirement age—actually past retirement age—Sergeant Grady wasn't likely to be fooled by a killer masquerading as a doctor, or a nurse, or an orderly. That only happens in movies and on TV.

Right?

"Well, dear," Mother said, turning to me, "let's see how our patient's doing."

Quietly, we entered Peggy Sue's room. Though the window blinds were closed, light filtered in, slashing white across Sis's form in the slightly cranked-up bed. Her eyes were closed, an I.V. stuck in one hand, oxygen tube lodged in her nose. One temple had been sheared to allow tending of her wound, including bandaging.

I whispered, singsongy, "She's not going to be *happy* about her *hair*."

Mother whispered back, not singsongy, "Well, she could stand a new hairdo, at that."

"I dunno," I replied, "another year or two, that pageboy *could* come back in style. Stranger things have happened."

Peggy Sue's eyes popped open like a mad killer at the end of a slasher movie, and both Mother and I jumped.

"I *can* hear you, you know," she said.

"Uh, hi, Sis . . . you feeling all right? They treating you okay?"

"Yes, darling," Mother purred, "do tell us how you're holding up."

Peggy Sue pulled herself upright a little, supported by a pillow. "You mean after suffering the insults of my loving family?" She didn't wait for any lame response, but went on defensively, "And there's not a *thing* wrong with my hairstyle—I get compliments on it *all* the time."

Dr. Tillie's voice played in my head: *Keep her quiet . . . no undue excitement. . . .*

"I'm sure you do," I soothed. Best not point out that the side of her head was shaved like a prisoner headed to the hot squat.

But Mother chirped, "And don't worry about how hideous it looks now . . . it'll grow out in a month or two! At which time, why, I could even style it for you! After all, remember the nice job I used to do, cutting Brandy's hair when she was a little girl?"

Peggy Sue and I traded looks. Mother would have been fired from a military base barber shop for undue cruelty to recruits. Her assaults on my head of hair were an indignity I put up with till I was old enough to fight her off.

With a pointed look at Mother, I said, "Let's move past the warm family reunion to what happened last night. I want to know what Peggy Sue can remember."

Mother tilted her head at me and gave me a mildly scolding look. "We are here visiting your sister because of her injury and to show her our support, and there's no reason to upset her by rushing into all of that unpleasantness." Then to Sis, she said, "What *do* you remember about last night?"

Peggy Sue shrugged. "Not much. I recall going downstairs for a sleeping pill."

Mother prodded, "And?"

"And . . . that's about all."

I asked, "You don't remember being slugged?"

"Really, I don't. Just waking up here. What *did* happen?"

I let Mother reconstruct what we knew about the attack, which she described with considerable melodrama and great theatrics. I will spare you. Don't say I never did anything for you.

After the curtain had come down, a tight-lipped Peggy Sue glared at me. "Let me get this straight. . . . I'm lying on the floor, unconscious, bleeding to death, and *you* leave *me* to take Sushi to the vet?"

Put that way, perhaps my actions did seem a little questionable. And even then, I'd known I would pay for it, for a long, long time.

Still, my response was eloquent and to the point: "I . . . ah . . . I, uh . . . I. . . ."

Her chin rose. With her bandage and I.V. and nose-threaded oxygen tube, she looked like the survivor of some major disaster. "You chose a *dog* over *me?*"

Mother came to my defense. "Now, darling, it wasn't at all like that. *I* was there tending to you. And the little doggie *had* been hurt."

An eyebrow arched—Leonard Nimoy couldn't have done it better. "As bad as me?"

Now I rushed to my own defense. "Hey! Sushi had stopped breathing. And, don't forget, she got hurt protecting you!"

"There were two victims," Mother said grandly, "and two of us. Do the math, dear!"

Peggy Sue lowered the eyebrow. "Okay . . . maybe I am being overly sensitive."

"No, sweetheart, you just weren't awake to understand the needs of the emergency. And Brandy only took the dog to the vet when I commanded that she do so."

"Okay," Peggy Sue said.

But I was clearly still in the doghouse. So to speak.

Mother placated: "Didn't everything turn out all right? Both you and the little doggie are going to be just fine." She patted Peggy Sue's shoulder. "Now, get some rest, dear—you could have an important visitor, you know, any time now!"

"*Who?*" Sis and I blurted simultaneously, if with different intonations—her, interested; me, alarmed.

What had The Madwoman of Chaillot cooked up this time?

"I called Senator Clark," Mother announced

proudly. "I thought he should be aware of what transpired."

"*What!*" Sis and I said—this time we were both on the same alarmed wavelength.

"Mother," I moaned. "Why did you do that? You *know* the election is just a few weeks away—"

A livid Peggy Sue cut in, sitting up so straight now, she was pulling at the tubes. "What if the media finds out about our relationship? Edward might lose his seat in the Senate!"

Mother, on the defensive, said, "I thought he had a right to know that you had been seriously injured—in light of the fact that you and he produced Brandy."

That sounded like I was a play.

In a reassuring tone even I didn't buy, I said to Sis, "Maybe he won't come. I could try to head him off—call him right away and say you're much better."

Sis glared at Mother. "*Where* on earth did *you* get his private number?"

Mother folded her hands. Looked at the floor. Then sneaked a glance at me.

Eyes wide, I spread my arms. "*I* didn't give it to her! I *swear*. She must have gotten it off my cell phone."

Mother's smile was girlish. She raised a single hand and said, "Guilty as charged."

"Get *out!*" Peggy Sue shouted. "Both of you!"

And with her I.V.-free hand, she grabbed the pillow and threw it. The thing sailed between us and plopped off the wall onto the floor.

"*Out!*"

As Mother and I beat a hasty exit, a tissue box hit me in the back. (Could have been worse—could have been a bedpan.)

Out in the hall, Sergeant Grady gave us a quizzical look, as if we were two junior high kids who had turned up a block away from a storefront window breaking. "Everything all right, ladies?"

"Why, couldn't be better," Mother declared. "It would appear that our darling Peggy Sue is back to normal."

After dropping Mother off at the house, I steered the battered Buick downtown to keep my late-morning appointment with Brian at the police station.

Downtown proper was four streets, cut into a grid by four intersecting streets, containing just about every kind of business a modest community like ours might need. The main thoroughfare was (natch) Main Street, regentrified Victorian buildings with little bistros, specialty shops, and antique stores.

The modern redbrick building of the combination police station/fire station perched at the outer edge of the grid, kitty-corner from the courthouse, that grand old Grecian edifice Mother heartily defended whenever the powers-that-be threatened to tear it down.

"Over my dead body!" was her battle-cry, and to some a tempting offer. In any case, she would inevitably swing into action—action that more than once had landed her in the county jail.

I pulled into a visitor's spot in the HQ's parking

lot, walked through an open atrium to the front entrance, and inside the small waiting room, approached the female dispatcher, sequestered behind bulletproof glass. I spoke into the little microphone.

"Brandy Borne, to see Chief Cassato—I mean, Chief Lawson . . . er . . . Acting Chief or Interim Chief—*Brian Lawson.*"

This flustered speech made no discernible impression upon the fortyish woman (short brown hair, glasses), who merely told me to take a seat. She would let the chief know I was here.

I took my usual chair next to the corner rubber tree plant, whose care and grooming had come to rely upon regular visits by Mother and me. The only difference between us was that I did not sing the appropriate excerpt from Frank Sinatra's "High Hopes" while doing my pruning.

But I had barely begun my dead-leaf-picking when the dispatcher announced that the chief would see me. Soon I was buzzed through the steel door into the inner police sanctum, where I walked down the beige corridor, its walls lined with photos of boys-in-blue of bygone days, passing the detective's room, the interview room, and other offices. All of which had become way too familiar to me in the last eighteen months or so. . . .

Whenever Mother made it past the steel door, she was escorted by one of the officers. *Out of respect,* she would say. *To keep you from snooping,* I would reply.

The chief's office was the last room on the left, next to an outside door (for a speedy exit, I supposed), and across from the break room (to keep an eye on the men, I figured); but it was odd, even strange, approaching the office where Tony Cassato had dwelled the last few years.

I half expected him to be sitting behind the desk, with his barrel chest, square jaw, gray temples, those bullet-hard eyes boring into mine as if to say, "Why don't you grow up?"

But sometimes those eyes would soften, as he handed me his handkerchief to wipe my tears and blow my nose. It was then I could see a different man behind the cold steel exterior of Tony Cassato. Yet I loved—and needed—them both.

"You doing all right, Brandy?" Brian asked, his brown eyes filled with concern.

He met me at the door, wearing his own take on the top-cop's uniform: light blue shirt (not Tony's white), pattern tie (not Tony's solid), black slacks (not Tony's gray), casual shoes (not Tony's Florsheims). Do you think I still had Tony on my mind?

"I'm fine," I said from the hall.

That the other ex-beau of the last several years had taken over Tony's job made this all the weirder. Wasn't having Vivian Borne in my life enough surrealism for one girl to stand?

He gestured to the visitor's chair in front of the desk. "Please, have a seat. . . ."

As I did so, he got behind the desk, settling into the swivel chair. But it didn't squeak when he did, like for Tony.

"I'm glad the reports on Peggy Sue are so encouraging," he said, businesslike but not without warmth. "How's Sushi?"

"She dodged a bullet, too. The vet says she can come home tomorrow."

"Dr. Tillie?"

"Yes."

"Good man. If he ever retires, Serenity will be the lesser for it."

"No question."

His expression turned serious. "We interviewed Peggy Sue earlier this morning, when she first came around, and apparently she didn't see who hit her."

"You think she was hit from behind?"

"Yes. That means whoever did it realizes Peggy Sue didn't see him, or her. So . . . with any luck, your sister isn't in any danger of retaliation." He paused, adding, "Still, we'll keep an officer at the hospital until she's released."

"Thanks. Maybe a car outside the house, too, for a day or so?"

"We can manage that."

"I realize Peg probably poses no threat to the assailant, but thank you for the added protection."

He nodded.

I shifted in the chair. I couldn't help feeling uncomfortable. Was it simply being in Tony's old office . . . or because Brian and I had once been an item? And yes, before Mother asks, I will tell you right out—we *had* been intimate.

He was saying, "Brandy, you have to promise me you'll stay out of this matter. None of this silly *Murder, She Wrote* stuff from you or Vivian."

I didn't answer immediately. If Mother had been here, she'd have been defensive, reminding

Brian that we had helped clear up a number of matters that the Serenity PD otherwise might have fumbled.

But I merely said, "I can try, Brian . . . but I can't promise. You know Mother."

He cocked his head, and a lock of sandy hair fell across his brow. He *was* a cutie-pie. Sorry if that makes you sick, a woman my age thinking about a man in such childish terms. But he was. A cutie-pie.

"You mean," he said delicately, "because your mother will get you involved whether you want her to or not?"

In the past I would have said, "Or whether you want her to or not . . . but I'll try."

But instead I replied, "Brian, someone almost killed Peggy Sue, and Sushi. Which *Jaws* movie was it?"

"Huh?"

"Where the poster said, 'This time, it's personal'? Well, this time, I'm afraid it is. Personal."

Brian's puppy dog eyes tightened into a pit bull's, and he leaned forward. He shook a finger. "Listen, Brandy, you just stay out of it. Whoever killed Jim Bob, and broke into your home, is obviously a very, *very* dangerous person."

All I could manage was "Yeah, well."

"You and your mother have been so damn lucky in the past, not getting yourselves killed, meddling in police business."

Now I cocked my head, ignoring being called a meddler, instead thinking about what he'd said before. "Sounds like you think the events were connected. Almost like . . . Brian, do you already *know* who it was?"

He held up a crossing-guard palm. "I don't know who it was. . . ."

"Brian . . ."

"But . . . I *do* know the kind of company Jim Bob McRoberts kept, back in Texas, before he returned to Serenity."

"What kind of company is that?"

He shrugged. "What do you think? Bad company."

"Maybe a little more specific?"

Now a sigh. "Drug dealers, petty thieves, ex-convicts. . . ."

"So . . . something from his past came home to roost?"

I took Brian's silence as a yes.

"But what would the killing have to do with *our* break-in?" I frowned. "There *has* to be a connection. . . ."

"Does there?"

I leaned forward. "Maybe the killer thought we'd seen something the morning of the auction—something that meant we could later identify him."

Brian winced. "Such as?"

Such as a white utility van. But I didn't say it.

"Brandy, are you holding something back?"

I just shrugged.

A guy Brian's age shouldn't have been able to summon such a weight-of-the-world sigh. "Brandy, for God's sake . . . for your *own* sake . . . please, *please* stop playing detective. Let the professionals handle it. Please?"

He was begging. This is a place where Tony wouldn't have gone, and it wasn't particularly attractive, cutie-pie or not.

But it worked on me, at least a little.

"Okay," I surrendered. "I'll try." Then, "Is there anything else?"

"No, Brandy." Another sigh. Merely weight-of-Serenity this time. "That's all."

I stood.

Brian left his chair, came around the desk, and faced me.

"Actually," he said, "there *is* one other thing. . . ."

I raised my eyebrows.

He gave me that boyish smile—the one with the dimples. "What would you think about having dinner with me sometime?"

I thought it over.

"How about it, Brandy? Old times' sake?"

"Just dinner? Nothing more?"

"Nothing more."

But I knew what would happen. I'd drink too much wine, and then we'd go back to his place, where I wouldn't be able to resist those dimples, and . . .

"When?" I asked.

I got home around noon, finding Mother in the kitchen making egg-salad sandwiches.

. I sat on a red 1950s step stool and told her about my meeting with Brian (but not our as yet unspecified dinner date, knowing she would view that primarily as an opportunity for me to wheedle info out of the acting chief).

Mother said thoughtfully, "You were correct to wonder about Big Jim Bob's past, my dear. Why *did* he come back to Serenity? Perhaps he was running from something."

"Or someone. Maybe someone who caught up with him."

Wiping her hands on a dish towel, Mother said, "Come . . . I want to show you what I found."

I followed Mother to the music room, where in my absence she had repacked the storage unit items, except for the stack of correspondence, which she now held in her hands like a devout churchgoer with a hymnal.

"Your instincts were correct, dear," she said, underplaying for once. "These have proved most interesting reading."

"Really? What are they, letters?"

"Got it in one, dear. Mostly love letters, yes— written during the Vietnam war . . . to 'Anna' from 'Stephen.' But that's not the most important discovery."

She wanted me to ask.

So I did. "Okay, Mother, what was the most important discovery?"

"Thank you for asking, dear. Among the missives was a contract for a storage unit."

That perked me up. "A storage unit? Her storage unit? *Our* storage unit?"

She nodded, smiling in that cat-that-ate-the-canary way of hers.

"So do we have a last name, to go with Anna?"

Mother nodded again, eyes and nostrils flaring. "*And* an address."

"In Serenity?"

"No. But nearby."

"Where?"

Why was she dragging this out? But I knew—Mother was an unbridled ham, and I was her audience.

"The Quad Cities, dear. We'll leave right after lunch."

Anna Armstrong's address was in Davenport—one of the five large burgs that made up the Quad Cities (don't ask). Specifically, we were heading to an area just east of the downtown, known as the Gold Coast.

On the half-hour ride, Mother gave me chapter and verse regarding this historic neighborhood of once-grand homes with magnificent views of the Mississippi River, established during the Civil War by wealthy German immigrants who had played such a large part in shaping the city.

During the 1970s, this fabled area began to lose its luster as the wealthy moved to greener pastures in the suburbs. The predictable steady decline followed, the once-grand homes left to rot and crumble, many becoming tenements, with (as Mother put it) "an unsavory, even criminal element" moving in.

In the last decade, however, various restoration and historical groups had begun buying back the properties, giving the old homes much-needed facelifts, and finding new owners who could restore the neighborhood to the magnificence of its past and its Gold Coast name.

"Turn left here, dear," Mother said.

I steered the Buick away from the downtown, up an incline lined with shade trees whose leaves shimmered in the early-afternoon sun with vibrant reds, oranges, and golds.

At the top of the hill, I turned right and drove along a similarly tree-lined street, passing refurbished homes of grandeur—some, still works in progress.

"Slow down!" Mother commanded, sitting up with the enthusiasm of Sushi out for a drive. "I want to see, I want to see!"

Leaning forward, she peered through the windshield, pointing at each passing house. "Greek Revival . . . Second Empire . . . Italianate . . . Queen Anne . . . Gothic Revival. . . ."

Mother was an acknowledged expert on architecture (acknowledged by her).

Suddenly she exclaimed, "Oh, a *stick!*"

I slammed on the brakes. "*What* stick?"

Was there a tree branch in the road?

"No, dear, upper-case *Stick* . . . not lower-case stick . . . as in architecture. It's a Stick-style house. Pull over!"

I eased the car to the curb. We got out, then positioned ourselves on the sidewalk to best stare up at the old mansion. With its towers, turrets, and balconies, the place looked like a combination Swiss chalet and medieval castle.

I said, "I'll bite—why is it called 'Stick?' "

"Because of its stickwork, dear. The exposed wood and timber?"

Which indeed gave it that Swiss chalet look.

Mother was saying, "Do you see that scaffolding on the side? Some nincompoop had dared to desecrate this work of art with"—she had trouble getting the word out, spitting it like a seed—"*siding*."

Only the one side remained to be restored.

Mother went on. "Whoever did that should be taken behind the barn and horsewhipped!"

She was old-school. But I saw her point.

Impatient to get on with the investigation, I asked, "Are we just admiring the architecture, or is this actually the right address?"

Mother shot me a look of rebuke. "Dear, it's not every day one has the opportunity to see the outside of a Stick house, let alone get *inside* one." She started up the old cracked steps. "But yes, yes, yes—this is the address in question . . . right here on West Seventh Street."

I followed her to a cement stoop with latticework overhang, where a weathered wooden door greeted us. Next to the door, on an exposed timber, were four black mailboxes with corresponding buzzers. No names were affixed to the boxes, just the street number, followed with letters A–D.

"Which one?" I asked.

"C."

But when I moved my finger to the correct buzzer, Mother grasped my hand and pulled it down like a lever.

"Let's just try the front door, dear."

She was afraid we might get turned away, and then she wouldn't get to see the inside.

"But that's breaking and entering. . . ."

"Not if it's *unlocked*."

So I tried the knob. It turned, and I pushed the door open.

We stepped into a large entryway, originally

used as a receiving hall, and I guess serving that same purpose again.

To the left—perhaps leading to the home's former parlor—was a newer door, marked "A." To the right, a similar door, "B," which could once have opened to the library. Ahead, a wide staircase with ornately carved banister yawned up to a windowed landing, then continued to the level where apartments "C" and "D" awaited.

At the bottom of the stairs, I asked, "Mother, would you like me to see if anyone's home in 'C'?"

"A few stairs won't hurt me, dear—I'm not an invalid."

But when a winded Mother leaned on the wall at the landing, I hurried on ahead.

And what I saw at the top stopped me in my tracks.

"I'm afraid we're too late," I told Mother as she reached me.

Because while the letter on the door of Anna's apartment was indeed "C," it had been revised to an "X" of crime-scene tape.

A Trash 'n' Treasures Tip

To find out where and when storage unit auctions are to be held, check local newspapers, Internet Web sites, and the schedules of individual auctioneers. Or—like Mother—you could phone the owners of the storage facilities, daily . . . at least until, like Mother, you get on their do-not-call lists.

Chapter Five

Good Neighbor Policy

As Mother and I stared in disbelief at the yellow-and-black tape, someone behind us spoke, and we turned to see a tall, slender man framed in the apartment doorway across the hall.

"Can I *help* you?" he asked, repeating himself pointedly.

Anna Armstrong's across-the-way neighbor was about fifty—judging by the gray hair winning over the brown—with an oblong face, long nose, and bushy eyebrows overhanging puffy-pouched eyes. Conservatively dressed in brown slacks and an argyle yellow-and-navy sweater, he regarded us with understandable suspicion.

Mother said, "We stopped by to see our dear, sweet Anna"—she gestured to the tape, then touched her bosom—". . . only to find this disturbing sight."

The puffy eyes narrowed skeptically. "'*Our*' Anna? You mean, you're related?"

I glanced at Mother—wondering why she had implied as much—and waited for her next move. She was the actress—let *her* do the improv.

Mother raised a hand to her forehead, moaning, "Ohhh, I feel *faint* . . ."

I couldn't remember Mother ever claiming to feel faint before, at least outside of a melodrama at the Playhouse—not even when we'd stumbled onto the occasional corpse.

But taking her cue, I slipped an arm around her waist, and asked the neighbor, "Could we come in for a moment? I'm so sorry to impose, but Mother needs to sit down. . . ."

The man hesitated, but then Mother's pitiful if put-on state turned his suspicion to compassion, and he replied, "Why, certainly, ladies."

"That's very kind of you," I said. But I wasn't sure I liked being thought of as a "lady" by a guy twenty years older than me.

He stepped aside, and I assisted the apparently distressed Mother (overplaying her part but apparently getting away with it) across the threshold and inside, revealing much if not most of a tidy apartment—a small parlor and large bedroom separated by a lattice archway.

The neighbor motioned to a brown leather couch—the only modern furniture among Victorian antiques—and as we sat, Mother asked ludicrously, "Could I trouble you, dear sir, for a glass of water?"

"Of course," he replied graciously. "I'll only be a moment."

When he had disappeared through the bedroom,

to a room beyond, Mother whispered, "Just so you know, dear, not wanting to alarm you . . ." And this she mouthed: "I'm faking."

"What a relief," I whispered. "Here I was ready to find the nearest ER."

She brightened. "Really?"

"Give me a little credit, you big ham."

She ignored that and went on, sotto voce: "We must get as much information as possible out of our benefactor during our short stay. I believe he's rather taken with me."

I shut my eyes, wishing for a swift, merciful death.

He was returning.

"Follow my lead," Mother whispered.

"Like I have a choice."

Our host came over and handed Mother the glass of water, which she downed no more greedily than some desert nomad stranded for days on the sands of the Sahara. Four glugs later, she handed the empty glass back with a great sigh and a brave smile.

"Thank you, Mr. uh—?"

"Anderson. John. I own the house."

"Well, it's a lovely old structure," Mother said. "I do so admire Stick architecture."

He brightened. "Yes. It's unique. I'm happy to have the chance to restore it."

She sat up straight, a little too quickly, reality edging out performance. "Then Anna was your tenant?"

He nodded. "That's right. Place is half-empty because I'm gradually getting rid of my tenants."

Mother blinked at him. That got my attention, too.

His smile was warm and embarrassed. "Forgive the poor choice of words. I'm just not renewing leases. You see, once the outside renovation is complete, I plan on turning this wonderful old place into a bed-and-breakfast."

Mother clapped, once, making me jump a little. "What a delightful idea!" she burbled.

His eyes narrowed again; perhaps he was just a trifle suspicious, thanks to Mother's miraculous recovery. "I'm sorry. . . . You *are* . . . ?"

"Oh, how silly of me!" Mother gushed. "How rude! I'm Vivian, and this is my youngest daughter, Brandy."

She left "Borne" off, though I wasn't sure why. Possibly she feared our prior escapades might have made the local news, since Serenity was only thirty miles south of the Cities. Or maybe she was just reluctant to leave a trail.

Mr. Anderson, taking an old wood-and-leather captain's chair opposite us, asked, "And how are you girls related to Anna?"

We were girls now, not ladies. I was fine with that.

His smile took a little of the edge off, when he added, "I'm afraid I don't recall her ever mentioning you."

Mother shifted on the couch. "Oh, we're *distant* relatives . . . from a shirttail branch of the family tree."

I crinkled my nose, and tried to smile cute—I was a "girl," remember. "More like a twig."

His eyes remained narrowed and suspicious, but his voice took on a surprisingly gentle, oddly tentative tone. "So, then . . . you didn't know about Anna?"

Mother seemed about to say, "Line!" to someone offstage, so I said, "Know what about Anna? Is it something to do with that crime scene? Was she robbed?"

Following my cue this time, Mother managed, "I certainly hope she hasn't been injured!"

"Much worse, I'm afraid. I hate to be the bearer of bad tidings, ladies. . . ."

Ladies again.

". . . but Anna passed away recently."

Genuinely surprised, Mother said, "Oh my!"

" 'Passed away' is, I'm afraid, a misguiding euphemism. She was . . . murdered. I had assumed you knew."

"Goodness no!" Mother said.

"We've been out of the country," I offered. "Italy."

Which would have been fine, if Mother hadn't simultaneously said "Russia."

"First Italy, then Russia," I revised. "It was a tour. One of those special packages?"

He was trying to make sense out of that when Mother asked, "Mr. Anderson, when did this happen?"

Our unlikely tour forgotten, or at least shelved, he said, "About a month ago."

I sat forward. "But the crime scene tape—why is it still there? Surely after that much time. . . ."

Mr. Anderson shrugged. "I left it in place as a deterrent. A good number of Anna's things are still in the apartment. She died intestate, and my attorney is working to see how her estate might be settled. You're the only relatives who've shown up."

This may have explained why he'd viewed us with some suspicion, after Mother implied we were related to the late Anna. And it put us in an awkward place right now. . . .

Maybe I wasn't an actress, but I didn't want to leave this to Mother's improvisational skills, which would have her drawing on everything from Agatha Christie novels to *Gaslight.*

So I said, "We're only relatives by marriage, and distant at that. I can't imagine we'd have any claim. We only looked Anna up a few years ago because we'd wound up in the same part of the country."

"Yes," Mother said too eagerly. "Same part of the country."

Was I just digging the hole deeper?

"Well," he said, "before you go, I'll give you my attorney's contact information. You might as well put in for the stuff. There are a few nice pieces. I believe there are some other things, probably of no particular value, in a storage unit somewhere."

With too much expression, even for her, Mother said, "Really? Isn't that interesting."

What was interesting about it?

"Well, it's a shock to hear about Anna," Mother said. At least she had the sense to get us off this track and back on the other. "Simply terrible. I hope she didn't suffer. I *had* heard this area became infested with crime, but I thought it was under control as of late."

Mr. Anderson sighed. "We've made significant

strides—with the help of watch groups and the police—but that kind of thing can't be completely eradicated."

I asked, "Was it a burglary?"

He nodded, and his expression grew overtly sorrowful. "And Anna woke up. Hard not to—just not that big an apartment."

Mother asked, "How did the burglar get in?"

Something close to anguish crossed Mr. Anderson's face. For a long moment, he didn't answer.

Finally he said, "The scaffolding . . . for the remodeling? It was beneath her window at the time."

"Oh, my," Mother said softly.

His pain was palpable, and I felt compelled to comment. "You mustn't blame yourself."

"But I do. . . ." He stood abruptly, walked over to a watercolor picture of the house framed on the wall, and stared at it. "You see, Anna and I . . . we were going to run the B and B together."

This last was spoken so softly, it might have been to himself. Had he been in love with his neighbor?

Mr. Anderson turned with a sigh. "I don't think she suffered. Apparently she heard sounds, and went to see what they were . . . perhaps she was headed to the door, to come get me. I'll never know."

I asked, as gently as possible, "She was . . . struck a blow?"

He nodded. "From behind. You hear that phrase all the time on television and in film—a 'blunt object.' When the police used those words, I almost smiled at such a cliché."

Somehow I knew he hadn't smiled.

Our host was gazing at Mother, his expression pleasant now. "You're feeling better, I see."

"I . . . I *think* so."

What was that about?

He checked his watch. "I'm afraid I must ask you to go. I teach an adult education class in an hour, and have preparations to make."

Mother nudged me with her foot, which I took to mean *stall.*

Feigning interest, I said, "Adult education. That's such a positive thing." *That's such a banal remark,* I thought, then asked, "What is it you teach?"

"Accounting."

Nowhere to go with that subject; my checkbook hadn't been balanced for years. And if I said, *Oh, that's interesting,* he'd know I was a liar. Even accountants know accounting is boring.

Vamping, I said, "You know, this house seems strangely familiar. . . ."

Actually it did.

"You may have seen it on TV. Or somewhere in the local media."

"Really?"

The owner of the Stick mansion smiled. "The old place is a landmark to folks around here."

"Why's that?" I asked.

Mother had quietly left the couch to go behind Mr. Anderson; I could see her snooping through his mail on a table by the door.

He was saying, "This house was built by Charles and Louise Beiderbecke."

"Oh," I said, and smiled unconvincingly.

"Beiderbecke?" he prompted. This time I was the one who needed to be fed a line from offstage.

Then I got it. Anybody who lived in this part of the world knew the name Beiderbecke, which belonged to one of the most famous jazz musicians of all time, and who was Davenport's favorite son.

This time I didn't have to fake it when I said, "Oh! Were they Bix Beiderbecke's parents?"

"Grandparents. Bix grew up in a house on Grand Avenue, which is still there."

Bits and pieces of information from articles and short news stories on local TV came flooding in. "Is it true that his parents disowned him because he loved to play jazz?"

Mr. Anderson was about to respond, but Mother cut in with, "Dear! I think you've taken up enough of this gentleman's time—he doesn't need to be pestered with all your foolish questions."

"Sorry," I muttered. Just *once* couldn't *she* be the shill?

I rose, and our host said, "It's really no trouble. I'm quite interested in Bix."

Mother came around and said, "As am I, and I can fill my daughter in without imposing on you any further, and making you late for class."

We thanked Mr. Anderson for his hospitality, then departed, heading down the grand staircase and out to the street.

Behind the wheel of the Buick, I looked at Mother.

"*Russia?*"

"Dear, you know I've always wanted to go to Russia."

"Since when?"

"Why, I've mentioned it many times. You know I'm fascinated by all those dolls within dolls. You just don't listen. And for that matter, why Italy of all places?"

Lamely, I said, "I do like pasta."

"Well, I admit that tour was a nice save, dear. All in all, quite a successful mission. Nice old gentleman."

John Anderson was easily twenty-five years younger than her.

I said, "You sure took a chance implying we were related to Anna. You dug us quite a hole."

"Pish posh. *Everyone* is related if you go back far enough. Now, drive around the block, then pull over."

"What for?"

"Because we're going back as soon as Mr. Anderson leaves for that class of his."

"What for?"

"Why, to search our late relative's apartment, of course."

I twisted toward her. "I'm not climbing any scaffolding!"

"No need, dear." Mother smiled. "While you were keeping Mr. Anderson busy . . . ? I found *this*."

And she waved a key attached to a round white tag that read "C."

We waited on a side street until Anderson—still in his distinctive yellow-and-navy sweater—glided by, apparently none the wiser about our lingering presence.

"Mother," I said, wide-eyed. "He's driving a white van."

"Yes, dear," she answered. "My glasses may be as thick as Coke bottles, but I can see that! You know, when Coca-Cola switched to plastic, they really ruined the flavor—their product tastes so much better in glass."

"Mother—could we stay on point? You do remember the white van at the storage facility? Possibly watching?"

"If that *was* him yesterday morning, then he would have recognized us."

"Maybe he did."

"He didn't appear to."

"Mother, people have been known to be deceptive when it's to their advantage."

"When you make sarcastic remarks, dear, you wrinkle your brow, and that will have a lasting effect, if you're not careful."

But I kept wrinkling. "If he knows who we are, why didn't he out us? Why play games?"

Mother shrugged. "For the same reason we pretended to be relatives of Anna's—to gather information." She opened her car door. "That class may only last an hour or so. Let's get started."

Soon we were back at the Beiderbecke house, slipping in the front door, sneaking up the grand staircase.

Quickly, Mother undid the crime scene tape across apartment "C," then inserted the borrowed key in the lock, and we stepped into a dark, musty room.

Groping for a light switch, I found one, and we stood surveying our surroundings.

Anna's apartment mirrored Anderson's—combination parlor and bedroom—and was similarly furnished with Victorian antiques. Heavy drapes were drawn across the windows, except for one, which was boarded up. Where the burglar had broken in, obviously.

I asked, "What are we looking for anyway?"

Mother, already going through papers at a quaint writing desk, said, "Anything of importance."

"Like what?"

When she didn't answer, I walked over to an easel in front of the boarded-up window—sunlight bleeding through the cracks—and peered at the watercolor landscape Anna had been painting, and would never finish.

Mother let out a low cry. "Ah! Now *this* is significant."

"What?"

Again she didn't answer, stuffing whatever she had found into her coat pocket.

It was no fun being Watson, not the Nigel Bruce one anyway.

I wandered back through the bedroom area, where a closed door led to a modern kitchen—most likely another transformed bedroom. Unlike the messy parlor, the kitchen had been straightened—no dishes in the sink, or food on the counters; one area had been used as a workspace, with a laptop computer.

I turned the machine on to check Anna's e-mail, but when asked for a password, I got no further. And swiping the computer didn't seem like an option worthy of pursuit, even if I did know somebody who might be able to plumb its depths.

A quick search through a small wastebasket beneath the counter—filled mostly with junk mail—

did produce an interesting letter. Which *I* stuffed in *my* pocket.

"Dear . . ."

I jumped.

Mother, behind me, said, "Sorry, dear . . . didn't mean to scare you."

"What?"

"My intuition tells me we must go. . . ."

And Mother's intuition was rarely wrong.

I followed her back through the bedroom to the parlor where she stood for a moment looking around.

"I think everything is how we found it. . . ."

I asked, "You have the key?"

She nodded.

"How will we get it back to Anderson?"

"You'll see."

We slipped out, locking the apartment door behind us, Mother carefully replacing the crime scene tape, which had enough stick-'em left to do the trick.

Just outside John Anderson's door, Mother knelt down, then slid the key beneath, giving it a good push along the polished floor.

"Think that'll fool him?" I asked skeptically.

Mother shrugged. "He'll never know for sure whether we took the key, or he accidentally dropped it. Brandy?"

"Yes?"

"Small problem. I can't get up."

I took Mother's elbow and tugged, helping her stand. Nice when Watson could contribute to the cause.

On our way down the staircase again, I commented, "There *is* another way the burglar could have gotten in to Anna's apartment besides using the scaffolding, you know."

"Which is?"

"That key."

Mother paused on the landing. "You mean our friend Mr. Anderson?"

I nodded.

"But, why, dear? He clearly loved the woman. She painted that watercolor of this place."

"Love's a great murder motive. We've seen that enough. Could be unrequited love . . . jealousy . . . lover's quarrel gotten out of hand. When love's around, things can go wrong."

Mother had no comment, but her eyes were narrow with thought behind the thick lenses.

On the porch, I said, "So this old house is connected to Bix Beiderbecke. Isn't it a funny coincidence that an old beat-up horn was the only thing stolen at our break-in?"

"But I've had that horn for ages, dear. It had no connection to the storage unit. Anyway, don't you think the horn was the blunt instrument used on your sister? And that the miscreant took the evidence with him to dispose of?"

That made sense.

But so, suddenly, did something else.

"Mother—we *do* have a trumpet that came out of that storage unit! It's in our garage."

"Well, that's right, dear." Then, as if she'd seen a ghost, she gripped my sleeve. "But it's not a trumpet, it's a cornet."

"Does it matter?"

"It may matter a great deal."

"Why?"

"*Bix* played cornet."

In the car, on the side street, Mother withdrew a photo from the pocket where she'd stowed it. She handed it to me—a picture of a man and two teenage boys.

"Isn't that Milton Lawrence?" I asked. "A lot younger than I ever remember seeing him. But isn't that him?"

The photo had been taken decades ago—late 1960s, judging by the boys' mod clothes and Beatle haircuts.

Lawrence, now in his early eighties, was Serenity's wealthiest citizen, thanks in part to the money his wife had left him. I had no knowledge of when or how she'd died; I just knew she'd inherited plenty from ancestors who had made a fortune in logging in the early 1800s when Serenity had been known as Bloomington.

"That's Milton, all right," Mother said.

So she was on a first-name basis with the wealthy coot. I did not detect any hint of intimacy, however.

"How about the two boys?" I asked her, not recognizing either.

"His sons. One died in Vietnam . . . the other lives in Canada . . . though, as far as his father is concerned, he might as well be dead, too."

"What?"

"Nothing, dear." Returning the photo to her pocket, she asked, "And what did *you* find? I could tell by your self-satisfied expression that you struck gold."

"Fool's gold, maybe. Anyway—this letter."

Which she took from me, reading aloud, " 'Dear Miss Armstrong, I'm sorry I missed you the other day. I hope you'll reconsider my offer. As you will discover, I don't give up easily when I set my sights on something. I hope to hear from you soon. Sincerely, Waldo Hendricks.' "

"Who the heck's that?"

Mother dropped the letter in her lap. "Oh, you know, dear—that pompous poop who runs that ridiculous antique store in the Village of East Davenport."

"Oh! You mean, that guy who overprices everything and won't haggle?"

She nodded. "*Or* give us a dealer's discount."

Mother never forgot a slight—real or imagined.

"He's always such a jerk. Please tell me we don't have to go talk to him."

"You know we do, dear," Mother said. "We need to find out what he wanted so badly from Anna."

The redundantly named Antiquarian Antiques, with its faux-weathered WALDO HENDRICKS, PROPRIETOR sign in the window, was lodged in a three-story Victorian brick building on the corner of Mound and East Eleventh.

Parking was free in the East Village, and we found a place right in front of the shop, where we quickly entered, a tinkling bell above the door announcing our presence.

Mr. Hendricks—late forties, mustached, wearing a dark pinstriped suit more befitting a banker—was seated at a tidy desk just inside the door. He looked up from his *Antiques Trader* with bored eyes, and intoned, "Oh, it's you."

Since I had rarely been in the shop, and exchanged perhaps a dozen words with him, the owner's displeasure was clearly aimed at Mother, suggesting they had a history of which I was only a small part.

At any rate, Mother tossed her head and said, "And how very nice to see you again, too, Waldo."

"Always a pleasure, Vivian," he said, his tone implying the exact opposite. Then, after a perfunctory, barely audible, "If I can be of any help," he returned to his magazine.

I prowled around, taking in the merchandise, knowing it would reflect the owner's taste in antiques, in this instance lots of red velvet chairs, massive mahogany beds, and overly ornate lamps with fringes and tassels—what Mother terms Victorian Bordello (and I call San Francisco Whorehouse).

Mother had moved on, through the front room to the second, larger one, where more of the same (to me) tacky furnishings awaited. I caught up with her in front of the last, not terribly large room, entry blocked by a metal turnstile.

A sign posted said:

BIX BEIDERBECKE MUSEUM
Recommended Donation $5.00

Affixed to the wall was a padlocked wooden box with a slit for donations, under a sign stating that all proceeds would benefit the Bix Philanthropic Society.

I asked Mother, "Just who or what *is* that society?"

She grunted. "You just saw him."

"Waldo?"

"Waldo."

And she pushed through the metal gate without paying.

As museums went, this one was pretty darn sparse, running to photos of the young musician (circa the 1920s), some sheet music, and a few old-time records—in various glass display cases, of course. There was even a rather embarrassing store manikin dressed in a twenties tux meant to represent Bix, but Madame Tussauds had nothing to worry about.

Still, one display had earned Mother's attention—an old, gold cornet, labeled with a white placard: SIMILAR TO THE CORNET USED BY BIX.

"And isn't *that* similar to the one *we* just got?" I asked.

"*Now* we know what Waldo wanted from Anna," Mother said.

She turned abruptly, and I had to hurry to catch up as she made a beeline back to Waldo Hendricks.

"*We* have Anna's cornet," Mother told him, laying all her cards on the table.

Hendricks looked up again from his periodical; but his eyes were not so bored this time. "Indeed? And where did you get it?"

With admirable lack of embellishment or melodrama, Mother told him about winning the storage unit auction, and running across his letter to Anna, although she did imply the missive had been among the contents of the unit.

Hendricks sat forward, elbows on the desk, hands tented. "Tell me—what kind of cornet *is* it? The brand name, I mean. . . ."

Mother didn't miss a beat: "A Bach. Stradivarius."

Hendricks sat back, the bored eyes returning. "It's of no import, now. My museum already has a Bach Stradivarius. When Miss Armstrong wouldn't part with hers, I found one on the Internet."

Mother was not good enough an actress to disguise her crestfallen reaction.

I tried to salvage the situation. "The one we have is in better condition—almost good as new, without the dings and dents. How much had you offered Anna for it?"

"Two hundred fifty."

Something jumped in Mother's eyes. She had that expression whenever she'd connected the dots. "What if that horn belonged to Bix himself? It came from the Bix mansion, after all!"

The dealer's expression could not have been more bored, his eyes lidded, his response almost drowsy. "That is not the 'Bix mansion,' Vivian, it's Bix's grandparents' home. And in any event, it did not come from there."

"Well, it certainly did!"

"It came from Anna Armstrong, who told me it was a gift from an old boyfriend. She was merely a woman with an old cornet who happened to live in a home with a connection to Bix Beiderbecke."

The dots disconnected and Mother's eyes lost their spark. Momentarily. Then they and she came alive again, and she blurted, "You can have it for two hundred! It's *still* a better example than the one you have."

His mouth moving as if trying to taste the memory of a meal, Hendricks contemplated our offer.

"Well," he said slowly, "I'd have to *see* the cornet first. I might be in the market for a *nicer* example. Can you bring it in tomorrow morning?"

"Certainly!" Mother chirped in a high-pitched manner worthy of Curly Howard.

And then she did something silly but very much in character: she saluted him.

And before she could do further damage, I pulled her out the door by her sleeve.

Out on the sidewalk, Mother asked, "Why the long face, dear? If Waldo takes our offer, we'll have doubled what we paid for the storage unit on that one item alone."

"I know . . . I just thought . . . after that Bix house? That we'd get more. And I thought we'd figured out what the valuable item was that our intruder was after—*and* Anna's."

Mother put a finger to her chin. "It *does* seem like we should get a better price—collectible cornets aren't exactly plentiful, having gone out of fashion when Harry James traded his in for a trumpet."

I mused, "What do you suppose it *would* be worth, if it had belonged to Bix?"

Mother thought for a moment. "I would imagine quite a lot. Why, the right Bix Beiderbecke collector might pay a small fortune for such a thing—perhaps thousands. You know, some of those antiquing people are bonkers!"

We arrived back in Serenity by early dusk, an orange harvest moon hanging low in the sky, having usurped a yellow sun.

The first thing I did was head to the garage to retrieve Anna's cornet, which I then brought into the music room.

Mother appeared and, taking the gold-plated horn from me, said, "You know, I used to play a pretty mean 'Boogie Woogie Bugle Boy of Company B.' "

I had heard this proclamation a hundred times, and so far had been able to avoid any such performance. This time, however, I decided to put an end to it.

"Go ahead," I challenged her, settling into an armchair.

Mother immediately backpedaled. "Of course, it *has* been a while . . . the old embouchure ain't what she used to be! That's 'lip,' dear, in musician speak."

"Oh . . . I think you still have *plenty* of lip left."

Ignoring that, she said, "Well, here goes. . . ."

She brought the mouthpiece up and blew into the little horn.

Nothing came out.

Not even a sour note.

"Maybe the valves are in wrong," Mother said.

She unscrewed the trio of cylinders, and withdrew them one at a time, checking.

"No," she said, puzzled. "They're in correctly. They could use some valve oil, but they're in, all right."

"Try again," I encouraged. "Blow harder."

Mother did . . .

. . . and two projectiles flew out of the horn's bell.

I bent over them, where they landed—pieces of folded paper, one small and yellowed with age, the other white with the appearance of stationery.

"What are those, dear?" Mother asked. "Music?"

I picked them up, unfolding the white one first.

" 'November 25, 1969,' " I read. " 'My darling Anna, please keep this cornet for me until I return. It once belonged to the great Bix Beiderbecke, and it may have some value one day. It sure holds sentimental value for me, thinking of the nights we spent listening to old jazz 78s in the rec room. I hope to come home on leave for Christmas. All my love . . . Stephen.' "

Mother's jaw hung loose by its hinges, her eyes wide and wild—and if my expression mirrored hers, I wouldn't be surprised.

She pointed excitedly to the smaller paper in my hand. "And that?"

I unfolded it.

"It's a receipt for the horn," I said, "from a music store on West 48th Street in New York." My jaw dropped. "And signed by Bix himself!"

"Good Lord," Mother cried, then spat, "Two

hundred bucks, my sweet patootie! Darling, we've hit the jackpot!"

"Yeah," I said, my smile morphing into a frown. "And the murder motive. . . ."

A Trash 'n' Treasures Tip

Keep in mind that many delinquent storage unit tenants often wait until the last minute to pay their back rent, which is why it's best to plan on attending several different auctions. Mother calls this hedging a bet, but I call it not wasting your time.

Chapter Six

A Snitch in Time

Vivian speaking, or that is, writing. Today I will be doing some investigating on my own—and you're invited! Brandy will be occupied with bringing Peggy Sue home from the hospital, and Sushi back from the veterinarian. More of that later. . . .

But before we begin our inquiries, I must digress momentarily to defend myself from unfair accusations and depictions, and set a few things straight with you, dear reader.

First of all, I would like to thank those who have taken of your precious time to contact our publisher requesting that more of my literary stylings be included in these volumes. As of this book, however, I am *still* confined to one paltry chapter (not counting the half chapter at the start that I managed to finesse), so keep those e-mails and letters a-comin', friends and neighbors!

(And you will be relieved to learn that I am no longer to be restricted to a strict word count. Honestly, who counts words! As the old saying goes, it's the thought that counts, and besides, it's not as if a few meager sentences would save a tree. What good was accomplished by cutting me off in mid-sentence in *Antiques Flee Market?* I ask you!)

Secondly, some of the glass-half-empty types among my followers wrote to express disappointment when—after four books—I was *finally* allowed to complete my hilarious, heartwarming story about little Billy Buckly, whose grandfather was one of the Munchkins in *The Wizard of Oz* (standing right behind Judy Garland in "The Lollipop Guild" number). Well, much as it pains me not to please you, surely you can understand that the buildup over so long a time was simply too much for the story to live up to your great expectations. (To make amends, I have another trolley tale—even more amusing—which I will soon share with you . . . without interruption!)

Thirdly, I do not feel that I am responsible for the departure of former chief Tony Cassato. How could I have guessed that the story I concocted and disseminated throughout our community might accidentally contain elements of truth? Who could have guessed that the New Jersey mob really *did* have a contract out on the chief? Certainly not *moi!*

I'd merely been trying to flush out (and flesh out) the mysterious past of that tight-lipped enigma, and had no intention of putting him— much less Brandy—in any real danger, or even to bust up their romance. My goodness, don't you think I would have *relished* having that balding Brando (middle period) for a son-in-law? Why, I get all goose pimply just thinking about the classified police information I could have pried out of him via Brandy!

Yes, if it came to that, Brian Lawson would also make a good son-in-law (should his renewed relationship with Brandy ever come to fruition), and he treats me with (marginally) more respect than his predecessor. Plus, he would make a passable permanent chief of police—ripe for putty-in-my-hands molding, though Vivian Borne would much prefer more of a challenge.

For those of you reading this book in a creative writing class (what a wretchedly redundant name for such a class—*of course* it's creative!)—keep in mind that what I've written here so far serves two purposes: backstory and characterization. Any complaints that I'm not moving the story along fast enough *(Brandy)* are balderdash (a perfectly good word not used near enough these days).

On this beautiful, warm Indian summer day, I quickly dressed in one of my colorful fall outfits (can't go wrong with Breckenridge!) (particularly not if you go to Ingram's Department Store on Wednesday Senior's Day, plus take a coupon, *and* use their store credit card, getting 20% off 20% off 20%—it's worth admitting you're over sixty-five!).

I packed a large orange tote with a few items, then headed out the door to catch the gas-powered trolley due momentarily, just down the block.

The reconverted trolley car (sponsored by the downtown merchants to fight customer exodus to the mall) was a fine, free way for me to get around without being beholden to Brandy. Everything of

importance in Serenity was within a four-block ra-
dius: the magnificent old courthouse and city hall,
the new police station and fire department, the
newer county jail. But today, I wasn't interested in
any of those municipalities.

Like any good detective, I was on my way to get
the latest skinny from my snitches.

The trolley ran a tad late, and as I stepped on-
board I could see that the driver, Maynard Kirby,
looked a little grumpy, so I chose not to berate
him for his tardiness.

Maynard had been through much personal
strife these past few years. When his wife, Phyllis,
lost his fish-hatchery pension playing blackjack on
the gambling boat, he was forced to take a post-
retirement job driving the trolley. Then a few
months later, Phyllis won a bundle on a slot machine at a casino, and he was able to quit the trolley. But soon she lost *that* money playing on-line
poker, so after so much financial yo-yoing, it was
no wonder poor Maynard was down in the dumps.

Maynard—late sixties, bespectacled, his salt-and-
pepper hair matching a trim beard—eyed me war-
ily as I took a front seat (most likely fearful I might
ask him the favor of deviating from his designated
route to drop me somewhere or other).

But I merely said, "Main Street . . . Hunter's
Hardware, to be specific."

He nodded curtly, and closed the trolley door. I
settled back for the picturesque drive down Mulberry Avenue, and soon we were passing some of
the grandest old homes in Serenity, their manicured lawns speared with colorful trees, porches
bedecked with potted fall mums.

The trolley was nearly empty—just a few people in the back—so I felt it well within my purview to raise my voice a trifle over the motor rumble and say, "I heard Phyllis made another killing."

Maynard took his eyes off the road for a second. "You heard right."

"Casino, was it?"

"Lottery."

"So will you be leaving the trolley again?"

"No. She already lost it all."

"Heavens to Betsy. How?"

"Roulette."

"My goodness, she certainly likes a *variety* of the games."

"Not really . . . When she loses at something, I make her promise not to play that again."

"Shrewd."

"But that just means she tries something new." He paused, then risked another glance. "Can't be many games left for her to run through. . . ."

I thought a moment. "There's still craps, dice, horse- and dog-racing, plus all those sweepstakes that come in the mail. What you need is to get a more specific promise out of her!"

We had arrived on Main Street, and as Maynard eased the trolley to the curb in front of Hunter's Hardware, I stood, then disembarked with this parting advice, "Get Phyllis to promise she won't play anything except bingo!"

(I didn't mention that I knew a woman, who, playing multiple cards, lost five C's in one week.) (A "C" is detective talk for one hundred dollars.)

The trolley pulled away with a little belch, which I didn't take personally, and I entered the hardware store, a little bell above the door winning an angel its wings and announcing my presence.

Hunter's hadn't changed since I was in bloomers (figuratively speaking, since of course I am not of an age ever to have worn bloomers), with the same scratched wooden floor, painted tin ceiling, and ancient fans keeping the stale air circulating.

The elongated store was a uniquely Midwestern aberration: while the front section sold everything one might expect of a modern hardware business, the rear was given over to a small bar, offering hard liquor to hard workers who came in for hardware.

Once in a blue moon, someone would imbibe too much before stumbling home and putting their purchases into practice, with an evening of drinking and woodworking coming to an unfortunate finish (and not in the furniture sense). The most recent incident had to do with a table saw and a missing index finger, by which I do not mean the finger had gone missing, just gone. Despite this, Hunter's had only rarely been sued and its various owners never contemplated closing the hardware store-cum-bar.

Ironically, Hunter's was owned and operated by a middle-aged married couple—Junior and Mary— who'd bought the establishment with money Mary received in a settlement some years ago after losing a leg in a freak accident visiting the *Jaws* attraction at Universal Studios.

Mary, who had quickly mastered her prosthesis, had slaved in the hardware end of the business for years, while goof-off Junior took the relative easy task of tending the bar. But last month, Mary finally put her foot down (so to speak), and announced that she'd had enough of the hardware trade, and was going to stay home and live a life of leisure, i.e., watch the Game Show Network.

Now Hunter's had a new employee running the front end, a young male veteran recently back from Iraq, who was a lot easier on the eyes than Mary. He, too, had lost a leg and did a jim-dandy job with his prosthesis (unfortunately, his loss of limb hadn't been the moneymaker Mary's had, since his had been lost in defense of his country and not at a theme park).

"Hello, Matthew," I greeted the ex-soldier. He was in his late twenties with cropped blond hair, tanned face, neck the size of a tree trunk, muscles straining at his tan work clothes. I report these details merely by way of good reporting and intending in no way to objectify this sweat-pearled hunk, that is, young man.

" 'morning, Mrs. Borne," he answered, looking up from a display of wrenches he was stocking. "Need anything today?"

"No, Matthew. My supply of duct tape and epoxy glue is holding up just fine, thank you."

"You still claim you can fix anything with just those two items?"

"I do. But don't tell your other customers, or Hunter's will be out of business in a fortnight."

He smiled, but also frowned a little. It was just possible he didn't know what a fortnight was. Nor did I, but I've always liked the sound of it.

I breezed on through to the bar, where Junior was polishing glasses behind the old marred counter.

Junior—fifty years ago his name might have been

more befitting—was a paunchy, rheumy-eyed, mottled-nosed gent who made a great bartender but a low-grade gossip, continually getting his facts mixed up. (Not wanting the good people of Serenity to get the wrong idea, I asked Junior to help spread the word that Brandy was going to be a surrogate mother, and he told everyone *I* was having the child.)

At this early hour, the bar was empty but for Henry, whom I considered more of a fixture than a customer. In his mid-fifties, slender, with silver hair, a beak nose, and his original set of teeth, Serenity's favorite barfly had been a prominent surgeon until one day, after slightly anesthetizing himself with bourbon, he expertly removed a patient's gallbladder—unfortunately, his mission had been to remove an appendix.

Unlike Junior, Henry had for years been a gold mine of information, giving up one glittering nugget of gossip after another. Lately that mine had been shut down, however. You see, not long ago I had made the mistake of sobering him up, and Henry returned from his decades-long stupor with a clear mind . . . including clear of much of his memory.

I took a tattered leather stool one down from Henry, who was still a constant customer here at Hunter's, only now he nursed not a whiskey but a nonalcoholic beer. He was neat as a pin in a yellow sport shirt and rust-color slacks and he had some tan left from getting back out on the golf course. Yes, he'd crawled out of the pit of despair and back into society's good graces. (He'd never practice medicine again, but his family had money.)

Happy as I was for Henry, the loss of a good snitch is a painful one for the amateur detective.

Junior was shaking his head. "Terrible about Big Jim Bob, just terrible. Getting shot like that, poor fella."

"He was struck a blow from behind," I said.

"Shot in the back, you mean."

"No, Junior. Jim Bob was hit on the head."

He frowned. "I thought *you* got hit on the head."

"No. That was Peggy Sue."

"Oh my God, Vivian! I didn't know! When was the funeral?"

"Peggy Sue was knocked out, Junior. She wasn't killed, but I do appreciate the sentiment."

You see? Worthless.

"Give me the usual," I said.

"Sure thing, Viv."

"And make it a double!"

Junior's bushy eyebrows climbed his forehead like caterpillars heading across a sidewalk to high grass. "Okay, Viv, if you say so. . . ."

While he turned his back to prepare my special concoction (and this, at least, he was capable of doing very well), I turned my attention to Henry.

"Hello, Henry."

He smiled and nodded, his eyes distressingly clear. "Vivian."

Oh well. One must always try, even in the face of hopelessness.

"Henry, were you by any chance acquainted with Big Jim Bob?"

Henry gazed for a moment into his glass of O'Doul's, perhaps looking for an answer, or contemplating diving in. "I knew him years ago," he said. "It's pretty vague. Apparently we were friends."

"Oh?"

"Not that long ago, he sat next to me here and we talked and he drank and I"—he lifted his O'Doul's—"drank."

"I was wondering why he'd returned to Serenity after all these years."

Junior set my double-tall, double-cherry Shirley Temple in front of me. (One of my classes at the School of Hard Knocks had taught me not to mix alcohol with my bipolar meds.)

"I don't believe he *returned* as much as he . . . hightailed it from somewhere else. From *something* else."

"From where? From what?"

"In a way, himself. He commented, after more beers than is prudent, that he was running from his past."

In a clear-eyed, clear-voiced, clear-minded manner (that I admit I found unsettling) the former souse shared with me his barroom conversation with Big Jim Bob.

Here is the gist: two days before his murder, Big Jim Bob confided in Henry that a business venture—another storage unit facility, in fact—had gone "south" in Texas, his partner accusing him of skimming off profits. The partner had tracked Big Jim Bob to Serenity, and was making threats. Details of those threats—whether in person or by phone—were not shared with Henry.

"That's it, Vivian. That's all I have for you."

I grasped his shoulder. "You are reinstated as a

snitch in good standing, Henry! Junior, put his next six nonalcoholic beers on my tab!"

Henry thanked me, then winced in thought. "I have a feeling Big Jim Bob was a fairly shady character, back in the day. But you know my memory is pretty fuzzy, presobriety."

With Henry's well of information having gone as dry as he was, I asked Junior, "Would you happen to know where the Romeos are having lunch today?"

The Romeos (Retired Old Men Eating Out) were an informal club of senior men who had been another good source for information for me over the years. A collective snitch.

Junior shifted uneasily behind the bar. "Can't say, Viv."

"*Can't* say, Junior? Or *won't?*"

Junior seemed like he might cry. "They made me promise not to give you their whereabouts no more."

"Oh, fiddle faddle!"

An excellent snack, by the way, Fiddle Faddle (free cartons of the delicious popcorn confection can be shipped to us care of our publisher for this unsolicited but most sincere endorsement).

I went on: "Those old billy goats will simply bray with delight upon seeing me, in hopes of finding out what dirt *I've* discovered! They're just a bunch of old gossips and you know it."

But Junior only shook his head, saying, "You're a good customer, Viv, but so are they, and I promised. A bartender is only as good as his word."

Henry said, "Riverview Café."

"You know, Henry," I said, "I'm starting to *like* you sober."

"Yeah," he said with a funny smile. "Me, too."

The Riverview Café, with its charming riverboat theme, specialized in wonderful old-fashioned comfort-food meals that older folks grew up on, and shouldn't be eating anymore; but that didn't stop the Romeos. (Yo, Guy Fieri! Bring *Triple D* to Serenity! We'll show the Food Network how to eat!)

I found the Romeos sequestered at a round table for six in the back, sipping cups of coffee, waiting for the ol' clock on the wall to strike eleven, the official time when patrons could put in their orders for the Blue Plate Special.

Once a hardy group of about fifteen, the Romeo numbers had dwindled due to the Grim Reaper . . . and Vivian Borne, who inadvertently caused them to disband for a while (see *Antiques Flee Market*).

But the Romeos were staging a comeback, having added a few new retirees, whose wives were more than happy to get them out of the house.

I pretended not to notice the group, and slid into a booth, my back to them, busying myself with examining a menu.

If you think the biggest gossips are women, think again! Men are so very much worse—just slightly more covert about it. Take these old codgers, whose appetites for the Blue Plate Special didn't compare to their craving for dirt. In less time than I could say, "I'll have the chicken fried steak with extra gravy," the Romeos had sent a point man.

" 'lo, Vivian."

I looked up from the menu, registering surprise. "Why, Harold! How delightful seeing you. It's been too long."

I may have fluttered my eyelashes, which are mine, I'll have you know (I have the receipt).

Harold, an original Romeos member, looked vaguely like the older Bob Hope (it took some squinting), and once upon a time, the ex-army sergeant had asked me to marry him. Having no desire to *hup-two*, and/or be permanently assigned to KP duty, I'd politely declined.

Harold was saying, "We have an extra chair, Viv. Would you care to join us?"

"Oh, I don't know," I demurred, "I wouldn't want to make anyone uncomfortable . . . I *know* I'm not Miss Popularity with you boys these days."

"Nonsense, Viv. Forgive and forget."

"I wasn't aware I'd done anything that needed forgiveness, Henry."

"Well, just leave it at 'forget' then. . . . We've certainly forgotten all about that unpleasantness last winter."

Ha! Like these old elephants ever forgot *anything*.

"You know what they say," he said with a silly grin. "Let bygones be bygones."

I smiled sweetly, burying my irritation at being made an outcast over doing my civic duty and (SPOILER ALERT!) exposing a murderer.

"Suits me fine," I said.

Gathering my orange tote, I trailed Harold back

to the round table, taking a seat between two other original members: Vern, a retired chiropractor, who reminded me of the older Clark Gable without the ears sticking out (but *with* the false teeth); and Randall, ex-hog farmer, who looked like a less sophisticated Sidney Greenstreet. (Since Randy had sold his hog farm, it was no longer necessary to sit downwind from him.)

There were several new old faces, including Gordon, whose top half (eyes, forehead, hair) looked like Ronald Colman, and bottom half (nose, mouth, chin) Stewart Granger (if you can work that math). Gordon was a second-generation heir to one of Serenity's famous pearl button factories, but don't any of you older gals out there get any ideas—his four ex-wives had bled him nearly penniless.

Then there was Wendell, a dead-ringer for Leo Gorcey (and for those of you younger readers who don't know what Leo Gorcey looked like, you have the options of a., looking him up on the Net, or b., counting yourself lucky). Wendell was a former river barge captain whose career abruptly came to an end one balmy summer day when he fell asleep at the helm and ran the *Mississippi Belle* up into the boat club parking lot, crashing into the side of the building, the riverboat's calliope playing at the time that ragtime favorite, "Bim Bam Boom."

"Hello, boys," I greeted in my best Mae West impression.

I received friendly nods, and hellos back, but mostly the Romeos were staring at me as if *I* were the Blue Plate Special. Since they'd sent their scout to fetch me, there was nothing negative about this reception—they were merely eager to find out what juicy morsels I was serving up today.

Harold cleared his throat, no louder than a cannon going off, then said, "What's new with you, Vivian?"

As if he hadn't already heard the scuttlebutt.

Before I could answer, a shapely waitress in her mid-thirties appeared, red hair piled on high, asking a collective, "What can I get you young fellas?"

Shocking how short the attention span of a man can be—with the promise of sex and food standing there in a blue uniform, it was suddenly as if Vivian Borne didn't exist. Ah, well.

Not surprisingly, I was the only one who didn't order the Blue Plate, opting for a spinach salad, chicken fried steak a mere will-o'-the-wisp. In a world where waitresses roamed, an older gal had to work to keep her figure, especially if she wanted to play the likes of the Romeos like a cheap kazoo.

While we waited for the food, I gave the eager group what they wanted: a play-by-play of the discovery of Big Jim Bob's body, and the break-in at our house; but I avoided any mention of Anna Armstrong, much less Bix B. While the information I provided wasn't anything that they hadn't "hoid" through the grapevine, I gave it the proper dramatic reading and that immediacy one gets only from the horse's mouth (as they say).

The food arrived, and as the men dug in, I picked and poked at my salad, and casually changed the subject. "I hear our esteemed Milton Lawrence is finally getting ready to retire."

Randall, mouth full of meat loaf, nodded, saying, "Gonna close his office in the bank building end of the month."

I smiled. "Ah! Maybe you can get him to join the Romeos."

Harold shook his head. "Naw. He's leaving Serenity. Bought a condo in Sun Valley, I heard."

Newbie Gordon commented, "Besides, he's not exactly the Blue Plate Special type."

Wendell, the other newbie, added, "I say good riddance."

Their comments surprised me, and I said, "Why so negative, gents? I thought everyone admired Milton, even if they didn't like him."

When that brought scoffs, I went on. "He's done so *much* for this town—built the new bank building, not to mention improving that entire block."

"All for the betterment of himself," Vern said.

"*And* on the back of his poor dead wife," Harold added.

I frowned. "That's a trifle unkind."

Harold cocked his head toward me. "Look, Viv, everyone knows Uncle Miltie was a male gold-digger who built his fortune off of Lillian's money."

"Is that right?" I asked, pretending I hadn't heard the same rumors, but hoping for something more substantial.

Vern frowned, puzzled. "Viv, you were around in the 1970s. Don't *you* remember?"

And sadly, dear reader, that was my problem: I had only a sketchy recollection of that period, thanks to the medication I was taking. And when I wasn't taking it, I had my mind on more important matters. Like gathering all the doorknobs in the house to mail to then-President Nixon.

Gordon was saying, "If you ask me, Lillian died of a broken heart after Milton disinherited Stephen—"

"*James*," Harold corrected. "Stephen died in Vietnam, James was the draft-dodger son who booked it to Canada."

The ex-army sergeant said this with no particular malice, having admitted to me long ago that he felt Vietnam had been a mistake. Of course, the shrapnel in his rear quarters may have contributed to that opinion.

"You know something funny?" Wendell said.

"What?" everyone said, including me.

"I hear the draft dodger's back in town. James."

Gordon said, "Huh! You don't say. . . . After all these years! I wonder if he's tried to get in touch with his old man."

"I doubt Milton would even see him," Vern said, then shook his head. "Still, I can't believe the old boy wouldn't want to make amends—after all, if the government pardoned all those draft dodgers, why shouldn't he?"

"Because," Harold said softly, "he'd have to admit Stephen, his other son, gave up his life for nothing."

Everyone digested that sobering thought, along with their meals.

Vern, digging out his wallet to pay for the check, said, "Something that's always bothered me—I know for a fact that Lillian kept in touch with James . . . she and I were friendly. Worked on some charity boards together. Anyway, certainly she would have left him money when she died—but I heard she never even made a will."

I thought of someone else who hadn't made a will: Anna Armstrong.

"Can you imagine?" Vern said. "A woman with that kind of fortune, married to a big successful businessman . . . and she didn't have a will? Strains credulity is what it does. Strains the hell out of it."

Soon chair legs were screeching as the Romeos stood; Harold, ever the gentleman, assisted me to my feet.

But it was Wendell who gave the parting shot: "Maybe Lillian *did* make a will, and somebody . . . guess who . . . suppressed it. Ever consider that?"

I actually hadn't, I'm embarrassed to say.

"Vivian," Vern said as we stood at the register, "you're thick with old Wayne Ekhardt, aren't you?"

"Wayne's still our family lawyer," I admitted.

"Isn't that old workhorse ever going to retire?" Vern grinned and shook his head. "Well, if you're interested in this subject, you ought to ask him about this. I'm pretty sure, back around that time, that he was the Lawrences' lawyer."

NOTE FROM BRANDY: Because Mother was not given a word-count limit, she wound up writing a double-length chapter. In order to preserve my sanity (and yours), I have divided it into two sections. This will give you the opportunity to (a) put this book aside, turn off the light and go to sleep, (b) toss cold water in your face and dry off and mentally prepare yourself, (c) self-medicate, preferably a nice glass of White Zin, or (d) press on after taking a deep breath. You're welcome.

Mother's Trash 'n' Treasures Tip

Usually, the best items in a storage unit are in the back, often hidden from view—that's why I bring a floodlight and stilts.

Chapter Seven

(A.K.A. Chapter Six)

Wayne Ekhardt occupied an office atop the venerable Laurel Building, an eight-story Art Deco edifice just a hop, skip, and jump away from the Riverview Café. (Figuratively speaking, that is—not much literal hopping, skipping, and jumping these days, with these artificial hips!)

At one time, the successful trial attorney had owned the entire shootin' match, using all but the first floor for his flourishing practice (although he'd never taken on a partner, Wayne's world had once swarmed with legal secretaries and interns). Then just as the city's most famous criminal attorney seemed to be easing into semiretirement, Wayne sold the building to an engineering firm with the stipulation that he be granted a lifetime lease of the eighth floor at one dollar a year—possibly the worst business deal the engineering firm ever made, considering that Wayne was still practicing at nearly ninety.

I entered the refurbished lobby, took the modern elevator up (whatever happened to those original Deco fixtures?), then stepped off on the eighth floor . . . and back into time.

While the other floors had been remodeled into typical office building sterility, this one retained its original flavor: scuffed black-and-white speckled ceramic-tiled floor, scarred-wood office doors with ancient pebbled glass, antique scone wall lighting, even an old porcelain drinking fountain (still functioning).

One could imagine Philip Marlowe in a trench coat and fedora pausing halfway down the hall to light up a Philip Morris! (Or is that Philip Morris pausing to light up a Philip Marlowe? Afraid I'm no expert on the hard-boiled detective field.)

Wayne—long since a one-man operation—had retained only a few choice clients (myself included) and perhaps ten years ago had pared his business hours back to only one afternoon a week, which luckily enough happened to be today.

As I walked down the long corridor to his riverview corner office, I tried the doorknobs of the ancient offices on either side of the hall.

Curses!

Still locked and inaccessible. One day Vivian Borne would get inside those treasure caves and find a trove of antiques: rolltop desks, oak swivel chairs, coat trees, ancient typewriters, banker's lamps and who-could-say what Art Moderne booty.

Arriving at Wayne's office, I rapped on the pebbled-glass door; receiving no answer (nor having expected to), I tried the knob, which turned, then went on in and found the inevitable.

Wayne was seated behind his grand old desk, head tilted back, eyes closed, mouth open, looking even more frail than usual in a suit that had become too large. More than once this sight had given me a start, as I assumed my friend had finally passed into that Great Court of Last Resort. But I could see his nostrils quivering, so I still had representation.

I coughed loudly, and when Wayne didn't stir, I simply said, "Ah-*hemmm!*"

His eyes fluttered open, and he struggled to focus on his guest.

He tried to speak. Coughed. Coughed some more. Then found his voice. And a smile.

"Why, Vivian, my dear," he said. "Is there any more pleasant sensation than awaking to look into the eyes of Vivian Borne?"

He was always more flirtatious when I wasn't accompanied by Brandy.

"Hello, you rascal." I took one of two visitor chairs opposite him. "I don't have an appointment, and apologize for dropping by . . . you did once say I was always welcome."

Pulling his shrunken self up into his suit, he waved a bony hand. "And you are. No appointment necessary, Viv. I always have time for you."

I smiled slyly. "The feeling is mutual, Wayne."

At one time, after both our spouses had passed away, I'm confident I could have snagged Wayne—he'd always had a thing for me. But a criminal lawyer's wife stands in the wings, and I'm more comfortable center stage.

"What's on your mind, Vivian?"

"There are those who would say asking me that question is a dangerous one."

"I've survived a lot in this career of mine. Please be frank."

"Glad to hear you say that, Wayne, because I may be overstepping."

"Nonsense."

I drew in a breath, let it out, smiled again, not slyly. "You represented Milton and Lillian Lawrence at one time, didn't you?"

He frowned in surprise. "Heavens. Why do you ask?"

"Oh, you know how it is. The Romeos and I were just having a gab fest, and—"

"Ah," he said, beaming, "you and the Romeos are speaking again . . . splendid. I hated to see your . . . public spiritedness, in that unpleasant matter last winter . . . get in the way of old friendships."

I waved that off. "Water over the bridge. At any rate, you know how those boys like to gossip, and something came up that I find intriguing."

"Oh?"

"We were wondering if it's true that Lillian never made a will . . . and if so . . . why?"

Wayne studied me so long and motionlessly that I almost thought he'd drifted back to sleep.

Then he said, "It's been ages since I represented the Lawrence family—thirty years, at least."

"That was a lawyerly response, Wayne." I gave him a tiny teasing smile.

Another long moment. "There's such a thing as client confidentiality."

"Lillian is gone."

"Milton isn't." He sighed. "Let's just say Milton and I disagreed on whether or not his wife needed a will."

"And you thought she *did*."

"Yes. Certainly. Ridiculous with that kind of wealth not to. And . . . there was another reason."

I felt I knew. "The estranged son, you mean. James?"

He nodded and sighed. "The boy who went to Canada to avoid the draft. Milton assured his wife that he would do the right thing by the boy, and showed her his own will, with a generous provision for James, to convince her. Anyway, Milton could always bully his wife into doing things his way, for business reasons."

"But you thought doing the 'right thing' by a draft dodger meant one thing to Lillian and another to Milton."

"I felt confident that if Lillian preceded Milton in death that, yes, Milton would remove the boy from his will. He'd already cut him off from any kind of supportive funds."

"Oh dear. And is that what Milton finally did?"

Wayne shrugged. "Frankly, I don't know. Milton did me the favor of finding another family counsel. But my guess is that James has been removed from his will, and as for Lillian? If she did have a will, none was ever found."

I rose and reached a hand across the desk and he took it. We didn't shake hands—more of a clasp, a warm one.

"Thank you for your time, Wayne." At the door I turned and said coquettishly, "Be sure to bill me, now!"

"Of course, Vivian."

But he wouldn't, because he never did.

As I've mentioned before, Brandy and I maintained a booth at the antiques mall, which was housed in a yet-to-be-restored Victorian building at the tail end of the shopping district, just before Main Street rose into the bluffs where the rich of Serenity once dwelled (some still did).

The building had an ornate facade, a unique corner entrance, and a notorious reputation, several murders having taken place there, which did not seem to bother antiques hunters looking for a bargain. In fact, the old building's history only attracted tourists and antiques fiends. (Fiends in the collecting sense, not homicidal.)

The current owner, Ray Spillman, was a short, spry, slender fellow in his late seventies with thinning gray hair, a bulbous nose, and a slash of a mouth.

At the moment, he was busy with a customer behind the center circular counter, so I went to check on our booth, hopeful we'd had some sales, October being a good month for antiques shoppers. Something about the cool, crisp air brings them out.

I surveyed the booth, noting with relief that among the happily missing were the brass spittoon, a Roseville vase (Clematis pattern), a Honey Bear cookie jar (rough—meaning chipped), and a small Whiting and Davis silver mesh evening bag, that didn't hold squat.

However—Brandy insists a sign of a bad writer is

if he/she begins a sentence with "however," saying that word belongs in the middle of a sentence, though I could care less (Brandy also insists it's "couldn't care less," which just doesn't sound right) (but I digress)—*however*, much to my chagrin, one item had been added to our inventory: a bright yellow smiley-face bedside clock.

I snatched up the item, marched over to the counter where Ray—having finished with his customer—was now tinkering with an old sewing machine.

Placing the demonically grinning clock before him by way of accusation, I demanded, "And what is *this* doing back in our booth?"

Ray looked at me sheepishly, then muttered, "Brandy returned it. She figured out you bought it yourself, Viv, just to . . . you know."

"I *do* know, Ray. To get rid of it."

The clock had been with us from the beginning of our antiques booth, one of Brandy's early acquisitions—which I'd advised her against. Even after marking the clock down to a measly simoleon, we couldn't get rid of it.

I said reproachfully, "You were supposed to throw the wretched object away, so Brandy wouldn't find out!"

Ray shrugged his slight shoulders. "She found it out back—in the Dumpster."

I *harrumped* my annoyance at this bit of information, though one aspect did please me: Brandy—always one to haughtily refuse to go through trash with me looking for treasure—had finally joined the ranks of us Dumpster-divers!

Returning to the booth, I retagged the clock at

five dollars, and placed it in a prominent spot. Then I dug into my orange tote bag and brought out Bix Beiderbecke's cornet. Carefully, I removed the protective tissue from around the instrument and—finding just the right spot on the pegged-board wall—hung it amidst the clutter.

What better place to hide a treasure, than out in plain sight, among trash like the smiley-face clock?

To discourage anyone from *playing* the cornet, I removed the mouthpiece (Bach, no. seven) *plus* the center finger valve. And to discourage anyone from *buying* it, I marked the cornet at a firm five hundred.

The sales receipt and letter of authentication from Stephen to Anna would go into my safe deposit box, along with the mouthpiece and valve.

I had another reason for "hiding" the cornet in our booth: I could get to it at any time I wanted, twenty-four-seven, because I had kept a key to the mall from when I'd filled in for Ray while he was recouperating from a hernia. Plus I knew the code to the building's security system. Knowledge is power, they say. And they're right.

Pleased with myself, I returned to Ray, who was bent over the dissembled sewing machine, an oil-can coroner performing a mechanical autopsy.

I said, replacing my irritation with sugar and cream, "Ray, my darling? A favor?"

Ray looked up like a puppy recently spanked for piddling, sensing an opportunity to get back in good graces. "You name it, Viv. Feel like I let you down with the clock incident."

Men. So easy to handle in the short term, such a burden over time.

I said, "I want to know the name of anyone—and I do mean *anyone*—who expresses interest in the cornet I just put in the booth."

Ray knew better than to ask why. "You got it, Viv."

I turned to leave, then glanced back.

"Say, Ray?"

"Yes?"

I turned back to him. "Did you ever happen to do any business with that fellow Big Jim Bob?"

"The one that got killed?"

"Yes. *That* Big Jim Bob."

"Whose body you and Brandy found?"

"I believe we've established the man's identity, Ray."

He frowned, suspicious now that he realized I was on another murder inquiry. "What *kind* of business, Viv?"

I gestured around us. "Antiques? Did he try to sell you any?"

Ray thought about it, hesitant to get involved in murder; but finally he nodded. "He *tried* to sell . . . but I didn't buy."

"Why not? Too high an asking price?"

"Actually, no . . . almost the opposite. It was a damn bargain, pardon my French. But he couldn't provide me with proof of purchase."

"Ah."

"He had some nice things, but no provenance."

Meaning the antiques most likely were stolen.

I bid Ray adieu, then paused out on the sidewalk, to review my findings, also because my corns were killing me.

Usually, I wore Brandy's soft UGG boots for my

field investigations, but she'd hid them after I got blood on them (not mine) (the spot came out with a little Oxi-Clean). Just then, a horse and buggy came crawling by. *No,* I wasn't hallucinating, and *yes,* I was current on my medication. Inside the buggy cuddled a bride and groom, while outside, a white-tuxedo-clad driver held the reins.

The attraction-for-hire was popular among Serenity's newlyweds, offering a romantic spin around the picturesque downtown and riverfront.

I fell in step alongside the buggy. "Would you be so kind as to give a poor woman with bunions a lift to the First National Bank?"

And before the startled couple could utter a word, I climbed aboard, scooching the bride over to make room. She seemed a little put out, but after all, I'd only make their ride more cozy.

The groom—a baby-faced youth of perhaps twenty—started to protest, but I crinkled my nose, saying, "It'll make a cute story for the kids. And their kids!"

We rode the three blocks in silence, a few pedestrians gawking from the sidewalk at my addition to the bridal party. As the buggy drew near to my destination (honestly, I could have crawled faster) I climbed off, with a "Have a nice marriage!" (Instead of "Have a nice day," get it?)

But as sullen as they'd been on the ride, I didn't hold out much hope for them.

The first thing I did inside the modern three-story redbrick bank building was deposit the Bix papers in my safe deposit box, along with the cornet's mouthpiece and valve. I took a few minutes to reacquaint myself with the other contents—my will, abstract to the house, wedding ring, and so forth. Then I headed back to the lobby and caught the elevator up to the third floor, and Milton Lawrence's office.

I pushed open the glass door to step into a modern reception room, where Lee Hamilton—Milton's longtime assistant / secretary / chauffeur / gofer—was busy at a desk equipped with every state-of-the-art gizmo a major domo might need.

Lee was in his late fifties but looked much younger, at five-foot-six or so, blessed with an energetic boyishness, with a slim physique, hair still ungrayed brown (only his hairdresser knew for sure), and a nicely chiseled face, well-tanned but not orange like that more famous Hamilton, and I don't mean Alexander.

I knew Lee from the Playhouse, where he sometimes acted in smaller roles (he never seemed quite right for a romantic lead). But his real gifts lay in the realm of set design—often incorporating antiques from his own extensive collection—and in making the costumes (what that boy could do with a handful of sparkles and a roll of tulle!).

Lee beamed and said, "Well . . . Vivian! What a pleasant surprise. Nice to see you."

I beamed back. Nodding toward his natty navy suit, I said, "You're looking as spiffy as ever—is that Armani?"

"Hugo Boss," he said with a catty smile. "Like my cologne—Armani is *so* last season."

"And I *adore* your shirt—takes a man secure in his masculinity to wear pink polka dots."

"I suppose so." He cocked his head. "When are

you coming back to the Playhouse, dear? We miss you."

I had been the artistic director for a while, but quit over creative differences with the board.

(It had nothing to do with the real live horses I brought on stage for the revival of *Annie Get Your Gun.* Could I help it if they got frightened and bolted? And I was hardly responsible for feeding them whatever it was that had caused them to decorate the stage in so appalling, and slippery, a fashion. Anyway, I'd promised the real live horses would be a showstopper, and they were.)

I said, "Afraid I'm far too busy to be involved with theater right now."

"Ah, yes," he said. "From what I read in the paper, I would imagine you're in the thick of another murder mystery. Any leads?"

I shrugged. "Just getting started, gathering data, you know. Like Holmes said, 'Data, data, data, I need bricks to build a wall.' "

"I think that's clay to make bricks."

"I prefer my wording. Is Milton in?"

I said this as casually as if I regularly dropped by to see Serenity's wealthiest magnate.

Lee made a sour face. "He is . . . but in such foul mood. I doubt he'll see anyone today."

"Well, *try,* would you? It's important. Milton and I go way back, you know."

"All right," Lee said doubtfully, and touched a button on the intercom. "Sorry to disturb you, sir . . . but Vivian Borne is here—"

"*I have no desire whatsoever to see that old battle-ax! Send her away!*"

Lee cringed. He mouthed, *Sorry!*

I took no offense—the stock market *had* been bearish—but replied, loud enough for Milton to hear, "Tell the lovely man that the battle-ax has brought him a sampling of her world-famous chocolate mint brownies."

Half a beat, then: *"All right . . . send her in—and bring me coffee!"*

Silencing the intercom, Lee smiled. "I marvel at your foresight."

"Everyone has a weakness. And I know what Milton's is. Or at least one of them."

As I headed toward the door to Milton's inner office, Lee spoke. "Vivian?"

I turned, expecting him to ask me what *his* weakness was (fine clothes and furnishings), but he merely asked, "How about one of those brownies for the guardian at the gate?"

"Anything for you, dear boy."

And I brought out the tin from my orange tote.

Chocolate Mint Brownies

Brownies:
½ cup butter (softened)
1 cup sugar
4 eggs
1½ cup chocolate syrup
1 cup flour
¼ tsp. baking powder

Cream butter with sugar, add eggs and beat well. Add syrup. Combine flour and baking pow-

der, then add to wet mixture. Bake in greased
11x16 pan at 350 degrees for 30-35 minutes.

Frosting:
2 cups powdered sugar
2 Tbsp. milk
½ cup butter (softened)
½ tsp. green food coloring
½ tsp. peppermint extract

Cream sugar, milk, and butter, add food coloring and extract. Spread on cool brownies. (If
brownies are still warm, spread frosting, then pop
into freezer to set.)

Glaze:
1 cup chocolate semi-sweet chips
6 Tbsp. butter

Melt chips and butter over low heat, stirring
slowly. Cool. Spread on top of frosting. Let set before cutting. Calories: Y.D.W.T.K. (You Don't Want
to Know).

As I entered Milton's inner office, Serenity's
wealthiest citizen didn't bother to get up from behind his large mahogany desk. Once a handsome
man, his features had been hardened by years of
worshiping Mammon. He, nonetheless, still pos-
sessed a commanding presence—tall of stature,
with a full head of silver hair, and a striking pair of
dark blue, sharply intelligent eyes . . . which at the
moment were locked in greedy anticipation upon
my tin of brownies.

"Milton," I said, "you're looking well."

He grunted only, "Vivian," never one to acknowledge (much less return) a compliment.

I sat in the black leather visitor's chair in front of the desk, then opened the tin, allowing the chocolate-minty aroma to waft teasingly toward his helpless nostrils.

Punching an intercom button, Milton snapped, "Lee . . . where is that *coffee!*"

"*Almost ready, sir. . . .*"

"Hurry it up. And, uh . . . fetch a cup for Vivian, too."

I called to the intercom, "Black, please!" Then to Milton I said, "You must treasure that man."

"Why?"

Because he was a saint to have worked for so long for such an egomaniacal taskmaster.

"Oh," I said, "as the saying goes, 'A good employee is a thing of beauty.' "

He frowned. "Who ever said that?"

"Well, I did. Just now."

Before this meeting went entirely to heck-and-gone, I placed a gooey brownie on a colorful leaf-print napkin and passed it over to Milton—a sacrifice to a grouchy god.

"I'm not here just to shoot the breeze, Miltie," I began. "Or to fatten you up. I *do* have important business."

(Once I made the mistake of calling him "Uncle Miltie," and he threw me out of his office. Some of you may be old enough to remember the television comedian Milton Berle, who was America's Uncle Miltie for a time. But as that Uncle Miltie was a raucous comedian who often dressed in drag, comparisons were not necessarily flattering to a stuffy old coot like Milton Lawrence.)

Of course, there was nothing stuffy about the way Milton took a big bite of that brownie, his eyes rolling back in his head orgasmically.

A tasteless overstatement? You've never had my brownies, then! I have been told on good authority that my brownies are better than sex.

(Note from editor: *The above passage may offend some of our readers; please soften.*)

(Note from Vivian: *But it's the God's honest truth . . . both Harold and Vern said so—of course, their memories may be failing them. How about, "My brownies are better than a roll in the hay?"*)

Milton, mouth brimming with brownie (his second), dark frosting smeared above his upper lip, asked pointedly, "What do you want, Vivian? What are these brownies costing me?"

Before I could answer, the door opened and Lee came in balancing a tray like a waiter—impressive, but I'd seen him do that in our production of *Weekend at the Waldorf.* He set the tray down on the edge of the desk and then, with the same flourish as on stage, poured coffee from a pot into two cups, adding cream to Milton's, and leaving mine black.

After Lee had departed, I reached into my tote once more, and withdrew the love letters from Stephen to Anna, which I placed upon the desk.

Milton picked up the stack, studied them, flipped through them like he was shuffling cards, then asked sternly, "How do you come to have these, Vivian?"

I told him about winning the storage auction on

Anna Armstrong's unit, concluding with, "I thought you might like to have them, now that the poor woman has passed."

His answer was another unreadable grunt.

"Were you close to her?" I ventured, bringing the coffee cup to my lips.

Milton set the letters down. "She was around our place a good deal when she and Stephen were dating," he said. "But after his loss, we . . . drifted apart."

I remained silent, hoping the brownies might have loosened his tongue. A sugar rush has its value.

"I did have *some* contact with Anna," he continued, "not terribly long ago. She wanted me to invest in a bed-and-breakfast."

I sat forward. "The Beiderbecke home in Davenport?"

He gave me a surprised glance. "Why yes. She and the owner—a John Anderson, I believe—were looking for seed money." He paused, then went on. "At first, I wasn't interested . . . but then Anna mentioned using the downstairs parlor room as a Bix museum."

In competition with Waldo Hendricks!

Gently I asked, "Did you?"

"Did I what, Vivian?"

"Invest?"

He shook his head. "No. Before it went any further, she was gone."

She was murdered.

He was saying, "And, of course, without Anna, I lost all interest in the project."

He took on a melancholy mien, and I wondered if he might not have been in love with Anna himself.

Milton suddenly sat straight in his chair. "Tell me, Vivian—did you happen to find an old cornet among the items in the storage unit?"

Why deny it?

"I did . . . along with the original sales receipt."

"Then you know"—those dark blue eyes glittered—"*know* that it once belonged to Bix himself."

I nodded.

Milton laughed once, silently, then shook his head, and he seemed to drift off somewhere, somewhere not in this room.

He said, "I bought that cornet for Stephen when he was a boy—he played the trumpet in the school band and was quite good. Especially jazz. He had a real interest in jazz, and my old 78s."

I gestured to the stack of letters. "Apparently he and Anna would listen to them together. In your rec room?"

The sharp eyes narrowed. "What are you planning to do with the cornet?"

"Why, sell it to the highest bidder, of course," I said. "That's the little business I'm in with my daughter, you know. That's why we bought that pig-in-a-poke storage unit."

"You had no idea that horn was in the unit?"

"None," I said, and that was technically true, though Big Jim Bob had indicated the unit might hold something valuable.

Then I added, "I do hope you're not going to challenge my ownership. I won the bid on the unit in good faith, and possession is nine-tenths of the law." (Ten-tenths in my case. Eleven-tenths.)

He seemed to melt back into the chair. "No, Vivian, of course not. Although I could challenge you on the fact that—if I remember correctly—the cornet was given to Anna not as a gift, but for safekeeping." He sighed heavily. "I might consider making you an offer. But I'll need to reflect on that—considering the cornet is something that would bring back sad memories."

I risked bringing up another memory. Perhaps not sad, but bad. "I apologize for asking, but . . . is it true your son James is in town?"

Milton's face hardened, and he responded tersely, "If he's here, I've had no contact with him."

"Don't you think you should? Isn't it about time that—"

"Vivian." His body stiffened. "Your brownies will only buy you *so* much goodwill. . . ."

I raised a finger. " 'The weak can never forgive . . . only the strong.' "

"Who said *that*? *You*?"

"Mahatma Gandhi."

He closed his eyes. He opened his eyes. "Vivian, I think it's time for you to go."

" 'Families are like fudge . . . mostly sweet with a few nuts.' Unknown."

"*Go!*"

In the outer office, Lee was at a side desk, working on a computer, the beginnings of a letter on-screen.

I asked the back of him: "What are *your* plans after Milton's retirement?"

He swiveled, his expression pleasant. "I'm taking mine, too."

I raised my eyebrows. "Aren't you a little young for that?"

"Mr. Lawrence has been very generous with my salary over the years . . . so why not take a permanent vacation? I'm thinking about either San Francisco or Key West."

"San Francisco in the summer," I suggested, "Key West in the winter."

"Nice notion. And if I get bored, wherever you are, there's always a community theater."

I chuckled. "You won't leave town without saying good-bye, will you?"

"Never. Expect a theatrical exit."

"Ha!" I smiled at the dear boy. "Do come by the house, anytime. Well . . . ta-ta!"

I simply had to find just the right girl for him.

It was late afternoon when I stepped out of the bank building, the autumn sun low in the sky, bright rays spreading a ribbon of gold across the Mississippi waters. (Not bad, huh?)

I hoofed it two blocks to a park bench in front of our beautiful Grecian wedding-cake of a courthouse to wait for the trolley.

As promised, I will now tell my even-better trolley story. There was a spinster in town who bought a chimpanzee to keep her company, and one day she wanted to take it with her on the trolley, but since the driver (the one prior to Maynard Kirby's most recent return) wouldn't allow pets on board, she dressed it up as a little girl, complete with a Goldilocks wig. Well, everything was fine until

(Note from editor: *Vivian's strict word count has been reactivated.*)

Trash 'n' Treasures Tip

If you are serious about making money from storage unit auctions, be consistent: attend as many as possible. Not just when the mood hits you (like Mother).

Chapter Eight

Scandal, Us?

With Mother off to terrorize downtown Serenity, I took advantage of the solitude around the Borne homestead to indulge in a warm, leisurely shower. Relaxed, even refreshed, I dressed in DKNY jeans and a new burgundy Three Dots tee (which I'd snagged on-line 75% off), slipped into some leopard-print Sam Edelman flats (another sale), and grabbed my mustard-yellow Hobo hobo-style bag. (It's so liberating that nothing has to match anymore—although Mother sometimes takes this to a what-did-she-do-dress-in-the-dark extreme.)

Before I continue, however, some reality checks are needed after Mother's marathon chapters: 1) The calliope was playing "The Merry-Go-Round Broke Down"—the Looney Tunes theme—at the time of the Boat Club ramming, not "Bim Bam Boom," which I'm not even sure is a real song, 2) she got catsup from a hotdog on my UGGs, not blood—and she is still forbidden to wear them, and 3) the unruly horses and their unbridled bodily functions had *everything* to do with Mother's dismissal as director of the Playhouse.

(Note from Vivian: *It's criminally unfair that Brandy gets to challenge my comments when I don't have another chapter in which to mount my rebuttal. The calliope was indeed playing "Bim Bam Boom"—a very real and quite catchy song. And I would never put catsup on a hotdog, as I'm a mustard gal all the way—with a little relish. As far as the horses and my Playhouse status are concerned, that is a matter of opinion.*)

(Note from editor: *Ladies, if you do not stop this squabbling, I will edit out* all *of your asides.*)

(Brandy: *Okay.*)

(Mother: *Ditto.*)

With a beautiful fall day awaiting, I left my jacket in the front closet, grabbed a few things Peggy Sue would need for her release from the hospital (change of clothes, small suitcase), then headed out to the battered Buick.

What I wanted to do first was retrieve Sushi from the vet; but considering how Sis reacted to my perceived favoritism toward Soosh, post-home invasion, I figured I better rank the human being over the canine.

So I steered the car toward the hospital, and on arrival I took the elevator up to the second floor, stepping off to see—at the end of the hall, in front of Peggy Sue's room—something that gave me a start.

Two very official-looking men with short hair and dark suits stood a few feet apart, in separate solemn conversations with their respective cell phones. I knew they weren't policemen, not Serenity ones anyway—the local gendarme didn't exist with whom Mother and I hadn't already tangled.

Iowa Bureau of Criminal Investigation maybe? Federal agents?

Whatever, I dropped the small suitcase and broke into a run—nearly knocking over a medical cart—seized by the sense that something terrible had happened to Peggy Sue!

At the door to Sis's room, a dark-suited man with a bucket head and crew cut put a "stop" palm up.

"No admittance," he said in a midrange monotone.

"I'm Brandy Borne, her sister! What's happened?"

The man spoke into his lapel, putting one hand to his ear. "The sister's here. Should I let her in?"

I didn't wait for a response from his lapel, before shoving my way into the room, my heart in my throat, not knowing what to expect—an empty room, Peggy Sue kidnapped . . . or even her lifeless body bludgeoned, our home intruder having returned to finish the job!

But there was Sis, in her cranked-up bed, hair coifed against plumped pillows, make-up perfect, looking rested and lovely in a satin crème-colored robe, its V-neck presenting a generous touch of cleavage.

My imagination—fueled as it was by DNA inherited from Vivian Borne, a theatrical diva capable of transforming a paper cut into an amputation—had run away with itself. Like those loose-boweled horses on the Playhouse stage.

And seated next to Peg, holding one hand, was my biological father, Senator Edward Clark.

Movie-star handsome—think Paul Newman in his early sixties, the light blue eyes and all—the senator was wearing his usual on-the-stump outfit: tailored navy suit, crisp white shirt, red tie, and flag lapel pin. Red, white, blue—not so subtle, huh?

My anxiety flared into irritation. Didn't the senator realize what he was risking, making this particular hospital visit, with the election a mere month away?

Sis said sweetly, "Why, Brandy, what a nice surprise!"

That was the kind of thing she said to me only when other people were around.

She nodded toward the seated senator, like I might have missed him. "Look who's been thoughtful enough to come see me."

I managed a tight-lipped smile and a nod. "Senator."

"Make it 'Dad,' " he corrected, flashing me the charismatic smile that had won over many a voter.

Me, I was more in the mood for a recount.

I said through clamped teeth, "Might I see you a moment . . . *Dad?*"

And turned on my heel.

Soon, in a little alcove across the hall, I stood facing the senator. His political advisors—not men from U.N.C.L.E., as I had suspected—kept a watchful eye, if a respectful distance.

"What are you *doing* here?" I demanded.

He frowned but just a little, keeping his cool. "Just what you see—visiting Peggy Sue."

"How did you even know—"

"Vivian got word to me."

Why had I asked?

I sighed. "And how are you planning to explain your presence to the media?"

He raised his eyebrows, doing an innocent act that really didn't suit him. "Your sister's been working for my campaign . . . and I care about my people."

He called her my sister, but "Dad" knew damn well she was my mother. Biological mother.

"You really think that explanation will satisfy the twenty-four-hour news cycle bunch?"

"Why shouldn't they accept it?"

I lowered my voice. "How long till some would-be Woodward or Bernstein finds out Peggy Sue was once a just-out-of-high-school campaign worker that you got pregnant . . . and that *I* am the evidence?"

Nonplussed, my father put a hand on my shoulder. "Brandy, since finding out about all this a few months ago, I've made no effort to hide any of it."

"Well, you should!"

His smile was unsettling in its humanity. "We both know that sooner or later the truth *will* out."

"Can't you make it later than sooner? You're going to lose, if this gets out."

The senator was up against a formidable opponent this time, and the poll percentages were closing fast.

"You surprise me," he said. "I hardly thought *you'd* have a rooting interest in my reelection."

"Maybe I just don't particularly relish being at

the center of a scandal! Peggy Sue is still reeling from her husband's tragic death, and our mother is a fruitcake who doesn't need Christmas to come early this year, if you follow me. *And* I have a young son of my own who I don't particularly want to subject to seeing his mom turned into an unwilling reality star."

He listened patiently to me rant and rave, then bestowed a fatherly smile. "Brandy, please trust me. Not my first time at the rodeo. I do know what I'm doing."

I felt suddenly sick at the pit of my stomach. Was this some kind of fourth-quarter play by the good senator to grab headlines? Could he play our twisted little family soap opera for sympathy?

He was reading my mind, or at least making a good guess, patting the air with upraised, calming palms.

"Brandy," he said, "I *was* going to wait for a better time to tell you this, because I really do want your support . . . your blessing. . . ."

I frowned and spat a word: "*What?*"

". . . but you'll hear it soon enough from Peggy Sue." He paused. "We're going to be . . ."

My Medusa expression had frozen him, and I heard myself completing his thought: ". . . *married?*"

He nodded, rather embarrassed.

Stunned, all I could do was crank my gaping mouth closed again. But my eyes were so wide, they were burning.

The bucket-headed aide intruded tentatively. "Senator . . . we have to go, if we're to make the next event on time."

His boss waved a dismissive hand, and the aide backed off.

My father's attention shifted back to me. "You seem less than . . . ecstatic at this prospect."

I got my mouth working again. My tone was about that of William Shatner reporting a gremlin on the wing of the plane to a stewardess. "Isn't this . . . *union* . . . a little sudden? I mean, you only found out this summer about Peggy Sue having a kid . . . having *me*. . . ."

He smiled patiently. "Brandy, in recent days, I've gotten to know Peg well enough to see that she'll make a wonderful wife."

"Really? She strikes you as a genuine, warm human being?"

"She strikes me as . . . an ideal politician's wife."

At least he was being honest—not so common in his game. And he was right—Peggy Sue would be brilliant in that role.

But I didn't see anything like love entering into the equation anywhere. And I had a right to wonder about that. After all, I was their love child, wasn't I?

He touched my arm and his smile wasn't the practiced, charismatic one. "Brandy, I do have to run now . . . but we'll talk again soon, all right? We have decades of catching up to do."

"I'm more concerned about right now," I insisted.

"Of course you are. You're a pragmatist. Like your mother."

For a moment I thought that was gibberish—who ever thought Vivian Borne was a pragmatist? Then I realized he meant Peggy Sue.

And at that moment, he leaned in and kissed me on the cheek.

Numbly, I watched the senator and his two aides walk down the hallway in military lockstep, then disappear toward the elevator.

Shell-shocked, I shuffled back to Peggy Sue's room.

When I entered, Sis was reading *Harper's Bazaar*—a fashion magazine too rich for my blood—and I took the vacated chair next to her.

She smiled at me as she set the magazine aside on the nightstand, next to a huge vase of red roses, most likely sent by the senator.

"What's the matter?" she asked.

"Whatever could be the matter?"

Never one to look too far under the surface, she took me at my word.

She inhaled deeply, breasts rising and falling, then cooed, "Isn't he just grand?"

"You can cover those up now," I said, nodding to her cleavage. "He's off to his next stop."

She ignored that, her eyes sparkling, probably with visions of the diamond ring that would soon grace her finger. "Brandy, I have some wonderful news! You will never guess."

"You're gonna marry the senator."

Her eyes flared. "Edward *told* you!"

I nodded.

She clasped her hands as if in prayer or maybe in anticipation of a feast. "Isn't it *marvelous?* Imagine, *me,* a senator's wife! . . . You seem less than overjoyed for me. I would think you'd be thrilled."

"Should I be?"

She frowned. "What's wrong?"

"What's wrong? Don't you realize if this gets out before the election, you'll be married to an *ex*-senator?"

She smiled teasingly. "Not jealous, are you?"

"Jealous! Of what? Of who?"

"Of me."

"Don't be ridiculous. I wouldn't be you for *any-thing*."

Normally, such a caustic remark would have sent Peggy Sue into a conniptions fit. But she was flying too high.

"Can't you just be happy for me, Brandy? If Edward loses the election, so be it—he and I will be together, and we'll *all* be able to come out of the closet."

"I *like* it in the closet! I like being nutty Vivian Borne's daughter. What I don't like is being part of some smear campaign launched against your precious senator. Peg, I've got a son. You've got a daughter. What are you *thinking?*"

She was staring at me with this peculiar smile, like she was trying to make out what I was saying but I insisted on speaking in Pig Latin.

Finally she said, "What's the matter with you, Brandy? Haven't we been closer these past few months than ever before? I was even starting to think we liked each other."

There was some truth in that. But had I only been able to feel closer to Peg because she'd been knocked off her high horse, and brought down to my undignified level?

"Sis," I said, "normally *you're* the one who's worried about what people might think. Can't you see the dangerous line you and the senator are trying to walk?"

Her smiling expression was almost Madonna-like, and I thought I understood, though perhaps Peggy Sue herself couldn't have articulated it: *Even marriage to a disgraced senator, an ex-senator, was a step up from her current condition. She would have status, perhaps slightly tarnished, but status, and money, and a nice house again, and . . .*

Sis was saying, "If I'm willing to take Edward for better or for worse, I'd like to know why you can't show me a little support."

I got up from the chair, and went over to the window to stare out at the fall foliage.

Suddenly I turned and mumbled, "Maybe you will get away with it."

"Get away with what?"

I half turned. "Living happily ever after."

"Brandy, you're talking nonsense."

"It's just that . . ." I returned to the chair, slumped into it. Sighed. ". . . well, you've always had it so *easy.*"

"Have I?" Her eyes flashed. "Starting when I . . . found myself in the family way, right out of high school?"

I rolled my eyes. "Oh brother. How did that shake down, anyway? Mother pretends I'm hers, you go off to college, marry Bob, get a big house, one perfect daughter, a country club membership, clothes, car, everything you could ever want. . . . Okay, sure, Bob dies and leaves you destitute, but then along comes Senator Clark on a white horse. Like I said, too easy."

"So . . . you want me to *suffer* more?"

"No. Not really. . . . well, maybe a little more."

"How *much* more?"

I shrugged. "Not *too* much. I'm *not* sadistic."

I let out a little smile and she returned it.

"Brandy, I can't change the past, and I'm sorry you got saddled with taking care of Mom—which couldn't have been easy. But you were always much better with her than I."

"Because she and I are alike, you mean."

"I didn't say that."

She didn't have to.

Sis sat up straighter in the bed. "Look, I'm no good to either you *or* Mom unless I get out of that house. When I'm Mrs. Senator Clark, I'll be able to help you financially, especially Mom in her later years."

I had to admit she was right.

"Do you love him?" I asked.

"Yes, of course."

That had come a little too quickly.

A haggard-looking female nurse's aide appeared. Heavy-set, wearing white slacks and a teddy-bear-decorated smock, she was holding the small suitcase I'd dropped by the elevator, and forgotten completely about.

"I believe this is yours," the woman said, handing it to me. She had the weary tone of the overworked and underpaid.

I thanked her and she departed.

Peggy Sue frowned. "*That's* what you brought for me? *Hello Kitty?*"

I looked down at the pink vinyl suitcase with the iconic Japanese cartoon cat. When I was little,

Mother bought it for me for those occasions when she would come into my bedroom in the middle of the night, saying, "Pack your little kitten bag, dear, we're going on an adventure!"

(Sometime I'll tell you about the "adventure" where Mother drove her car across a cornfield, with me and Hello Kitty in the back, and a trunk-full of butter.)

I said, defensively, "Well, I didn't think you'd want to lug around a *big* suitcase."

Sis muttered, "You might as well have brought a sack."

"Couldn't find one."

"I can't walk out of here carrying that! I'm going to be a senator's wife! What did you bring for me to wear? . . . I hesitate to ask. . . ."

I placed the pink bag on the bed, unzipped it, and yanked out some jeans and a sweatshirt. "Figured you'd want to be comfortable."

Her expression soured further at the sight of the clothes. In her defense, they *were* a little dirty, having been hamper-bound—the only casual things of hers available.

"And," she said, put upon, "I suppose you drove your dented-up car and not my Cadillac?"

Now *I* was put upon. "Don't tell me, Sis—you can't go home in it because you're gonna be a senator's wife."

She gestured with an upturned palm and wiggling fingers. "Give me your phone."

I dug in my purse, gave my cell to her.

She punched in some numbers, then: "Veronica? This is Peggy Sue. . . . Yes, I'm fine. Are you busy? . . . Good. Could you take me home from the hospital? I can't seem to reach Brandy. . . . Great. Oh! And would you bring something of yours for me to wear? All I have are nightclothes."

Peggy Sue handed the cell phone back, with, "Veronica just got a new BMW, and wears Lauren's Blue Label."

"I'll put her on speed dial."

She pursed her pretty pink lips. "I don't mean to be ungrateful, but I have to start thinking about appearances."

"I think you started thinking about appearances maybe forty years ago."

"Brandy. . . ."

"I'll see you at home."

A sigh. "Yes. I already have the hospital release papers. . . . Brandy?"

"Huh?"

"Help yourself to any of those flowers on the windowsill—anything but these roses . . . Edward brought them, and I'll take them home myself."

I crossed over to the window, and picked up a fall mum arrangement. "Say, this is lovely. Who's it from?"

"James Lawrence," she said. "You don't know him."

I set the mums down, and turned. "No, but I know *of* him. His brother was Stephen, the Lawrence boy who died in Vietnam."

Sis looked almost confused. "That's right—how did you know about that?"

Suddenly it dawned on me that we hadn't yet told Peggy Sue about the valuable cornet Stephen had given to Anna, which wound up in our possession, and most likely was the cause of her hospital stay.

So I took the chair by her bed again.

When I'd filled her in somewhat, she said, "Look, if you're thinking James had anything to do with our break-in, you're loopier than Mother. James is an old peacenik who's been living in Toronto since college."

"And who is back in town, obviously. Did he send these flowers, or come to visit?"

"He came to visit."

"Did he say when he got back to Serenity?"

She frowned in thought. "A few weeks or so, I believe."

"Right." I gave her a told-you-so smile. "And why did he come to see you, if not to find out whether you would recognize him from the assault?"

"Oh, Brandy, that's ridiculous."

"Is it? Why *did* he visit you? Did you know him from childhood? Did you go to school together?"

"How old do you think I *am*, anyway?" she asked, offended. "I didn't go to school with either Lawrence boy—Stephen was eight years older, and James six. But everyone in town knew the two well-off Lawrence boys."

I pulled up the chair. I wasn't surprised Sis would keep track of rich prospects, even at an early age. "What were they like?"

Sis settled back against her pillows. "Stevie was a dreamboat, so handsome and smart . . . I hated the fact that I was too young to date him."

"Okay. What about James?"

"Jimmy was the complete opposite. Oh, he was almost as cute as his brother, but more in a James Dean kind of way, always in some kind of trouble. A real Peck's Bad Boy."

I didn't know the latter reference, but got the gist, though how James Dean evolved into a harmless peacenik, I had no idea.

Sis was saying, "When he was eighteen, and I was twelve, something happened between us."

I raised my eyebrows.

"Not *that* kind of 'something' . . . just something that happened, where I kind of helped him out of a jam, and he appreciated it and was always nice to me after. Despite our age difference, we stayed in touch off and on, even after he left for Toronto to avoid the draft."

"Is that all there is to the story?"

She glanced at her watch. "Veronica will be here soon, and I have to fix my face."

"Looks fine to me. Spill."

"Maybe later. At home. Now go."

Reluctantly, I got up from the chair and headed to the window to collect the mum arrangement from the mysterious James, when something occurred to me, and I turned.

"Please tell me you've been in touch with Ashley," I said.

My niece was at college out east, and I'd spoken to her briefly the night after the break-in. She'd been alarmed obviously, and I'd played it down, but I hoped Peggy Sue had called her to ease any concerns.

And she had.

Peggy Sue said, "Ashley wanted to come, but I said I was fine and didn't want her to miss any classes."

"What about this new wrinkle?"

"What new wrinkle is that?"

I winced; she was maddening. "The you-being-my-mother, me-being-her-stepsister, the senator-being-my-father, you-*marrying*-my-father-the-senator, all-of-this-maybe-coming-out wrinkle . . . ?"

"Oh. *That* one." She avoided my gaze. "Not yet."

"Well, you'd better do it before cable news does!"

She raised a surrender palm. "I know, I know . . . it just wasn't the right time, over the phone. You've told Jake, naturally. I mean, he knows everything, right?"

"Uh . . ."

Sis looked at me with an arched brow.

"I'll call him as soon as I get home," I said.

"Brandy?"

"Yes?"

Was my biological mother about to say something tender, something loving to me, that would begin healing wounds?

"When you get home, please hide that old car of yours around *back* of the house . . . and leave the Caddie in the drive."

I gathered the flowers, picked up Hello Kitty, and headed out.

At the veterinary hospital, I waited anxiously for Dr. Tillie to bring Sushi out from the back, and when he handed her to me, she was so excited, the little fur ball piddled on my T-shirt—but I didn't even care. She was alive and happy and so was I.

"Any instructions?" I asked.

"She's fine," he assured me. "But if you have any concerns, you know where to find me."

I laughed. "Not in the middle of the night, I hope."

"I hope so, too," he admitted.

I paid the bill—*Yikes! The antiques booth better make a good profit this month.* Then I left with my bundle—the smell of the mums in the backseat helping to hide the *Eau de Sushi* I was wearing.

On the ride home, the little darling—normally content with sitting in the passenger seat—insisted on perching on my lap. Apparently, from a side angle, this made it look like she was driving, judging by the double takes we garnered from pedestrians along the way.

Inside the house, I released Sushi at the edge of the living room and she scurried around happily getting her familiar bearings. Meanwhile, I checked the answering machine for messages—particularly any from the police department that might report Mother's arrest on some downtown shenanigan or other.

All clear.

I turned to find Soosh sniffing at the spot on the wooden floor near the edge of the Oriental carpet where Peggy Sue's blood had pooled, even though I had repeatedly cleaned the area with disinfectant and bleach.

The little mutt had an incredible sense of smell, often surprising me, like the time she kept scratching to get under my bed, its low structure preventing her from doing so. I checked with a flashlight for an old bone or abandoned treat that might have tumbled down between the mattress and foot-board, but found nothing. Even a swipe with a broom brought out only dust. But Soosh wouldn't give up her pawing. Finally, I moved the heavy bed, and saw a tiny, tiny piece (more like a crumb) of a cookie (Girl Scouts peanut-butter sandwich) that I'd eaten in bed six months before while reading *Lucky* magazine.

While Sushi trotted off to her bed in the kit-chen, I got my cell phone and sat on the couch to call Jake, expecting to leave a message for him to call me when he got off school . . . but he answered.

"Hey, Mom. What's up?" He sounded older than twelve, boy beginning his journey into man.

"I'm surprised to catch you at home," I said. I didn't want to lay anything heavy on him in be-tween classes.

"Got out early. In-service day."

"Good, because I have something important to tell you, even though I'd rather do it in person."

His response was lightly sarcastic. "You gonna have somebody *else's* baby for them?"

"No, once was enough for me. This is about family, though."

"Okay. What?"

And as matter-of-fact as I could, I told him.

After a long silence, Jake asked, "Does this mean Grandma isn't my grandma?"

"She's really your great-grandmother."

"Oh. And Aunt Peg isn't my aunt, but my . . . *grandma?*"

"That's right," I said chipper, trying to sell it, so

wishing I could have done this in person. "And your cousin Ashley is now your . . ." What was she? Niece? Aunt? Stepaunt? You couldn't tell the players without a scorecard in this family.

Jake said, "What if I don't like these changes?"

"I'm sorry, honey . . . I felt the same way as you do, when I found out. If it helps, you can keep on calling them 'Grandma,' or 'Aunt,' like you always have. Nothing has *really* changed."

"I guess. Does Dad know?"

"No. I'll tell him later. I just wanted to make sure you knew about this, because it might get in the media."

" 'cause of that senator?"

"Right. Jake, honey . . . are you okay with this?"

"Sure. Look, I gotta go. I'm meeting some friends. . . ."

I didn't want to end the call, but said, "All right, sweetie—have a good time! And call me if you want to talk again."

I sat for a moment, mulling over the conversation, wondering if I'd handled it all right.

I was about to head upstairs to change my piddled-on top, when I spotted Peggy Sue in the driveway, getting out of Veronica's silver BMW, wearing her friend's tony clothes, and toting a borrowed Vuitton carry-on.

Shaking my head, I watched her pause next to the car, granting any paparazzi who might be lurking in the bushes or treetops a good photo pose, before sashaying up the walk.

Now there were *two* prima donnas living in this house—three, if you counted Sushi.

"Any sign of Chris Matthews or Anderson Cooper?" I asked, as Peggy came in the front door.

She gave me a disgusted look. "No, of course not. But I can't be too careful from now on—I'm not sure when Edward will announce our marriage. Have to look my best."

Sometimes, Peggy Sue took shallowness to new depths.

Abandoning the Vuitton in the entryway, she crossed the Oriental rug to sit on the Victorian couch.

"We have to talk," she said.

"Didn't we just do a bunch of that at the hospital? I'm tired and want a nap before dinner."

"A nap? Are you a child? Are you eighty years old? Brandy. Come. Sit."

She patted a spot next to her.

I sighed, then paddled over and sat. As an older sister, she'd always made me feel about seven years old. Now that I knew she was my mother, I felt five.

"First of all . . ." She sniffed the air. "What smells?"

I gestured to my top. "Sushi was excited to see me. Should I change?"

"No. Just . . . move down a little."

I did.

She tried again. "First of all, I don't want Mom to know anything about the marriage—not until it's formally announced. If she gets even the slightest whiff"—after the word *whiff,* Peggy Sue scooted farther away—"the news will be all over town."

"Mother does know how to use a computer, you know. It'd be all over the known universe. *Martians* would know."

"All the more reason to keep this from her as long as possible."

"She won't hear it from me," I promised.

"Good. Now, concerning that awful murder . . ."

Murders. Sis didn't know about Anna Armstrong—I hadn't filled her in on that part yet.

". . . you have *got* to keep Mom from looking into it."

"Right," I said with a smirk. "And how exactly am I supposed to do that? Short of nailing her feet to the floor."

"I'd loan you a hammer if I could," Sis said dryly. "Make Mom understand that it's better for the police to handle such matters. She has to stop snooping into these kinds of things or she's going to get herself in real trouble."

I gaped. "You absolutely have *no idea,* do you?"

"About what?"

"About stopping Mother from doing something she has it in her head to do." I spread my hands. "In case you haven't noticed, she's a force of nature. She's not going to listen to either one of us."

"Brandy, you need to *try.* . . ."

"Besides, I have a vested interest in this one . . . lest you forget, someone tried to kill you and Sushi." (I put them in the right order that time. I hoped Sushi wasn't listening.) "And who's to say our intruder won't come back?"

Peggy Sue set her pretty lips in a pout. "I can't have you two running around stirring up trouble! I'm going to be a—"

"I know! I *know! A* senator's wife." Before I lost it entirely, I switched gears. "By the way, what exactly is the rest of the story where you and James Lawrence are concerned?"

Before Sis could reply, Mother burst through the front door, out of breath, eyes wild, hair disheveled. She looked like the survivor of a dust storm, minus the dust.

"What a productive day!" she proclaimed. "And how are my darling daughters? Everything go all right at the hospital?"

We both nodded.

Mother came forward, gazing down at Sis. "You look a little tired, dear . . . why don't you take a nap? I'll call you in about an hour for dinner."

"I feel fine," Peggy Sue objected.

Mother put hands on hips. "I do think a little lie-down is in order, dear. Remember what you've been through."

Sis stood. "All right." She gave me a "Remember what we talked about look," and I was tempted to say, "What are you, a child? Are you eighty years old?"

But I didn't, and she headed for the stairs, defeated by Mother's strength of will. And this was the woman who wanted me to stand up to Vivian Borne and discourage her detective delusions?

Then Mother said, "Good, she's gone," and turned to me. "Come . . . to the Incident Room."

Earlier, Mother had dragged a large old wooden green-faced schoolroom chalkboard into the dining room, which meant that we would be eating on TV trays for the duration.

I parked myself at the table, while Mother began writing on the board.

MURDER VICTIMS:

Big Jim Bob
Anna Armstrong
Lillian Lawrence (?)

NEAR MURDER VICTIMS:

Peggy Sue
Sushi

SUSPECTS:

John Anderson
Waldo Hendricks
Milton Lawrence
Texas partner of BJB

"Who's Lillian Lawrence?" I asked.

"Milton's late wife—just a hunch."

Knowing not to question Mother's hunches, I said, "You should add James Lawrence under 'Suspects.'"

"Ahh," Mother said. "Then you *know* the prodigal's been spotted in town."

Having gotten nowhere with Sis on the subject, I asked Mother, "Were Peggy Sue and James ever close?"

Mother frowned. "A few times he gave her a ride home from school—he had a Corvette convertible back then. But I put a stop to that because she wasn't even a teenager yet, and he was in high school."

Was *that* the "thing" Peggy Sue and James Lawrence had had?

I said, "Back then, people weren't as suspicious
of an older boy driving a young girl around, I suppose."

Mother nodded. "That's true, but I didn't like
it—he was a wild one, and your sister was very attractive and precocious, and I felt she was playing
with fire. Your sister threw a fit when I forbade it,
of course, because I think she felt grown-up riding
in his car, and—What's going on out there?"

Suddenly, Mother's attention was drawn to the
front picture window. She tromped over to it.

"My goodness!" she exclaimed. "That's a lot of
activity!"

I left the table and followed her to have a look.

A TV van was parked at the curb, the female an-
chor from the Davenport nightly news climbing
out, followed by a cameraman.

"Oh my!" Mother exclaimed, eyes bugging behind her glasses. "It would seem my tweets have finally paid off."

Her tweets were more like quacks.

"What are you talking about?" I asked.

Mother, face flushed with excitement, said, "At
last the Fourth Estate has come to query us about
our successful sleuthing! I knew our light would
not be forever hidden 'neath a bushel."

"You *didn't*. . . ."

Mother put hands on hips. "It's about *time* they
took us seriously. How I wish I'd known! Is my hair
all right? Lipstick on straight?"

"You look perfectly demented."

"Good," she said, apparently hearing only "perfect." She smoothed her Breckenridge outfit.

I wagged a forefinger at her. "Just keep me out of this."

"Fine, dear—stay here, if you wish. But I'm going to drink in the limelight."

"You bask in limelight. You die drinking lime."

"That's lye, dear," Mother said. "You have such a tendency for malleable props." Then she hurried out of the dining / incident room, to face the media.

I trailed after her, but turned toward the stairs, opting to hide out in my room.

Only, then I paused.

How could I miss what would certainly prove to be one of Mother's stellar performances? If we solved this case, there would undoubtedly be another book in it, and Mother's hijinks seemed unaccountably popular with our readers, so . . .

I hung back in the entryway to listen behind the screen door.

By now, another local TV crew had arrived, and Mother made her grand entrance onto the porch, taking her position downstage.

The media—now *three* local crews—gathered at the foot of the porch steps, like groundlings, microphones extended, cameras going, asking questions all at once.

Mother raised a benedictory hand. "Now, now. Let's have some sense of decorum. . . ."

Uncharacteristically, the reporters fell silent.

Mother went on. "First of all, I would like to welcome you one and all . . ."

A couple reporters exchanged puzzled glances.

". . . and assure you that I will answer all of your questions until fully exhausted . . ."

Whether Mother meant herself, or them, or both, I couldn't be sure.

". . . but first, I would like to give you a little background about our sleuthing. It all began—"

The Channel 6 anchorwoman shouted, "How long has Senator Edward Clark been seeing your daughter?"

Startled by the question, Mother took a step back, out of the limelight. I felt lucky to be hiding in the wings.

It was starting. . . .

Mother looked as though she had prepared for one play, but wandered into another.

"Why . . . why," she stammered, "Peggy Sue has known the senator—"

"Not *that* daughter," a man from Channel 4 said, "the *other* daughter—Brandy—the one half his age!"

What?

Mother, going up on her lines, was speechless for once.

Channel 4 had an eight-by-ten photo in his hand. "Isn't that *her* the senator's kissing?"

He waved the photo at Mother.

I could see the picture of my father and me: a blow-up of the end of *our* blow-up in the hospital hallway, when he'd kissed me good-bye on the cheek, just a few short hours ago.

Fading back farther, I stepped on something: Peggy Sue's toes.

She yelped, then said, "What's going on?"

"I think your good news has broken. You should go out and relieve Mother."

Smiling, Sis headed out to face the media.

I grabbed Hello Kitty (conveniently still packed), slung my purse over my shoulder, then lammed it out the back to my car, silently thanking Peggy Sue for advising me to hide it back there.

A Trash 'n' Treasures Tip

To get the most out of selling storage unit items, use Internet auction resources like eBay, for the higher-valued finds, *if* packaging and mailing is cost effective. Bulky items can be sold via classified newspapers ads, flea markets, or Craigslist. Mother refuses to use Craigslist, however, because a boy named Craig was unkind to her at her senior prom.

Chapter Nine

A Loss of Trust

Feeling very much like a fugitive, I took refuge from the media storm by checking in at the Holiday Inn Convention Center, on the north edge of town, under my former married name, using a credit card still reflecting that status.

At the desk I picked up a few toiletries not included in Hello Kitty, stuffed with the set of clothes intended for Peggy Sue.

My room opened onto the indoor pool area, where right now no one was swimming or lounging. The scent of chlorine in my nostrils, I sat on the edge of the bed wondering who had taken the photo of the senator and myself, exploiting an all-too-private moment between father and daughter.

Somebody representing his political opposition, probably—somebody shadowing the senator, just waiting for the right time to grab an embarrassing or even incriminating time, without need of a camera, just a cell phone. What little privacy we'd all once had was long gone, courtesy of technology.

Right then my cell trilled, I.D.ing Sis, but I let it go to voice mail. A moment later, Mother tried, and I ignored her, too. Let diva and understudy bask in that limelight they both longed for. Then I shut off the cell.

While I didn't relish hiding out at the Holiday Inn at one-hundred-plus bucks per, I had few other decent options. I certainly couldn't impose on my BFF Tina and Kevin, now that they were dealing with BB (Baby Brandy), who was technically still a preemie (but gaining weight fast, thank goodness).

And, to be perfectly honest, I had been putting off visiting them because—while I was thrilled for Tina and Kevin—seeing the baby so soon would only break my heart.

My stomach growled. It was dinnertime (which is any point between four and six P.M. for us Midwesterners) and since I had trouble thinking on an empty tummy, I grabbed my purse with keycard, and made for the hotel's restaurant, exiting the sliding glass door onto the pool area. The hotel restaurant was just across the pool, and I decided not to swim there, taking the more roundabout route. I wasn't *that* hungry.

The Hawkeye Room had (not surprisingly) a sports-theme going, heavy on the University of Iowa's gold and black and images of their cartoon mascot, Herky the Hawk. Pity the poor Iowa State fan staying here.

I took a cozy table for two by a glass windowed

wall looking out at a large pond, where an assortment of ducks capered in the water, others sunning themselves on the lush green banks. Wouldn't it be nice to be one of them? Until duck season, anyway.

A pretty, plump waitress handed me a menu, and I studied the nutritious salads and heart-healthy meals, then ordered a breaded pork tenderloin with onion rings, which was more in tune with my disposition and the eating habits of farm country.

A few other people were dining early: a young couple drinking wine; two forty-something businessmen devouring steaks; and a sixtyish guy picking at a salad like he'd lost something in it.

Salad Guy—quite fit, tanned, and handsome with thick gray-sandy hair—caught me staring, and flashed me a smile.

Embarrassed, I nodded, then returned my attention to the lucky ducks.

After a short wait, my food arrived, and as I dug in, some of the ducks—either curious or hungry—waddled over to watch me eat, pressing their bills against the glass, as if to say, "How do *you* like it, somebody staring at *you?*" At least I was eating pork—my usual chicken tenders might have made me feel uncomfortable.

And even in Iowa, they don't let hogs loose outside restaurants to come guilt-trip you at the windows.

The last onion ring loaded with catsup was heading into my mouth when the plump waitress approached Salad Guy. She said, "Would you like me to charge this to your room, Mr. Lawrence?"

I nearly choked on the battered bite going down. "That'd be fine, Doris," he said to her.

James Lawrence?

Risking another glance, I could make out remnants of the boyish face from the photograph Mother had found at Anna's apartment.

Looked like I wasn't the only prodigal hiding out at the Holiday Inn.

After Lawrence had gone, Doris asked me if I wanted dessert and I said I did—they served a mean strawberry rhubarb pie, and I was in no frame of mind to watch my diet—and then I asked her how long "James" had been at the hotel, nice and casual.

She crinkled her brow, mildly suspicious.

I said, "He's from here. I don't think he recognized me, but I knew James years ago."

That should be just enough to sell it, but not too much to bog it down. . . .

She uncrinkled her brow and said, "Think he's been with us a couple weeks, anyway."

Which meant James *had* been in Serenity at the time of Big Jim Bob's demise, and our home invasion, and possibly even Anna Armstrong's murder.

Back in my room, I turned on the Channel 6 news, just catching the end of a report by Erica Paul, the local newswoman who'd been the first to arrive at the Borne homestead this afternoon.

She stood on the sidewalk with our porch and front door looming behind her, hand mic poised before her perfectly made-up face.

"There are now reports," she said animatedly, "that the young woman in the photo with Senator Edward Clark is *not* his young lover, rather an illegitimate *daughter*. I emphasize that this is as yet to be confirmed by our network news division . . ." She let the pregnant pause hang, then gave birth to this beauty: ". . . but one thing *is* certain: this news, coming at this time, cannot be good for the senator's reelection."

"You think?" I said to her, and shot at her with the TV remote, switching to pay-TV, where I spent the remainder of the evening watching a big dumb action movie followed by the new Woody Allen movie (they never come here), and putting a dent in the minibar, and I don't mean the nuts and Snickers bars.

The next morning I woke with a terrible sinus headache, or was it the flu?

All right!

So I was hung over. I don't drink that much, and I have had hangovers only rarely in my relatively young life, so when I *do* have one, it's two things: a) a shock to my system, and b) a doozy. You know that corny bit in the movies where people with hangovers experience even the most minor noise as exaggerated, an echo-chamber roar? Turns out that isn't a corny bit. Those were all documentaries, those movies. . . .

I found two stray aspirins in my purse, expending no more effort than running the last lap of a marathon race. Then I took a cold shower, toweled off, shivering like I really did have the flu, then dressed in the hamper-bound jeans and sweatshirt I'd unpacked from Hello Kitty. After using my lipstick as a cheek blush, trying not to look as sickly as I felt, I somehow exited my room and navigated around the pool on rubbery legs all the way to the restaurant, in hopes something on the menu wouldn't send my stomach bouncing.

And those damn ducks better leave me alone! Or I swear I'll . . . I'll . . . start crying!

I was about to be seated when I spotted James Lawrence across the lobby, heading for the revolving doors.

Curiosity trumping my hangover, I told the hostess I'd changed my mind about breakfast, and hurried to follow my fellow prodigal.

In the parking lot, James climbed into a black Jaguar with Ontario plates, and I hoped he didn't notice, in his rearview mirror, yours truly dashing over to my Buick, parked a few rows away. Mother would have been proud, as I followed him out of the hotel lot, onto the by pass, letting a car slip in between us, to give me some cover.

After a few miles, the Jag veered off at the Locust Street exit, and headed back into town. A few more miles later, break lights flashed, and he swung into the main drive of Greenwood Cemetery.

This destination wasn't user-friendly for somebody tailing a perp. (Well, I know he wasn't necessarily a perp, but I'm afraid TV and Mother have worn off on me.)

Nonetheless, I pulled in myself, taking a secondary drive running parallel to his, keeping his car in sight, hoping I wasn't too obvious.

Greenwood was Serenity's oldest cemetery, dating back centuries. You know the kind, like in horror movies—towering monuments throwing dark shadows, guardian angels warding off evil, and creepy crumbling stone crypts. In more recent years, the wealthy opted out of this ancient grotesquerie, however, in favor of storing their dearly departed in expensive mausoleums—ornate granite structures with stained-glass windows.

Years ago, when Mother brought young Brandy to Greenwood to visit Jonathan Borne—who I'd *thought* had been my real father—she would ask me, "Do you know how many people are dead in this cemetery?"

And young Brandy would say, "No. How many?"

And Mother would say, "All of them."

Which I thought was pretty funny at the time, and it did somehow take the edge off having to visit there.

As I drove slowly along, keeping the Jag in sight, the low morning sun shot through each passing monument like a strobe light, sending sharp pains through my already-throbbing head, accompanying the grinding of gravel under my car's wheels, which reverberated like one twenty-one-gun salute after another.

When James finally pulled his car over in front of a particularly grand mausoleum, I paused long enough to watch him exit his car, debating what to do next.

Mother would have come up with some ridiculous reason for being here *exactly* at the same time as James . . . but I had no patience with subterfuge, and limited talents of improvisation. So I continued on to the next cross drive, then drove back to where the Jag was parked, inching the Buick up to his.

In a brown corduroy jacket and tan slacks, James

was seated on a cement bench in front of the mausoleum, his back to me, and when I shut the car door, he craned his neck, his somber expression turning to surprise.

"Well, hello," he ventured.

"Hi," I responded as I walked toward him through freshly cut grass.

He looked up at me. "Weren't you in the hotel's restaurant yesterday evening?"

"That's right."

His eyebrows raised and maybe that was a smile. ". . . and weren't you all over the news this morning?"

"Oh yeah. Belle of the ball."

"Hiding out at the Holiday Inn, huh?"

I nodded.

"Not very dignified, is it?"

"Not when you raid the minibar and pay for it in the morning."

That made him laugh. "Well, I don't blame you for ducking the media. I've had my own share of bad publicity. I don't think anyone will think to look for you in a cemetery."

That was a smile, and it was nice—mischievous. I liked him already.

I nodded toward the mausoleum. "Visiting your mother?"

"Yes." He patted the cement seat next to him. "Please, sit."

I did. "I guess you know who I am. If you were paying attention to the news, anyway."

"I know you're my friend Peggy Sue's sister. Or should I say daughter?"

"It's like that scene in *Chinatown*," I said. " 'Sister, daughter, sister, daughter' . . . without the slapping, thankfully."

"Nice to meet you, Brandy Borne." He extended a hand.

I shook it—warm, firm, not show-offy strong. "Nice to meet you . . ."

Should I admit I knew who he was?

"James Lawrence," he said, like somebody in the wings prompting Mother. "But don't you know that? I mean, you *did* follow me out here."

"Spotted me, huh?"

He grinned. "Not till you ran that red light to keep up."

"It was pink. Not that running a light's *okay*, but there weren't any other cars, and . . . look, I don't normally follow men around, you understand."

"They probably follow you some," he said, having swiveled to look at me. "So what can I do for you, Ms. Borne?"

"First, you can call me 'Brandy.' " I took a breath. "Second, you can quench a sister/daughter's curiosity."

"I'm willing to try, within reason. And my friends call me Jim."

"Okay, Jim. You visited Peggy Sue in the hospital, either today or yesterday, not sure which . . . anyway, you brought her some flowers. I was just wondering what your relationship was."

His eyebrows raised. "What did Peg *say* it was?"

I shrugged. "She didn't. All she said was that there had been 'something' between you years ago. But the age difference makes anything romantic, at least back then, very unlikely. Hey, don't worry—I already figured out who my father is."

Again wearing an almost smile, he remained silent for a moment, gazing at the mausoleum, clearly wondering whether or not to tell me to mind my own business.

Finally he said, "It *wasn't* romantic. Only in the vaguest, someday-when-you're-old-enough-give-me-a-call kinda way. But I *was* a little wild when I was young—"

"A regular J.D., I heard."

"What's the phrase? Rebel without a clue?" He spread his hands. "Anyway, sometimes I'd give Peggy Sue a ride from school—I was a senior in high school, and she was in middle school. I had this Corvette convertible, and I'd see her walking those couple miles home."

"Back then, a neighborhood guy giving a girl her age a ride was no big deal."

"Right. And I was just being friendly. But, again, I'd lying if I said it didn't cross my mind that I wished she were older, because she was so beautiful."

And even at that age, Peggy would have known James was "so rich". . . .

"Well," he was saying, "one day, just before graduation, I was in a jewelry store downtown, looking at a gold necklace for my mom, when Peggy Sue came in to buy another charm for her bracelet— or some such thing. And while the owner was busy with her, I swiped the necklace."

"What? Why? You come from—" I couldn't find the polite way of saying it.

"Yeah, my family was stinking rich. Still are." He shook his head. "I don't know why I did it—I had the money."

Rebel without a clue was right.

"What happened?"

He shrugged a shoulder. "Peg must have seen me do it. Anyway, she comes running out after me, and really lays into me. Then she grabs the necklace out of my jacket pocket, and runs back in the store and says *she* swiped it."

"Really?" That didn't sound like Sis.

He went on: "She told the store manager that she did it on impulse, and she was sorry, and she wanted to give it back. She worked up a bunch of tears, too—probably was scared enough that that wasn't hard. Now the store manager doesn't believe her, not really, he *knows* I took it, just can't prove it. And anyway, the store got it back, and with a nice little kid like your sis involved, no charges were filed."

"You were eighteen," I said. "You'd have done time."

He nodded. "You are so right. And I already was on probation for something else stupid I did. So I owed Peggy Sue. I owed her a lot."

I gave him a half smile. "You don't think she was motivated by losing her ride in a Corvette with an older guy? Particularly a cute one from a wealthy family?"

He gave me the other half of the smile. "Well, there's that. She was a smart, pragmatic kid. But, nonetheless, it was a spunky thing for someone her age to do. Took spine. Took guts."

I had to agree.

"And for me, that incident was one of those life-defining moments, coming to that fork in the road you hear so much about. Turn one way, your life goes bad, the other way, good . . . or, anyway, *better*, in my case. Ever have one of those?"

"Oh, yeah." Like the night of my tenth high school reunion when I threw my marriage out the window for an old flame. A real bad fork up.

He seemed about to ask for details I didn't want to share, so I asked, "Jim, what brought you back to Serenity, after all this time?"

He nodded toward the mausoleum. "When my mother died in 1975, I couldn't make it home."

"Because you were in Canada."

"Avoiding the draft, yeah. You seem to know a lot about me."

I shrugged. "My mother, Vivian, is the twenty-four-hour news of local gossips."

His turn to shrug. "I'm not ashamed of being a so-called draft dodger. I operated out of self-interest, but I really did have strong feelings about the wrongness of that war. And I have never changed my opinions, especially since my brother ended his life facedown in a rice field for *nothing*."

His eyes were wet.

"Were you close, you and Stephen?"

"Very. Not all brothers *are*, you know. Especially when the father makes no pretense about favoring one over the other. But we were tight. Really tight."

"But your dad favoring Stephen . . . I suppose that's why you were so wild."

"Maybe. Or maybe I was just wired differently than Steve."

Like Peggy Sue and me.

I said, "You did all right. Everybody calls you a 'peacenik.' But you sure didn't *stay* a hippie."

He chuckled. "Well, I did manage to make a good life for myself in Toronto."

As owner of Lawrence Communications, one of the largest telecommunications companies in Canada, having gotten in on the ground floor of cable TV in 1975. (I looked him up on the Net.)

"Jim—mind if I ask you a personal question?"

His laugh was half cough. "Well, what have *these* been?"

I smiled. "Guilty as charged. . . . Anyway, I heard that your mother always looked out for you—maybe to offset your father's indifference . . ."

James took a beat, then nodded.

". . . but when she died, she didn't leave you anything."

"That's right—more local gossip, courtesy of Vivian Borne?"

"More or less. Didn't you wonder why she'd left you out in the cold? I mean, you hadn't made your own fortune yet."

He drew in a deep breath. Leaves in trees rustled with the wind, as if a physical manifestation of his thoughts.

Then he said: "I've come to look at it like this, Brandy—being cut off made me find my own way, make my own success. Besides, I'm not sure how well I would have handled the kind of money my mother said she was going to leave me."

"She indicated she was going to leave you money?"

"Oh yes. She and I stayed in touch. The money I started my business with came from what I'd saved from regular checks she'd been sending. And of course we spoke on the phone frequently. I was to be well taken care of. But somehow my father must have changed her mind. She was sick toward the end—Alzheimer's. Manipulating her wouldn't have been difficult."

I frowned. "Jim, you've been really nice, very generous, about answering my nosy questions . . . so I'll tell you something you might like to know."

"What's that?"

"Do you remember the Bix Beiderbecke cornet that belonged to your brother?"

"Sure! Steve treasured that thing. He was such a jazz buff, Steve."

"Well . . . I know where it is."

And I went into the whole song and dance about winning the storage unit and finding the provenance papers in the bell of the horn.

He was shaking his head, smiling in astonishment. "I always wondered what happened to that cornet," he said. "I hoped to someday end up with it. But I figured it was long gone."

"You'd like to have it because of its . . . value?"

"Yes, but not monetary value—sentimental. My interest in that item is strictly personal. You see, I have nothing to remember Steve by, really—just a few old photos that I took when I left home."

"Did you know Anna Armstrong had been killed?"

He nodded solemnly. "When I passed through Davenport on my way here, I stopped to see her. *Tried* to see her, anyway." His chin tightened. "I guess she died the day before."

We fell silent.

Then suddenly he leaned toward me. "Brandy—

would you—you and Vivian—consider selling the cornet to me?"

I said, "As a matter of fact we *are* planning to sell it . . . but when and how will be Mother's call. Vivian, I mean, not Peggy Sue."

He nodded, his expression one of understanding. "But you'll let me know, if you *are* going to sell? To give me a fair shot at it?"

"Sure. How long will you be in town?"

"A few more days, anyway. I have some meetings with the city planning commission. Now that my . . . father . . . is retiring and leaving town, I'm considering giving something back to the community that put up with me all those years ago."

"Cool," I said. "Hey, I'd like to see the bike path extended."

Even if my old Schwinn did have two flat tires.

"It's a possibility," he said with a smile.

He was thirty years older than me, but I could definitely understand what twelve-year-old Peggy Sue had seen in him. And it wasn't just his money.

I stood. "Well. See you around the hotel. Don't miss the meeting of the Prodigal Offspring Association at the stroke of midnight."

"Wouldn't miss it for the world," he said, and we shook hands again.

Then I left him alone with his mother.

Back in my hotel room, I risked calling mine.

"Brandy, dear . . . where have you been?" She sounded out of breath, and rather giddy. "You've missed all the hoopla!"

"That was the point. Have the reporters gone?"

"Yes, dear, they've scurried off, like rats off a sinking ship!"

Apparently she hadn't thought that one through, since that made our house the sinking ship. Or had she?

I said, "I find it hard to believe they aren't skulking somewhere in the neighborhood."

"No, they've gone, at least for now. You see, the senator and Peggy Sue are holding a press conference this afternoon to explain everything, and it's *not* here."

"Where then?"

"Channel Six in Davenport. They're the NBC affiliate."

So the senator was going public. Out of necessity? Or as some kind of PR stunt? I wasn't sure I cared anymore.

I said, "Guess who besides me is staying here at the Holiday Inn?"

"The national media!"

"No, Mother—James Lawrence."

And I told her about my morning conversation with Jim, emphasizing his belief that his mother had intended to leave him an inheritance.

"Good work, dear! I'm afraid I've allowed myself to get stars in my eyes, with all these cameras and microphones waving at me. It's just not *like* me."

"No. Not like you at all."

"I'd like to clear up this business of a will once and for all—Brandy, come pick me up. Toot sweet."

"Okay. Where are we going?"

"To drop in on Wayne Ekhardt."

"He doesn't have office hours today."

"I know. We'll beard the lion in his den!"

"Go to his house, you mean?"

"That's exactly what I mean!"

It disturbed me, realizing I was actually starting to understand almost everything she said. . . .

"Mother, shouldn't we *call* Wayne first?"

In all the time we had known him, the cagey lawyer had managed to keep Mother away from his residence, meeting only at his office.

"No! He might say not to come. We'll just surprise him."

"Do you think that's wise . . . he *is* almost ninety—"

But Mother had already hung up.

Half an hour later, with Mother riding shotgun, I guided our trusty, rusty Buick onto Park Drive—a picturesque neighborhood of well-tended old homes bordering Weed Park.

I know what you're thinking, and I apologize to those of you who've already heard this unlikely but very true explanation; but the park—ten acres of gently rolling, green-grassy land overlooking the river—was donated to the city by a family named Weed.

Years ago, the park had a zoo, including (but not limited to) a smelly snake house; a surly, peanut-shooting elephant named Candy; some marauding mountain goats; and the rudest orangutans this side of the Congo.

Then in the early 1980s, due to the soaring expense of maintenance (along with pressure from animal activists), the elephant shot its last peanut, and the zoo closed.

But, as Mother is wont to say, I digress.

"There's Wayne's house, dear," Mother said, pointing to a brick Tudor.

I pulled into a drive and up to the well-kept, two-story hugged by a tidy row of evergreen bushes. Next to the house, a tall oak loomed, spreading its vibrant-colored leafy limbs out for protection and shade. We exited the car, then walked a short distance to three cement steps leading up to a screened-in porch.

There was no buzzer, and Mother raised a bony fist to rap on the door, when I stopped her hand, spotting Mr. Ekhardt on the porch, snoozing in an overstuffed chair, feet stretched out on a matching ottoman. He looked pale and skeletal in his over-sized sweats. As usual, whether he was alive or deceased was a mystery.

"Don't startle him," I whispered.

Mother frowned. "How *else* is the dear man to know we are here?"

"Well . . . knock lightly, then."

She did.

He didn't stir.

Mother rapped harder.

He still didn't stir.

Mother tried the door, found it open, and went on in, while I hung back on the steps watching through the screen. Had the time finally come? Was the great lawyer standing before the biggest bench of all?

Mother went over to Ekhardt, bent as if at the bed of a slumbering child, then gave his slight shoulders a shake. "Wayne, dear, wakey wakey."

The attorney's creped eyelids slid open, blinked several times as he took in Mother's face, then closed again.

"What a strange dream," he muttered.

Did he mean Mother?

She shook his shoulder again, and the eyes opened again, this time in a wide stare.

"Oh, it *is* you," he said.

Unfazed, Mother replied, "Yes, dear, it is I, *and* little Brandy . . . come for a neighborly visit."

We were his neighbors like I was "little" Brandy.

He rolled a dry tongue around in his mouth for a moment, pulled himself up a bit, then, with a resigned sigh, asked, "What is it, Vivian?"

Mother sat down on the ottoman, scooching his legs over. I continued to watch all of this through the crosshatch of the screen door.

"Wayne," she began, "we've been friends for a long time . . . always truthful and honest with each other . . ."

Him: *possibly.* Her: *rarely.*

". . . yet I feel there's more to this business about Lillian and her will than you've told me."

Ekhardt, his face flushed, said tightly, "Vivian, as I've said before, there *was* no *will.*"

Mother shook her head. "I have it on *good* authority that Vivian told her son James that she would provide for him in the event of her death."

Hey! I had just risen to the rank of "good authority"!

The ancient attorney stared at Mother, his lips a thin, tight line, as if he were hoping she were a vision that would dematerialize.

When she didn't, a sigh began at his toes and

found its way out his mouth. Then he said, "You're not going to give up, Viv, are you?"

"No, dear. You *know* me."

The old boy did, because he surrendered with no more fight.

"Very well," he said. "I'll come clean, and frankly . . . it's about time . . . I've carried this around with me for thirty-some years."

I quietly opened the screen door and stepped in, not wanting to miss anything.

"There really never was a will, Vivian," he said slowly. "That much was true. Mine was a lie of omission."

"Whatever do you mean?"

"There *was* a trust set up by Lillian for James."

"Then . . . then it must have been *revokable*, if James received nothing."

Meaning Milton had been able to cancel it.

The lawyer said nothing, though his rheumy eyes spoke volumes.

Mother leaned forward, earnestly. "Don't tell me it was *irrevokable!*"

When Ekhardt did not reply, Mother gave a little gasp.

I couldn't help saying, "I don't understand."

Mother's head swiveled on her neck toward me, stopping just short of an *Exorcist* impression. "It's self-explanatory, dear. Irrevokable means James *should* have received his money."

I spread my arms. "Then where did it go?"

Mother made a "hush" motion to me, and that's when I noticed a single gleaming tear slide down the wrinkled hollow-cheeked face of our longtime lawyer.

Mother looked back at him. "You suppressed the trust, Wayne? Or . . . *allowed* it to be suppressed?"

As if there were a difference.

Ekhardt slowly nodded. "A few months before Lillian died, Milton found out about the trust . . . whether she told him, or he discovered a copy of it, I honestly can't say . . . but he wanted it undone, voided. When I told him that wasn't possible, he said he would contest the trust in open court . . . bring in medical information showing that at the time the trust was drawn up, Lillian was already suffering from Alzheimer's."

"Had she been?" I asked.

Ekhardt shrugged his slight shoulders. "My opinion was that Lillian knew what she was doing or I wouldn't have drawn up the trust." Another deep breath, another sigh. "But I had no doubt that Milton would have dragged her good name through the court. She was in advanced stages of her disease, and putting her on display . . . what a travesty, what a tragedy that would have been. She was still enough herself to have sensed the shame. . . . I felt it would have been sheer hell for her."

Mother said, "So you destroyed the trust agreement. But your reluctance to do so wound up losing you a very valuable client in Milton Lawrence."

The lawyer's nod was barely perceptible. "It's the only time in my entire career that I did something I was really ashamed of."

"You should have been disbarred," I said.

His watery eyes found my face. "Yes, I should. And I have lived with that knowledge every day since."

Ekhardt leaned forward, buried his face in his hands. Mother rose and went to sit on the arm of his chair, slipping a comforting arm around his shoulders.

And I slipped out to wait in the car.

A Trash 'n' Treasures Tip

Contents of a storage unit can sometimes be sold immediately after the auction by the winner to dealers who lost out, thus eliminating extra hauling. So be friendly and polite to your fellow bidders. Mother has on occasion paid dearly for having said, "Nah nah nah *nah* nah!"

Chapter Ten

A Rocky Homecoming

A good fifteen minutes passed before Mother emerged from Wayne Ekhardt's house, while I cooled my heels in the Buick, windows down, crisp fall breeze keeping me company.

"Is he all right?" I asked Mother as she settled into the passenger seat.

"My, yes. The old dear will be just fine."

I grunted. " 'The old dear' should be disbarred for suppressing that irrevocable trust."

Mother sighed. "Perhaps once upon a time, but at the age of ninety—with the infraction so far in the past—I scarcely think that will happen. Why, is it a point you would like to press?"

"Well, no. But that 'infraction' could still get him sued."

Mother was frowning at me, thoughtfully. "Are you going to share this information with James Lawrence?"

"I think I should at least suggest that he speak to

Wayne about it. Do you think the 'old dear' will come clean?"

Mother was nodding. "If I know Wayne, he will."

Starting the car, I mumbled, "Maybe you didn't know him as well as you thought. . . . Where to?"

"River Road—north."

She wasn't more specific, and I knew it was futile to ask.

I caught River Road on the other side of the park, then headed along the twisty two-lane that took us by the Lucky Four Leaf Clover, the storage facility looking benignly banal against a colorful fall-foliage backdrop, as if nothing out of the ordinary had ever happened there.

I expected Mother to tell me to pull in at the storage facility, but she had something else— somewhere else—on her mind. Mine was not to reason why, mine was but to do and drive.

As we cruised along, the Mississippi—looming too close for comfort on the right—glimmered with gold highlights in the early-afternoon sun. My stomach growled, and I wished we had stopped somewhere for lunch—even a stale hot dog (best with catsup and pickles, despite what Mother says about mustard and relish).

But Mother had no need for sustenance, fueled by her own obsessive energies, her eyes glued ahead in rapt attention, like single-minded Sushi anticipating a rare adventure away from home.

In ten minutes or so, we passed through the tiny town of Freeport, just a bump in the road with a two-pump gas station/bait shop amid a cluster of clapboard houses.

"Turn right," Mother said.

She knew where we were going, anyway.

I did as I was told, veering off the main road onto gravel that took us bumping across a railroad track, then down along a row of summer cottages built on stilts on a sliver of land begrudgingly given up by the river. Come spring flooding, the Mississippi would reclaim it.

"That's Big Jim Bob's house," Mother said, pointing to a handsome-looking tan single-story structure held up by cement block columns; stored in the space beneath the cottage, on a metal-frame trailer, was a spiffy speedboat.

Big Jim Bob was doing all right. Or . . . *had* been doing all right. . . .

I eased the Buick in beside an open stairway leading up several straight flights to a landing. We got out and—with Mother very much in the lead, not bothering with the railing (which I held on to for dear life)—we climbed to where a half-circle deck offered a splendid view of the water and shoreline beyond.

I stood taking it in. "Okay, now I get it."

"Get what, dear?"

"Why some people want to live here and fight the flooding every year."

The ambiance *was* quite relaxing, particularly if you factored out the mosquitoes and fishy smell.

"Yes, dear," Mother said, nodding like the wise guru she thought she was, also taking in the view, "it *is* rather like being on vacation year-round."

Then her meditative moment passed, and she was moving as quickly as if in dire need of a bathroom, heading toward the cottage door, which was centered between rows of windows. She tried the door, whose top half consisted of four glass panels, and of course it was locked.

"Check for a key, dear," she said.

There was a welcome mat (even if it didn't say "Welcome"), but no key was under it. I checked under a heavy planter. Nothing.

"Go back downstairs," Mother ordered, "and check for a rock key."

Everybody in the Midwest has a rock key—a fake rock that you hide among real rocks that look nothing like the fake one. Dutifully, I did as she asked. There was gravel down there, but not really any rocks, fake or otherwise.

Back on the porch, I reported my failure.

"Well, dear, we'll just have to break in."

"As in breaking and entering?"

"Well, in this case, you can't have one without the other," Mother said patiently. "And the owner is deceased, so he can hardly press charges."

"That's your understanding, is it? That it's legal to break into houses if the occupant is deceased? *You* may have a good time in jail, Mother, but I don't think *I* would."

"Nonsense. Just one small tap on that pane of glass, and you can reach in and unlock the door for us."

"No way."

"Very well," Mother said, disgruntled, "*I'll* do the dirty work. You are, at times, a most disappointing Watson."

"Yeah, well there are better Sherlocks, too."

She made a fist with one hand. "Now, you *do* know what to do, should I sever an artery?"

I sighed. "All right! Stand aside."

At least the cottage we were breaking and entering into was hidden from its neighbors by trees. This broad daylight home invasion would be less than subtle. . . .

Slipping off one shoe, I aimed the heel and gave the pane a quick hard *whap!*

Glass tinkled down on the inside. A few more whaps dislodged any remaining sharp pieces, then I reached a trembling hand through to unlock the door.

We stepped inside, our feet crunching glass shards, and stood surveying the front room, which was tastefully decorated with modern furnishings, if in a surprisingly feminine manner. Facing the river was a pastel floral couch and matching side chair, along with a couple of nice end tables and brass lamps. A card table and four chairs took up one corner, a jigsaw puzzle of the President and First Lady nearly completed.

"I always said Big Jim Bob had wonderful taste," Mother gushed. (I had the feeling she was referring less to BJB's decorating skills and more to his taste in female companionship . . . i.e., herself.)

"Uh-huh," I said, picking up a framed photo on an end table. "Did he also have an African-American wife and two equally African-American kids?"

Mother frowned as I showed her the picture of the happy black family—even Mother, with her poor eyesight, couldn't have mistaken the husband for Big Jim Bob.

"Uh-oh," she said slowly.

Through clenched teeth, I managed, "Can I quote you on that?"

"Perhaps it might be prudent for us to skedaddle."

"You'd be the expert on 'prudent,' right?" I was already heading toward the door.

"Just a moment, dear!" Mother said.

She was digging in her jacket pocket, producing a tiny pencil and a bridge score pad.

"What are you writing?" I asked, as she began to scribble. "Not our *names*, for pity sake!"

Mother harrumphed. "I'm not *that* feeble-minded! I'm merely explaining our error."

I grabbed the pad, which read: *A thousand apologies! We broke into the wrong house.* And tore off the note, crumpled it up, and slipped it in a pocket.

"Well," Mother huffed, "we should at least leave them some money to fix the glass."

"My purse is in the car."

"Run and get it."

"I have five dollars and a few coins. Do you think that's sufficient to repair that door?"

Mother sighed. "Very well, I'll use the emergency funds I always carry with me."

She kept a clump of bills in her bra. I believe she got the idea from the old TV show *Maverick* where James Garner pinned cash inside his vest.

Abandoning Mother to make her monetary amends, I scurried down the long steps to wait in the car, hoping no one drove by—like, say, the homeowners. I worked on a story I might tell them should they show.

After a few minutes, Mother came clomping down the stairs—what one would call beating a hasty retreat as opposed to making a surreptitious exit—apparently undaunted in the face of her (not our!) grave mistake.

She said, "I'm sure it's the cottage next door."

"You're sure?"

"I'm fairly sure."

" 'Fairly sure' doesn't cut it, Mother."

"Almost positively fairly sure. Absolutely."

"Okay. If we get caught breaking into the wrong cottage, or get nabbed for breaking into *this* wrong cottage"—I gestured to the scene of our crime—"*here's* the story."

"Story?"

"The story we tell the police." I took a beat. "You are off your meds—"

"I am *not* off my meds!"

"It's just the story, Mother. You are off your meds. I came looking for you and found you. You were confused about where you were and thought you were at home."

She goggled at me. "*That's* the 'story'?"

"Yeah. Pretty good, I think."

"Why would I be down here? Why would you think to come looking for me down here? What happens when they test my blood and find out I am indeed on medication? What—"

"Never mind." I had started the car and was backing it around. I really was terrible at improvisation. "I won't be breaking in this time . . . *you'll* have to do it. I don't care if you sever an arm."

"My, my, my . . . *some*body got up on the wrong side of the bed this morning!"

The cottage next door was actually some distance away, sheltered by a thickness of trees and brush. This structure, too, was raised on cement blocks, but not as high as the one we'd accidentally "visited." Also not as nice: smaller, with white peeling paint, no porch, and trash scattered on the ground. This time, Mother made no comment about BJB's superior taste, and neither did I.

And Mother didn't have to risk severing an artery *or* arm, because—after climbing the steps to a landing—we found the warped wooden door unlocked.

The inside was a mess, but not the mess of a slovenly home owner, rather the purposefully disheveled aftermath of someone searching for something—drawers open, cupboards ajar, cushions overturned. Each room was the same, from the small living area to the galley kitchen, from the single bedroom to a tiny bath. The extent of the damage gave me the impression that whoever had done this had *not* found what he or she was looking for.

Mother expressed the same opinion, but in her idea of detective speak: "Somebody tossed the joint!"

Soon we were standing in the bedroom where a mattress had been cut open, its stuffing removed and flung, exposing metal coils, the remains abandoned as an unsuccessful surgery.

I asked, "Did Big Jim Bob have a habit of hiding money in his bed?"

"How should I know, dear?"

"Well, I thought you . . . you know . . . had some kind of special relationship, and—"

"And thought I might have noticed if the mattress was lumpy?"

Okay, I was goading her, peeved how the day was going.

Mother put hands on hips. "Young lady, ours was not *that* kind of relationship! It was strictly a friendship, a platonic arrangement . . . and, all right, with a little heavy petting on the side."

Wincing, I quickly changed the subject. "What are we doing here, anyway?"

"Yeah!" a male voice behind us roared. "What *are* you doin' here?"

After we finished jumping, we turned to a figure standing framed in the bedroom doorway, a skeletal creature wearing a torn T-shirt, jeans, with tattoos adorning both arms. He was a wiry forty, his dark gray-streaked hair pulled back in a ponytail, his face a leathery tan, with a long nose and small dark dangerous shark eyes.

Were we in the presence of Jim Bob's killer? After all our silly shenanigans investigating the very serious crime of murder, were we finally in the kind of hot water we likely deserved?

Almost haughtily, Mother said, "I could ask the same of you, young man."

His response was a smirk.

Mother approached him tentatively, her tone turning pleasant. "You wouldn't by any chance be Big Jim Bob's partner? From Texas, isn't it?"

"Mebbe," he said, but the way he drawled it said yes.

"Vivian Borne," she announced, "a close personal friend of Big Jim Bob's."

Mother drew near enough to him to stick out her hand for a shake.

Which he wordlessly declined.

"I'm Brandy," I said lamely. "Her daughter? Didn't really know the man."

For this effort, I received an awkward silence.

Then, grudgingly, he said, "I'm Travis. Travis Taylor."

"Travis," Mother said, putting music into the name, "would there be somethin' to drink around here?" I cringed as she went all folksy. "I'm so dry I'm spitting cotton." (That was her favorite Bette Davis line—though "What a dump" would have been more fitting.)

Travis, still blocking the doorway, studied us for a long moment, then shrugged. "What makes you think I'm stayin' here or somethin'?"

"Well," Mother said, gesturing grandly to the mess, "you just walked in like you owned the place!"

As had we, but never mind.

"Well, I'm not." Then: "Knowin' Big Jim Bob, there's gonna be beer in the kitchen."

He turned, apparently to go there, and Mother and I wasted no time in getting out of the bedroom, following him into the front room, which at least gave us a shot at the exit.

While Travis was in the adjacent galley kitchen—getting beers, I reckoned (sorry), and not a sharp knife—I replaced the couch cushions so Mother and I had a place to sit.

He returned with three cans of beer (whew!), which we took, even though Mother and I had a mutual dislike for the beverage, me partial to white wine, and her up for nothing stronger than a Shirley Temple, because of her medication.

But Mother popped the top on the can like an old pro, took a greedy, slurpy sip, then produced the tiniest, ladylike burp.

While Travis had his back to us, righting a table chair for himself, I gave Mother's shin a quick kick with my foot so she would stop trying so hard. But she didn't seem to get it, mouthing a frowned, silent, "What?"

To which I could only roll my eyes.

Travis, seated with hands on knees (ready to spring?), said, "So . . . what did ol' Jim Bob have to say about his pardner Trav?"

Mother took another swig, then said, "Jest that you'd steal the stripe off a skunk."

Yes, she said "jest." Sue me.

Hairy eyebrows arched over the shark eyes. "That right? Sounds about like him."

She nodded, burped again, more naturally this time, then said, "That's why he left Texas, isn't it? Because you robbed him blind?"

Where was she getting all this?

"That's a damn lie," Travis said. "*He's* the one who stole from *me*, then hightailed it up here."

Mother shrugged. "Young man, I have no dog in this hunt—I am only reporting to you what Big Jim Bob told me. Because you inquired."

Tired of waiting for my cue, I asked, "What kind of business were you two in, anyway?"

Travis, tight-lipped, stared at me, then turned the tiny dark eyes on Mother. "Y'know, I don't feel much like jawin' with the two of you no more. You ain't explained what *you're* doin' here."

Ignoring that, I twisted toward Mother, giving her a wink Travis wouldn't see. "Didn't your friend Big Jim Bob say they ran an antiques shop together?"

"No, dear. It was an auction house."

"No, Mother . . . I'm sure you said *he* said an antiques shop."

Travis blurted, "Weren't neither of those! We was pickers."

Mother, feigning ignorance, asked, "Pickers? You mean like on the banjo or git fiddle?"

Yes, she said "git fiddle."

"No, Mother," I said. "Antiques pickers—like that TV show."

"Oh, yes," she said, and nodded. "That's where them city slickers go around and swindle good folks out of valuable antiques."

A scarlet flush was creeping up under the tanned leather face, turning him into a literal redneck. "*We* didn't swindle nobody. We paid good money for that junk."

I asked, "So what happened? Did Big Jim Bob run off with all the proceeds?"

"No!" Travis yelped in frustration. "It was *later* he diddled me . . . when we went into the storage unit game . . . and that ain't *all* he done."

"Do tell," Mother exclaimed, beer can on its way back to her lips. She was getting loosey goosey— the old girl could get looped on bourbon cake.

Travis, whose own beer had been left untouched on the floor, now reached for the can, and downed the whole thing in a series of interconnected gulps.

Well, chug a lug! I was impressed.

"You were saying?" Mother prompted.

"Huh?" Travis belched, putting Mother's efforts to shame, then crumpled the can in his fist.

"About the storage unit game?" I prodded.

"Oh. Yeah. That's where Jim Bob made off with the money in our checking account."

I said, "Did you go to the police?"

"No," Travis said glumly. "We was both signed on the account, so technically it weren't really stealin'."

"Oh my," Mother said. "Married couples who break up have that same problem, all the time. Still, I can hardly believe that about Big Jim Bob— he always seemed like such a good ol' boy."

Travis snorted. "That's what *I* thought, when I went into bidness with him. But that weren't the worst of it."

"Oh?" Mother asked.

"Yeah, he looted stuff from the renters' lockers—unbeknownst to me—an' fenced it."

I frowned. "How could he get away with that?"

"He was crafty 'bout it," Travis said. "Gotta admit. Hittin' the units of dead people that couldn't exactly bitch. Sometimes, if some relative got wind, he'd tell 'em a burglar broke in and done it." His eyes narrowed. "What really sucks is he done all that without cutting his own pardner in!"

"What a crook," I said with a straight face.

Mother, having drained the last of her beer, asked, "Do you think Big Jim Bob was up to those same crafty tricks here in Serenity? Stealing from the storage units, that is."

Travis nodded like a bobble-head doll. "And I bet he didn't work alone, neither."

I asked, "Why do you think that?"

"Too small a town—couldn't risk fencin' things on his own. Jim Bob was a cautious dude, if noth-

in' else. That's how come I didn't see him stealing
from me, in my rearview."

I said, "Is that why you trashed this place? To get
even? Or were you looking for something?"

"Who says *I* trashed it?"

We just looked at him.

"Ladies, place was like this when I come in.
Okay, I did poke around a bit—I got bills back in
Texas for that storage business, debts Jim Bob
owes just as much as me."

Mother said, "Then you *should* get some restitu-
tion. Do you have a lawyer?"

"I'm supposed to see a fella this afternoon."

Mother said, "So you'll be around the Serenity
area a while longer?"

"Not too long, I hope." He stood. "Any good
barbecue to be had?"

I said, "The Pitt on University. Across from the
car wash."

"Thanks." Travis headed for the door, then turned
with a sly smile. "Ah hope you girls find what *you*
was lookin' for."

Moments later I was at a side window watching
him climb into an unmarked van.

A white one.

Mother, watching also, said, "What do you
think, dear? Is he our killer?"

"Travis certainly had the motive and opportunity . . . but he's not the only one. He *does* have a
white van. . . ."

"Plenty of white vans in the world, dear."

"Why was he so chatty, do you suppose?"

"Obviously, because I had him twisted around
mah little finger!"

"Stop talking that way. Maybe he got as much out of that conversation as we did."

"Mebbe."

"Stop it!"

On the drive back to Serenity, as I approached a familiar side road, I asked Mother, "Mind if we take a quick detour?"

"Not at all, dear. Perhaps it will improve your overall disposition. Anyway, I wouldn't mind seeing Tony Cassato's old homestead myself."

The "homestead" of my ex-boyfriend (and Serenity's ex-police chief) was a modern log cabin whose location had been privy to only a select few.

I took my eyes off the road. "How did you know?"

"How did I know *what*, dear? That you wanted to drive by and reminisce? Or that I knew its location?"

"Both." I slowed down for the turn.

She laughed with the merry abandon a can of beer brought her. "I can see through you like a book, dear."

"Right, and read me like glass. Spill."

"Oh, I've known where Chief Cassato lived for quite some time—even though he guarded its location like a hound-dog does a ham bone."

This folksy thing was hard to get out of her system.

"*How* did you find out, Mother?"

"Oh, I followed you once."

"What, on foot?"

"Don't be ridiculous, dear. In my car, of course."

Mother did have a car—stored in the garage among the other trash and treasures, an old pea-green Audi that had seen more action than a military tank. What she did not have (anymore) was a driver's license.

"But . . . but I had the *tires* removed!"

After her third moving violation.

She laughed again, as if to say: *Silly you.*

"Dear, tires can go back on—it just takes a little time, and a few dollars to enlist a neighborhood youth. Now, if you make a left at the next gravel road, we can get there faster."

And Mother's route *was* shorter than mine, and before long we were bumping down a narrow dirt lane secluded by tall undergrowth, some of which had advanced boldly inward now that the cabin stood vacant.

Or was it?

Perhaps in the short time since Tony had gone, someone new had moved in. He might have sold it, after all, or rented it out. But as the cabin came into view, no vehicles were visible, nor any other sign of human life.

I parked close, got out, then took two steps up to the low wooden porch, and peeked in a window. What I saw brought a lump to my throat—everything had been cleared out, the cabin-style furniture, the fishing gear, Tony's collection of snowshoes, even the ancient rifle that had hung over the fireplace, in front of which we had spent many a cozy hour. . . .

But who had cleared out his belongs? And where did they go? Tony certainly hadn't had time to do all that before being whisked into WITSEC. I felt an awful emptiness, like a ghost haunting the place.

Mother was heading toward the barn; from the

porch, I could see its weathered red door ajar. She disappeared within, and as I left the porch to join her, she reappeared.

"Brandy!" she shouted. Her urgency was real, and not at all theatrical. "Come quickly!"

Since just about the only thing in a barn that might excite Mother would be an antique thresher—for which I had no interest—I took my good sweet time getting there.

"Hurry, dear," she beckoned again from the barn door, disappearing once more.

As soon as I entered, I saw him.

Not Tony (much as I might wish), but his trusty dog, Rocky, a black and white mixed breed with a distinctive black circle around one eye, K.O.-style, like the mutt in the *Little Rascals.* The animal looked half-dead, prone on his side in a small pile of hay.

Astounded, I said, "Surely Tony didn't *leave* him." I bent and stroked the dog, who began to whimper.

Mother bent, also. Her tone was gentle. "No, dear. Look at his paws . . . he's come a great distance."

"Then he must have gotten separated from Tony . . . or whoever had him . . . and come back to the only home he knew."

We've all heard the stories of faithful animals lost many hundreds of miles from home who found their way back. Maybe some of those yarns were true.

Mother said, "I'll get the bottle of water from the car. Dear?"

"What?"

"I can't get up."

"Never mind. I'll go for the water."

Which I did, finding an old plastic bowl along the way to pour the water in.

Together we got Rocky onto his feet—after I got Mother on hers, anyway—and the dog thirstily lapped up the dish's contents.

Since Rocky was too heavy for either (or both) of us to lug, I moved the Buick as close to the barn door as possible, and Rocky was able to hobble to the car, where Mother and I, working as a team (for a change), pushed him by his rear up into the backseat.

On the drive home, I worried not only about Rocky's health, but about Sushi's reaction to the inclusion of another animal in the house.

And with good cause—last year we'd temporarily taken in a dog named Brad Pitbull, and Soosh got her nose seriously out of joint, expressing her displeasure in an assortment of unsavory ways—like chewing up my favorite Stuart Weitzman shoes, and piddling on my pillow.

But when Rocky was led into the house and placed on an old blanket in the kitchen, Sushi seemed to sense that he was hurt, and transformed into Doggie Nightingale, licking his paws, even bringing him her favorite toy as an offering.

When Rocky showed no interest in a bowl of dry dog food, I got some sliced turkey from the fridge, and suddenly the animal forgot he was sick, and gobbled up all the tender white meat—Sushi joining in, too.

In the meantime, Mother was busy at the stove making a large pan of popcorn; when I asked if that was her idea of dinner, she reminded me of the senator's press conference, scheduled on TV in a few minutes. I reminded her that I had no interest in watching, to which she shrugged, saying, "Suit yourself."

Of course she knew my curiosity would get the better of me, and sure enough, there I was joining her on the couch in front of our little flat-screen, bowl of popcorn in my lap.

Mother must have gotten the time wrong (Eastern vs. Central always threw her), because the press conference was already in full swing as we tuned in, the senator standing in front of a podium, Peggy Sue at his side. They seemed to be in a ballroom—the Hyatt in Davenport?—with an assortment of media folks seated in chairs, armed with hand recorders and microphones.

My father looked maturely handsome, face bronzed, hair slicked back showing hints of silver at the sides and temple, Paul Newman blue eyes determined and focused. Peggy Sue looked stunning in an elegant champagne-colored silk shift, pearls at her throat, her auburn hair spilling to her shoulders in random sexy waves (no bald spot from the hospital stay, so she must have had extensions put in), her make-up polished, hitting the right balance between vixen and virgin, looking like the future Washington socialite and perfect senator's wife she was hoping to be.

Peggy Sue was saying, apparently in answer to a tough question, "I chose not to contact Edward when I discovered I was expecting, all those years ago. Although he was single at the time, I felt he might feel pressured to marry me. And that wouldn't have been fair to him—or me, for that matter, as I had plans for college."

A male voice asked pointedly, "Isn't it true that you were only *seventeen* at the time of conception?"

Sis said patiently, pleasantly, "No—I had turned eighteen, and graduated from high school. And I was very mature for my age."

A female voice asked, "Were you seduced?"

"Let me make perfectly clear," Peggy Sue said, that Nixonian phrase striking me as not the best choice, "that I was the aggressor in our brief relationship."

The senator jumped in. "I take full responsibility for my actions, and had I known, thirty years ago, that Peggy was with child, I would have taken care of her and our daughter, Brandy."

"What *about* your daughter?" someone shouted. "When did *she* find out you were her parents?"

Peggy Sue lifted a manicured finger. "You may ask anything about Edward and me, but please respect our daughter's privacy. Brandy was recently a surrogate mother for her best friend and husband, who couldn't conceive—the friend is a cervical cancer survivor—and Brandy is still recovering, physically and emotionally."

I muttered, "Nicely played, Sis."

Mother seemed to be watching Peggy Sue with a combination of pride and envy. "You know," she said slowly, "I may not be the *only* actress in this house."

"You're not even the *best* actress in the house."

She flashed me a frown, then returned her attention to the melodrama on screen.

I'd had plenty. Of press conference. Of pop-corn. I got up and headed to the kitchen to check on Rocky, who was sleeping peacefully on his side, Sushi snuggled against his belly.

Upon hearing me, Soosh raised her head and gave a low growl, as if to say, "Hey, dummy, don't wake him!"

So I tiptoed out.

Retrieving my cell phone from my purse, I dialed Brian's number, and he picked right up.

"How 'bout that date?" I asked.

"Tonight?" He sounded surprised, but pleasantly so.

"If you're not doing anything."

"Well, I'm a very popular guy, you know."

"I'm sure."

"But as it happens . . . I'm free."

"Your place?"

"Okay. Give me an hour. Do you want me to pick you up?"

"No. I'll find my way there."

"Brandy?"

"Yes, Brian?"

"I'm glad you called."

An hour later, freshly showered and pampered, wearing a green military-type shirt-dress, tan western booties, and a black leather jacket (mixing up styles keeps 'em guessing), I headed downstairs to tell Mother I was leaving, and where I'd be, in case Rocky regressed and needed the vet.

Mother was in the music room, straightening up. "What wonderful timing, dear."

"What is?"

"That you happen to be seeing Brian. I want you to do something for me. . . ."

I narrowed my eyes. "I'm listening."

"You must convince him to come here tomorrow at one in the afternoon—*precisely*."

"Why, *precisely?*"

"Because that, dear child, is when I will be gathering all the suspects—under the guise of auctioning off the Bix cornet—and will reveal who the murderer is."

I raised my eyebrows. "Then . . . you know?"

Because I sure didn't.

"Not exactly," she admitted. "But I do have a key witness in my pocket."

"Who?"

"Never mind, dear—I'll tell you later. Now, run along and don't keep the interim chief of police waiting . . . and remember, he *must* be present tomorrow to assist me in making the collar!"

Brian lived in a nice bungalow in a neighborhood of nice bungalows not far from downtown. I sat in the Buick out front, getting cold feet—this was no time to be renewing an old relationship, and there was the added pressure of Mother's request.

Several minutes must have passed, before Brian rapped on the window, scaring me just a little.

As I opened the car door, he said, "Hey, it's not *that* terrifying inside. I hope you weren't sitting there trying to decide whether to come in or not."

I smiled as I climbed out. "It's not that . . . I've just been through a lot lately."

"I know. But then it seems like that's always the case."

"Not by plan."

He took my arm. "You can unload on me, if you want."

"Thanks. I may take you up on that."

Inside, the living area had a hurriedly straightened up look, but was cozy and masculine, with brown faux-leather couch, tan recliner, and touches of sports memorabilia. A small gas fireplace was going, and an oak coffee table offered an assortment of cubed cheese and crackers, along with a bottle of white zinfandel (my fave, next to champagne).

Brian, in a pullover blue sweater and tan slacks, said sheepishly as I eyed the setup, "Too obvious?"

"Maybe a little," I said with a smile. "But flattering."

"We *could* go out for some dinner, only . . . I thought maybe you would want some privacy, after, you know . . ."

"The press conference?"

He nodded, puppy-dog brown eyes sympathetic.

"You got that right," I said glumly. "Not much fun being the little girl who isn't there."

I plopped down on the couch and helped myself to a tall glass of wine.

For much of the next hour, between bites of cheese and crackers and sips of wine, I did indeed unload on poor Brian, and when I had finally run out of steam, and was sitting there sulking, he asked kindly, "Anything *I* can do?"

I set the wineglass down. "Yes."

"Name it."

"You can shut me up."

"How exactly?"

"You might kiss me."

So he did, a kiss that started soft and sweet, then turned as hot as the flames dancing in the fireplace (okay, it had been a while since I'd been kissed).

But before things could get hotter, I drew back.

"Brian," I said, "there's one thing . . ."

"Yes?"

"It's about Mother. . . ."

He groaned and leaned back. "You always did know how to kill a mood. . . ."

I told him about her request to be at our house the following afternoon at one.

To my surprise, he said, "Sure, fine, great, I'll be there. I'll do that for her."

My eyes were popping. "*Really?*"

He nodded. "But *she* has to do something for *me.*"

And he told me about the single as-yet-unidentified print found on the steel cutter used to bludgeon Big Jim Bob, and how we could help him.

"Now," he said, slipping an arm around me, "can we stop talking about mothers and murders?"

"Absolutely," I said.

We kissed.

Fade to black.

A Trash 'n' Treasures Tip

Often, appliances and furniture found in storage units need repairs or refinishing in order to be saleable; that's when being a handyman (or woman) can be . . . handy. But if you don't have a knack for home repair, don't risk anything valuable with your early efforts. This is where I would insert a humorous anecdote about Mother, if the piece she ruined hadn't been so valuable. . . .

Chapter Eleven

Horn of Plenty

The morning of the gathering of suspects—under the guise of auctioning off the Bix Beiderbecke cornet—found Mother busy turning the library/music room into an unreasonable facsimile of Nero Wolfe's office.

I asked, "What happened to us being Watson and Holmes?"

"Holmes and Watson," Mother corrected. "Here's a trivia question, dear. In what story did the Great Sleuth of Baker Street *ever* stage a drawing-room who-done-it finale in his messy flat?"

"I can't think of one."

"Right. Holmes had attempts on his life in his digs, plenty of times—but never a gathering of suspects! That technique was perhaps best utilized by Christie's Poirot and by the movie version of Charlie Chan . . . though they never held those gatherings in their respective abodes, either."

"But Nero Wolfe did," I said.

"Yes! Almost always, his office at home was where he conducted his 'charades.' "

"So now I'm Archie Goodwin."

"That's right, darling."

"Just checking."

Still, Mother seemed excessive in her elaborate rearranging of the furniture, though I did understand that she needed a stage and props for what was to be the first-ever performance designed to trap a killer right here at the Borne homestead. I would have rather held it on an ocean cruise like Charlie or in some exotic locale like Hercule. But you take what you can get.

We moved the Oriental rug in from the living room ("The Persian simply won't do!"), and Mother—while less than overjoyed about it—consented to use the large library table as her/Wolfe's desk, with an overstuffed chair behind. The books on the built-in wall shelves had been rearranged in a more orderly, librarylike fashion, and her ragtag collection of musical instruments had been stored away . . .

. . . with one notable exception—the horn of the hour, the Bix cornet she'd retrieved from our booth at the antiques mall. She had reassembled it, returning valve and mouthpiece to their rightful position. The horn and its papers of authenticity she placed out of sight.

Mother got into a particular tizzy when she realized we had nothing handy to fill in for Wolfe's mammoth, magnificent world globe, until I remembered a smaller one languishing in the garage, among the hundreds of yard sale treasures patiently awaiting repairs.

When I brought the slightly dented globe in, Mother at first balked at the sight of it, wobbling on a thin pole (the globe, not Mother). Her first complaint was that the map was so old Israel wasn't a country yet, but I countered that by reminding her that Israel hadn't been a country yet in plenty of Wolfe novels.

"Mother, we are running out of time. You have to accept that this is not a Broadway production, and that you—like many a great actress—must use your gifts to make magic out of a few secondhand props."

I think I threw up a little in my mouth toward the end there.

"You are correct!" Mother said, raising a finger skyward much as she had when playing the world's tallest Mammy Yokum in the Playhouse production of *Li'l Abner*. "A great actress must make the most of it, no matter what the deficiencies of her stage crew might be!"

That wasn't terribly gracious of her, was it? But at least my tactic worked.

The only staging left to do was the manner of seating the suspects before the "desk." Specifically, the two well-known (to Nero Wolfe readers, anyway) leather chairs: one red, the other yellow, for important guests. Well, we didn't have any leather chairs, red, yellow or chartreuse. Again I solved the problem by covering a pair of Queen Annes with a yellow sheet and red blanket.

By this time I was exhausted by Mother's inane demands, and almost cried in happiness when she finally shooed me offstage so she could rehearse, closing the library doors behind me. If she really had a good idea who our killer was, maybe all this foolishness would prove worthwhile.

I went into the kitchen to check on Sushi and Rocky, the dogs having been kept out from underfoot, behind closed doors. Rocky was up and around, sniffing at the floor, no doubt finding a few errant Froot Loops that had escaped my cereal bowl; Sushi was curled up on the blanket, pooped from her stint as night nurse.

Since it was a warm, sunny fall day, I put the two dogs outside on separate chains that would no doubt get tangled as soon as I turned my back.

About a quarter to one, Brian arrived with his apparel as casually handsome as he was—sky-blue button-down with sleeves rolled up, gray slacks, and black shoes. He did have his revolver on his hip. Well, even men accessorize.

As I let him in the front door, he shook his head and said, "Wild one down at the station this morning—almost couldn't get away." Then: "Everything all right? You look like you fell off the back of a truck."

I cocked my head, smirking cutely (I hope). "Gee, you sure do know just the right thing to say to a girl, the day after."

He smiled sheepishly. "Sorry. Just trying to be funny."

"I'll do the jokes, thanks."

"But you do look frazzled."

"Don't I know it. I'm just a poor old clapboard house that got picked up and tossed around by Mother's tornado."

"Was that one of the jokes?"

"Shut up."

"Just wondering. Where is la Diva Borne?"

I nodded toward the library/music room. "Rehearsing for the matinee performance."

His sigh started at his belt buckle. "Well, I just hope this stunt of hers works . . . otherwise we've got nothing else to go on."

"Not a stunt—a charade. Like in Rex Stout."

"Who's Rex Stout?"

I liked him anyway.

As I went to inform Mother that Brian was here, I noticed out the window that the first of our suspects—that is, guests—had also arrived: Milton Lawrence himself. His black sedan, chauffeured by his secretary/assistant Lee Hamilton, was just pulling into the drive.

Mother, face flushed, flew out of the library like a flustered hen from a henhouse. And she was now wearing a pair of men's yellow silk pajamas!

Brian clutched my arm. "What the hell . . . ?"

"That's something Nero Wolfe wears," I said.

"Who's Nero Wolfe?"

Mother approached, gestured to herself, and quipped, "These are the *most* notable attire Nero wears in the books."

"Yeah," I countered. "To *bed!*"

Brian's mouth was hanging like the hinges had stopped working properly—he just had to be having second thoughts about being here, and particularly about endorsing Mother's charade. The Girl in the Yellow Silk Pajamas (watch for the new bestseller from Sweden) seemed to sense this, and latched on to his arm, before he could bolt.

To me she said, "Dear, escort Milton in, *after* I get Brian into his proper position." Then to no one in particular, she added, "Oh, I *do* wish we had our own Fritz to answer the door, dear, but you're needed as Archie. But then, I guess sometimes Archie *does* answer the door, when Fritz is busy. . . ."

As she hauled him away, Brian called back to me, "Who is—"

"Fritz is Nero Wolfe's cook/butler!" I said, "I'm Archie Goodwin, by the way. And before you ask, Archie is Wolfe's secretary and leg man."

Brian's expression was caught between tears and laughter. "I'm kind of a leg man myself," he said.

Hauling Brian into the music room, Mother called to me, "Don't forget, you're to join me when the last suspect arrives!"

Brian gave me the fish-eye before disappearing, and I went out to greet Milton Lawrence, whom Lee Hamilton was escorting up the front steps.

The elderly millionaire looked like at least a million—dark suit, gray shirt, and silver-and-red striped tie, conservative but beautifully cut. The assistant was allowed to dress more casually—a pale blue Ralph Lauren polo shirt and navy slacks and Italian loafers. Still pricey.

I instructed our wealthy guest to go on in, and as he did, his man Lee paused at the door to ask, "Any idea how long the auction will last, Brandy? I have some errands to run for Mr. Lawrence."

"Better allow an hour," I said. "You know my mother—she has her own way in mind of running it. Let's just say she has some . . . *entertainment* . . . prepared."

"Oh, I know." He grinned. "Where do you think she got the silk pajamas?"

I should have guessed.

He winked, then disappeared down the walk.

One by one, the rest of the guests arrived: John Anderson, owner of the Beiderbecke house and landlord of the late Anna Armstrong; Waldo Hendricks, antiques shop proprietor and Beiderbecke collector; Travis Taylor, ex-partner of Big Jim Bob; and James Lawrence, Canadian cable TV mogul and disinherited son of Milton.

There was enough time between arrivals for me to escort each guest individually to the library—Mother instructing them where to sit (Milton was to have the red chair, James the yellow). Consequently, the suspects only discovered who the other bidders were as I brought them in.

Some tension developed when Waldo Hendricks spotted the already-seated John Anderson—the antiques dealer stiffened and grumbled to himself, though neither man made a move to leave. The Bix horn trumped their animosity.

When the final guest, James Lawrence, was ushered to the remaining chair, Milton—seated nearby reacted at once. He might have needed Lee Hamilton to help him up the walk, but he sure didn't need any help flying to his feet.

He glared at Mother, and began to sputter: "You . . . you . . . didn't *tell* me . . . *he* . . . was coming!"

Yellow-pajamaed Mother, seated behind the library desk, in full Nero Wolfe mode, bellowed in a bassy male manner, "*Sit down, sir!* I prefer people at eye level. I do not confer with one guest to ask for the approval of inviting another. At any rate, this is a business transaction, the auction of a valuable collectible, and if it has inadvertently led to

an awkward family reunion as well, that is beside
the point. Now . . . this can take a short time, or a
long one—you decide."

Milton Lawrence, flabbergasted, sat. James
Lawrence crossed his legs, amused.

Mother leaned forward, elbows on the table,
tenting her hands. In her basso profundo, she said,
"Before we begin," and then she started coughing.
It lasted a while.

Everybody looked at each other, even Milton
and James.

Then Mother started again, in just as preten-
tious a tone but abandoning her efforts to sound
like a male.

"Before we begin," she said, "I would like to
offer refreshment. Will you join me? Archie?"

I gave her a sharp look. "Mother, I'm only going
to answer to 'Brandy.' "

She nodded. "Refreshment, Brandy?"

Now I was willing to pick up on my cue, which
was to pass out glasses of iced tea (for fingerprint
I.D., the reason Brian had been willing to go along
with the charade). I did this using a silver tray,
each guest taking the glass, except for Travis, who
declined . . . but I went out to the kitchen and returned with the tray and a bottle of beer for him,
and that he took.

(We had the beer on hand because Mother
wanted to empty a bottle to use as a prop, since
beer was Nero Wolfe's beverage of choice, and she
would on occasion pretend to take a sip from it.)

I took my place to Mother's right at an old metal
typing stand with a manual typewriter, meant to
represent Archie's desk.

A disgruntled Waldo Hendricks was saying, "Let's get on with it! I closed my business for the afternoon and drove down here for an auction, not these ludicrous theatrics."

"Yes," said John Anderson, "where *is* the cornet?"

"Confound it!" Mother roared, and everybody blinked. "*I* will ask the questions. The cornet will be revealed in due course."

Milton sneered at her. "I don't mean to interrupt your audition for the loony bin, Vivian—but what is the chief of police doing at this auction?"

Until now, no one had seemed to notice Brian standing quietly in the back corner; now they all craned their necks, Travis Taylor looking especially nervous.

"Silence!" Mother said. She looked at Hendricks. "Despite your impertinence, sir, the auction will begin shortly"—her slit-eyed gaze went to Anderson—"at which time the cornet *will* be produced." And to Milton, "Acting Chief Brian Lawson is here to safeguard the valuable antique that brings all of you under my roof."

Sufficiently scolded, the men fell silent.

Mother sat forward. "Before the auction begins, however, I feel it best to dispense with the elephant in the room."

Travis said, "You mean them yellow jammies?"

"No, sir! The murder of Big Jim Bob. We cannot have a murderer bidding on Bix's cornet—that would be neither dignified nor proper. So before we get to that, gentlemen, I will reveal who among you *murdered* Big Jim Bob . . . the same miscreant who broke into this house and assaulted my daughter . . . *and* possibly killed Anna Armstrong."

The guests began talking all at once: "This is preposterous," "I don't have to stay here and be insulted," "I'm leaving," and so on. All but James Lawrence, who seemed to be delighted by the afternoon's entertainment.

"Silence!" Mother bellowed again. "You can do this here with me, or down at the station with the constabulary. Isn't that correct, Mr. Lawson?"

Nice detail on Mother's part—Wolfe always called Inspector Cramer "Mr." Cramer during his charades.

"We can do that," Brian said.

Travis snarled back at him, "You ain't got no call to detain me."

"Don't I?" Brian said, underplaying his line in a manner that might have been instructive to Mother, if she were capable of instruction. "Perhaps you'd like to explain what you were doing in Jim Bob's cottage yesterday?"

Travis thrust a finger at Mother, then at me. "Them two was there before me!"

I said, "We're not suspects."

A pall fell over the library. The guests now knew: they were not guests at all.

They were suspects.

Skinny Travis seemed almost pouty as he said, "Fine. I'll stay as long as the beer holds out. Anyway, I got nothin' to hide."

"Good to hear," Brian said with an easy smile. His eyes traveled from suspect to suspect. "Can I assume everyone else here also has 'nothin' to hide'? If you're really interested in the auction,

you might as well just sit back and enjoy the pre-
game show."

When no one responded, Mother announced,
"Then I shall proceed." She leaned back in the
chair, tenting her fingers again. "Each one of you
had both opportunity and motive for the afore-
mentioned offenses. With your forbearance, I will
explain why everyone here is, as Archie, uh,
Brandy has pointed out, indeed a suspect . . . beginning with *you*, Milton Lawrence."

When the millionaire once again began to
protest, Mother barked, "I reiterate, this can take a
short amount of time, or a much longer, protracted
one, should you insist upon these continual inter-
ruptions!"

Milton fell silent, and Mother continued.

"You, sir, were aware that Anna Armstrong had
possession of the valuable cornet because your son
Stephen had informed you of the fact before de-
parting for Vietnam. Whether or not you approved
of his entrusting the cornet to his sweetheart is
unimportant, but at some point—possibly after
Stephen's death—you desired it back. Did you also
come to desire her as well, sir? And did she rebuff
you on both accounts? And then did your love
turn to homicidal hatred?"

Milton was leaned forward so far, he practically
made a right angle. "That's preposterous!"

"Quiet! I have not yet finished. When you discovered the cornet was not in Anna's apartment,
you surmised it must be in the storage unit she
rented near Serenity. You made your way there
only to find the contents had been sold. You argued with Big Jim Bob—accusing him of chi-

canery—and then, sir . . . you killed him, *after* learning who had purchased the possessions. And so you came here—to my house—to steal the cornet under the cover of night. Unfortunately, my daughter, Peggy Sue, interrupted your search, and you tried to silence her, much as you had Big Jim Bob."

"Vivian, you're a fool," Milton said. "This is slander! I will sue you into next *month*—"

"Sir, I do not accuse, I merely speculate."

"The hell!"

Mother, unfazed, gestured with an open palm. "If Mr. Lawrence insists upon his innocence, then who *did* commit these foul deeds?"

She leveled her gaze on John Anderson.

"You, sir, were also in love with Anna, but the affection was not reciprocated. And when she was visited by Milton Lawrence—a man who could offer her wealth—you became incensed, not only because you loved her, but because she had offered to bring him into your bed-and-breakfast enterprise. You realized that if this were to transpire, the two of them could tip the balance of power regarding any business decision. And so, one night, you confronted her. There was an argument, and you killed her, making your brutal deed look like a burglary."

Anderson was flabbergasted. "That's a damn lie!"

Mother continued unflustered. "You wished to find the historic, valuable cornet she had gone on and on about—it might prove a real asset to the Beiderbecke bed-and-breakfast. You knew it was in the storage unit because Anna had mentioned as much, and so you drove there, only to arrive too late for the auction, parking your white van on the highway, watching as we loaded up some of the murdered woman's belongings."

Anderson shifted in his chair. "I *do* have a white van, and I *did* arrive late, and watched from a distance. That hardly makes me a murderer. I agree with Mr. Lawrence—you are flirting with slander, Mrs. Borne."

"One cannot be sued for speculation!" Mother pressed on. "And so you followed us home, broke in at night, mistook *another* cornet for the Beiderbecke horn, and—upon encountering my daughter—struck her a blow upon her head."

Anderson spoke a single though compound word, its literal meaning related to what the horses had done on the Playhouse stage. Its figurative use was more pertinent.

"Still later that night," Mother said, narrowed eyes on Anderson, "you discovered your mistake, and returned to the storage unit where you hoped to find the *real* cornet among the boxes remaining there, and—"

"Don't tell me," Anderson interrupted acidly. "Big Jim Whozit caught me snooping around and I killed him."

"So you admit it!"

"No, I don't admit it!" Anderson snapped. "I didn't kill *anybody*. I not only did not kill Big Jim, I never *met* the man! The only thing you're getting right—apart from me showing up at the storage unit that morning—is that I indeed was in love with Anna. And Anna . . . I believe she loved me, as well."

Silence draped the room.

"Satisfactory," Mother said. She looked at Waldo Hendricks. "And now for you, sir."

Hendricks smirked. "I suppose you're going to claim that *I* was in love with Anna Armstrong."

"Quite the opposite," Mother said evenly. "You hated the woman. She rejected your offer to buy the cornet at what I would assume was a ridiculously low price—apparently you were unaware she knew its true value. Additionally, she was planning to open another Beiderbecke attraction at the bed-and-breakfast, which would overshadow your own museum with the addition of the cornet."

"Let me see if I have this straight," Hendricks said archly. "I broke into her apartment, killed her, went to the storage unit, saw you there, broke into your house, hit your daughter, went back to the storage unit, and killed Big Jim. Did I leave anything out?"

Mother stared. "In a matter as serious as murder, sir, it hardly pays to be flippant. These are very real and serious allegations."

"You're a moron," he said.

"That, sir, is a matter of opinion!"

She shifted uncomfortably, a little thrown.

"Travees Taylor," Mother said, and I realized she was lapsing into a French accent, "*you* had ze best motif for the killing of Big Jim Bob—ze former part-nère of yours in Texas, where together you engage in ze des-rep-you-ti-ah-bull bizness practiss . . . until you discover zat your friend, he has been swindling you."

"Mother!" I said. "Not Poirot. *Wolfe.* Not *French* . . ."

"Belgian!" she roared, but back in her Wolfean bellow, anyway.

God help us if she lapsed into Charlie Chan.

Travis, not knowing what to make of Mother's shift in characterization, seemed really rattled. On the other hand, several people were covering their faces with their hands. I was one of them.

"After Big Jim Bob fled Texas, sir, you tracked him here. When confronted, he offered to cut you in on his storage unit racket, by way of making amends for his prior financial transgressions against you. But you wanted cash, and you wanted it now, and this he claimed he didn't have. There was an argument and it escalated into violence. Sir, you killed him with a steel cutter, *but not before* he told you of a valuable cornet, and where it could be found. The rest you know."

"What was that French part about?" Travis asked, perplexed.

John Anderson frowned, apparently having followed Mother, alternating accents or not. "Where does Travis here fit in with Anna?"

Mother shrugged. "In that scenario, she doesn't. Her death remains a tragic loose end."

"An extra murder," Anderson said, "is a pretty major loose end, don't you think?"

"It is called the art of deduction, sir," Mother announced huffily. "Not the science! I must leave *something* for Chief Lawson to do."

James Lawrence uncrossed his legs. "Well, then, Mrs. Borne . . . that leaves me. I can hardly wait to hear how I did it." He laughed, shook his head, even slapped his knees. "Vivian, you haven't changed one iota in all these years."

"Thank you, dear," Mother said, without any Wolfe. Then she reverted to faux Rex Stout: "I *have* saved the best for last. For you have the most unusual motive—neither jealousy nor greed, not even profit . . . but sentiment. A desire to have something that had meant so much to your brother—the cornet—and which Stephen had promised to give you when he returned from the war . . . even though Anna had possession of it for safe-keeping."

James's expression of cynical amusement faded.

"The cornet," Mother said, "represented to you the last vestige of Stephen—a brother you loved and admired and lost—and your guilt for running away from an obligation which he heroically—"

"Stop it!" Milton was on his feet again. "Leave the boy alone. He had nothing to do with any of this."

Mother blinked. "Is that an admission of guilt, sir?"

"Certainly not!" And the millionaire sat.

Mother eyed the old man. "Very well. I've said my piece, and now all that remains is for the murderer to be taken away in irons."

I blinked. *That was it?* She had just accused everybody in the room except Brian and me of murder!

Anderson taunted her. "So then, which of us did it, Mrs. Borne? Where's your proof for *any* of these accusations?"

"Yeah, lady," Travis parroted, "where's your damn proof?"

Mother sat back, folded her hands over her

yellow-silk-clad tummy. "Gentlemen, I have no proof."

This brought an outpouring of outrage. I closed my eyes.

Mother raised a finger. "*But* . . . each of these scenarios is viable. And I *do* have a key witness, who indeed can identify the murderer." She swiveled to me. "Archie!"

I gave her a look.

"Brandy! Bring her in."

I left my little metal desk, disappeared from the room for a minute, then returned with our surprise witness in my arms.

Sushi.

"*That's* your witness?" asked Milton, incredulous.

"A *dog?*" said Anderson.

"Preposterous," spat Hendricks.

Travis howled as if *he* were the pooch.

But James Lawrence, twitching a smile, said, "This could be interesting."

Brian spoke from his corner. "While this may be a little unorthodox, the dog *did* come into contact with the burglar, who we believe to be the killer. She is, in fact, an eyewitness to the events in this house that night."

I put Sushi down in front of the semicircle of suspects.

Hendricks scoffed, "Look at those eyes! Your eyewitness isn't just a canine—the thing is blind. How's that going to—"

"Quiet!" Mother said. "The animal has a great sense of smell."

"Sushi," I commanded. "Find the killer."

In response, her little button nose began to twitch, and the unseeing eyes moved slowly from Milton Lawrence, to John Anderson, to Waldo Hendricks, to Travis Taylor, and finally, James Lawrence. One at a time, she trotted over to each guest and sniffed. It was beautiful, as if we had choreographed it—just perfect.

Except she didn't stop at any one of them.

"Sushi?" I prompted.

She turned toward me, yawned, returned to centerstage, scratched her side with a hind leg, then lay down and started licking a paw.

I looked at Mother, who stared back, chagrined. How could the little mutt *do* this to us? At least we had the fingerprints on the glasses to fall back on. . . .

A voice spoke from the library doorway. "Excuse me—did I miss the auction?"

Lee Hamilton was sticking his head in.

"I got back as soon as I could," Milton's assistant said.

And suddenly I got a whiff of the same thing Sushi did: a strong scent of men's cologne.

With a vicious little growl, Sushi scampered to her feet, and made a beeline for Lee, sinking her sharp little teeth into his ankle, hanging on with all her might, while Lee, yelping, tried to shake her off, doing an awkward one-legged dance.

Mother was on her feet, pointing. "*There's* your killer! Arrest him, Chief Lawson."

I had moved to pull Sushi off of Lee, but she had already dropped off him like a swollen tick, teeth dappled red.

"Are you all right?" I asked him disingenuously.

"No, I'm not all right!" Lee shouted.

"Good." I kicked him in the other leg. "And *that's* for Peggy Sue."

He fell backward against the French door, and in a nice piece of luck, pressed his hand to the glass.

Fingerprints.

While everyone watched in astonishment, Brian took Lee's arm. "I think we need a little talk down at the station."

Lee, trying to shake himself free, protested, "I'm not going anywhere."

"Oh, but you are," Brian said, asserting his grip. "You can call your lawyer from there."

I glared at Lee as I pointed to Milton Lawrence. "Did you do all this for him? Were you just carrying out your duties as usual, Lee?"

He spoke two words, neither worth reporting.

I realized Milton Lawrence was at my side. His expression was crestfallen. Then he said to me softly, "I swear I had nothing to do with this. And I have no idea why Lee would betray me so, after all these years of loyal service."

Then, astoundingly, Lee blurted the same two words at his employer. But now Milton's righthand man had tears in his eyes.

Escorting his suspect out, Brian looked over his shoulder, caught my eye, then nodded pointedly at the door where Lee had touched the glass. Brian wanted that protected.

And Archie Goodwin knew just what to do.

* * *

The auction, which took place after a brief recess, was anticlimactic in light of what had just transpired.

Travis Taylor decided to book it, before getting booked himself; but the others stayed. After an examination of the cornet and the papers by the bidders, the auction was over quickly, both John Anderson and Waldo Hendricks dropping out early, no match for the wealthy father and son.

Then Milton conceded to James—on purpose, I think.

How much did Bix Beiderbecke's cornet go for, you ask?

A lot. But the amount doesn't matter, because Mother announced then and there that the money would be donated to various charities that would help Serenity's less fortunate—allowing, however, for Peggy Sue's hospital bill, Sushi's vet expenses, a winter wardrobe for me, and some new bridgework for Mother. Apparently her teeth had been killing her lately.

"But you know me," she said, smoothing her yellow pajamas. "I'm not one to make a big production out of it."

As the group dispersed, Milton approached James.

"I guess that leaves me without a ride."

James nodded. "I'd be happy to drive you home, Dad. But I haven't had lunch yet. Maybe you'd care to join me? We have some . . . catching up to do."

"Yes we do, and I could eat." He touched his

son's arm. "And the check's on me, son . . . considering what you just spent."

Nice, huh?

A Trash 'n' Treasures Tip

In a small town, winning a storage unit auction may become troublesome if a friend or neighbor discovers you are selling their possessions. Mother has on numerous occasions allowed sentimental objects to be bought by relatives—at a modest price.

Chapter Twelve

Disposable Income

Mother: *Lest there be any quibbling over who is best disposed to write the concluding chapter of this real-life mystery, let me remind one and all (Brandy) that it was Vivian Borne who talked her way into the county jail the morning after our gathering of the suspects; yes, Vivian Borne who visited Lee Hamilton, and drew from him an explication of why and how he committed these reprehensible acts.*

Brandy: *Nothing doing . . . I will write the last chapter, just as I always have, and you can simply report to me what Lee Hamilton said, and I will share it with my readers.*

Mother: *Our* readers! *And you will miss all the nuances of my jailhouse visit. And you may well leave out something pertinent.*

Brandy: *What I'll leave out is everything that's not pertinent.*

Mother: *My rare digressions may not technically be per-*

tinent, but they add a richness and poetry to the proceedings that your more prosaic style (which I admit has its merits) (particularly your creative use of parentheses, dear) may not do this material justice. A single solitary creative writing class at a community college does not make you Jane Austen or Mary Higgins Clark.

Editor: *I have repeatedly asked the two of you to stop your bickering, and to settle your differences, and you have consistently ignored me. Therefore, I will make a Solomon-like editorial decision and divide this baby in two. Regarding this chapter: Vivian will write the front half; Brandy the rest. And I expect to be subjected to no more of your squabbling, understood?*

Brandy: *She started it.*

Editor: *I repeat*—understood?

Brandy: *Fine.*

Mother: *And have I mentioned what a lovely editorial job it is that you've been doing?*

Dearest ones! Vivian here, by popular request. The morning after my triumphant unveiling of the murderer—with a soupçon of help from our diabetic doggie—I awoke filled with vigor and vinegar, determined to bull my way into the county jail to see Lee Hamilton, who was remanded there pending charges. My performance as Nero Wolfe had clearly detailed how all of our suspects might have committed the crimes, and why. Unfortunately, I seem to have neglected the why and wherefore of the actual murderer.

The morning was sunny and crisp, the swallows gathering on the telephone lines making ready to wing their way to Capistrano, where I have never been incidentally, but hope to "fly" myself one day. San Juan, Puerto Rico, that is, not California . . . unless the Capistrano in this instance *is* in California, in which case I *have* been there, and it's nothing to write home about.

Editor: *Vivian, I reserve the right to reverse my decision, should you insist on these digressions.*
Mother: *I bow to your expertise.*

After arriving downtown on the trolley—

Mother: *Oh! Wouldn't this be a delightful place to insert my much funnier trolley story?*
Editor: *No.*

After arriving downtown on the trolley, I hoofed it over to the new county jail, and was in luck to find Sheriff Rudder in residence; I felt confident that he would acquiesce to my request to see the prisoner because we have a mutual admiration and respect for each other.

Brandy: *What you mean is, he would agree to anything to get you out of his hair.*
Editor: *There's always the option of canceling your book contract.*
Mother: *I will pledge not to interrupt Brandy in her half chapter if she will pledge not to interrupt me in mine.*
Brandy: *Deal.*

Within minutes of my brief powwow with the sheriff, I was moving through the lobby's metal detector—with a minor time-out when the pins in my knee set off the infernal gizmo—and then a female deputy named Patty, who'd been so accommodating during my most recent incarceration, escorted me through one locked door, then another.

Finally, in the small visitors' room, I sat awaiting Lee to appear on the other side of the Plexiglas. Assuming, that is, that he agreed to see me. After all, Brandy, Sushi, and I had exposed him as a two-time murderer.

Perhaps five minutes passed, and I was beginning to wonder if he might be holding a slight grudge, when a burly male guard escorted the prisoner to the chair on his side.

Lee had been forced to trade in his dress shirt and slacks for the familiar bright orange garb that I also had been issued not so long ago. Unlike *moi*—with a natural coloration enhanced by vivid fall shades (I recommend *everyone* have their colors done!)—Lee, minus his usual pastel finery, appeared a ghastly shade of pale.

We picked up our respective phones.

"How are they treating you, dear?" I asked with sympathy.

"It's not the Savoy," he responded.

He seemed rather morose.

"It must be simply dreadful," I said.

In reality, I'd had a *wonderful* time in jail organizing a theater group (see *Antiques Knock-Off*), and actually had been sorry to leave. But saying so in these circumstances would have been less than gracious.

"My dear," I said, "I thought I *knew* you. All those hours we worked together at the Playhouse. Please help me understand."

His eyes narrowed. "Understand what?"

"Oh, let's not play cat and mouse—we go back too far for that." I leaned forward to where my nose almost touched the Plexiglas. "Rest assured I'm not wearing a wire—this conversation is just between us veteran thespians."

"Vivian, I only said I'd talk to you because it was a change from that damn cell they have me in. If you think I'm going to open up to you, you're wrong."

"Really? We've been friends, Lee, perhaps not close friends, but fellow warriors in the theatrical trenches. And yet you enter my house, and almost kill my daughter? *Really?*"

"Vivian, that wasn't personal."

"It was *extremely* personal." My eyes met his, and to his credit he did not avert my gaze. "I *do* feel you owe me an explanation."

He said nothing for the longest time.

Finally he said, "Perhaps," shrugging with his face.

But if I thought a confession would come rushing out, I was mistaken. I would have to dig for these nuggets.

"My dear, what confuses me is that your future outlook was so bright. Why risk it?"

His laugh was small but towering with bitterness. "My future outlook was bright?"

"But of course! Think of your glorious retirement! When last we spoke, you were considering Florida, or perhaps California."

He laughed again, louder, humorless. "Viv, old girl, that would take a boatload of money, and I am left up shoot creek without a paddle."

(Although he did not say "boatload" or "shoot"— apparently a night in stir had already made a hardened criminal of him.)

I frowned. "Surely, working for the wealthiest man in Serenity, you must have had a generous retirement package."

He shook his head.

"Severance pay, then?"

Again the head swiveled.

"Why, that's simply dreadful!" I said, aghast. I was not acting—this seemed a travesty, after all the years Lee had put in as Milton's right-hand man.

"Well, dreadful or not, it's the case, Vivian. I was going to be set out on the curb with the rest of the refuse."

"But my dear . . . it's not as if Milton couldn't have afforded to give you such benefits. Surely you were shocked, after so much loyal service, and considering all of the sacrifices you must have made!" I shook my head, *tsk-tsk*ed. "Such shabby treatment."

And now I must admit I had moved into the acting realm. As shameful as it might be for Milton to have treated his major domo so poorly, that hardly justified Lee Hamilton's homicidal activities.

But my feigned sympathy had Lee's eyes filling with tears. What a pity that this, one of my finest performances, was presented to an audience of one. How I wish you had been there!

He dabbed his eyes with a tissue (a box was provided—apparently tears in the visitors' room were commonplace). Then he sniffled and said, "It wasn't the money. Not really."

"What else could it have been, dear?"

"It was the indignity! Of how disposable I was to him after decades of service and, I thought, mutual regard. Vivian . . . I *thought* I was like a son to the man."

Considering how Milton had cut off his real son James, maybe that should have been an indicator to Lee. But I kept this observation to myself.

I asked, "Hadn't Milton paid you a substantial salary over the years? I do remember you saying as much."

"Yes, he did, and he was more than fair. But I . . . I just don't know where it all went."

Here is where I might have said, "On fine clothes, expensive furnishings, and extensive travel?"

But I didn't.

Instead I said, "Surely it must have dawned on you that maintaining your lifestyle would be impossible after Milton's retirement. You must have known there was no retirement package."

"I assumed there would be some kind of gift, some lump sum that would take the place of that. But when Lawrence informed me that my services for him would soon terminate, I asked if there would be a bonus, and he said . . . well, he said yes."

"He did?"

"He did." Lee made a face as if tasting something nasty. "A one-thousand-dollar one."

"Is that when you decided to find some other avenue of securing retirement funds?"

Lee sighed and nodded. "Lawrence had mentioned, several times, having bought a valuable cornet for his late son, Stephen. Once owned by Bix. Beiderbecke himself. Recently I asked him what had become of it."

"And he revealed that Anna Armstrong had it."

Lee nodded glumly.

"So you went there one night last month, climbed the scaffolding, and broke-and-entered into her apartment."

His eyebrows climbed his forehead. "But I guess I made too much noise. I was a beginner, an amateur."

"No one's perfect, dear."

"And, well . . . she woke up and . . . there was an accident."

An interesting euphemism for killing a person.

I said, "You didn't find the cornet, did you? But did discover something that led you to the storage unit facility."

"An invoice for the rental, yes. I . . . I heard rumors that Jim Bob had a shady past, and I went to him to strike a deal. I told him the Armstrong unit contained some valuable antiques, and that . . . well . . . I knew a person in Chicago who wouldn't ask questions about where they came from, and we would split the proceeds."

"Had you really made contact with someone like that in Chicago?"

"Yes."

"Did you specifically mention the Beiderbecke horn to Big Jim Bob?"

For a moment, Lee didn't answer.

Then with a sigh he said, "Only that it was a collectible instrument that could bring in several hundred dollars." His eyes flashed. "Somehow Jim Bob found out it was worth much more. Apparently he'd arranged to have you buy the contents of the locker, and he intended to go to your home and take back the cornet."

"What a crook!"

"Wasn't he though? An untrustworthy, low-life S.O.B. When I confronted him, he insisted the horn had never been in the locker. That he'd done an inventory and it simply wasn't there. But I knew he was lying. We argued, and I was threatening him with that cutting tool when finally he admitted that he'd sent the horn home with you—but that you didn't know the instrument's value. He tried to convince me we should throw back in together, and go to your house to retrieve the thing . . . but I was having none of that, and we argued some more, and scuffled some more, and . . ."

"Another accident?"

He again nodded glumly.

That seemed about it; but I decided to try to tie up a loose end or two.

I asked, "What about Big Jim Bob's cottage? When did you go there?"

"After I discovered the cornet I took from your house was not the right one, I thought perhaps Big Jim had lied about you having it, and that it was really hidden at his place."

One detail remained unanswered.

"What happened to the boxes Brandy and I had left in the storage unit?"

He shrugged an apology. "Sorry, Viv. Bottom of the river, after I didn't find the cornet in them. I don't think there was anything very valuable, but I am sorry." He seemed more regretful about that than the murders.

He leaned closer to the Plexiglas, eyes pleading now. "You understand, don't you, Vivian? I'm really not a bad person. I lived a good life, working diligently for a man who treated me like a son and then cast me off like an old shoe. You do understand, right? That I was forced to do what I did?"

"Yes, dear," I said, "these things happen . . . just as the legal system will be forced to do what *it* has to do, no matter how much of an 'accident' it all was—but you do have one source of solace."

"I do?"

"Oh yes. You have the state to take care of your retirement plans now."

I replaced the phone and he was still sitting there, when I left.

Brandy back.

And let me say, bickering aside, that I can only admire Mother for the manner in which she got Lee Hamilton to open up and explain himself. Unfortunately for Lee, while Mother indeed hadn't been wearing a wire, all conversations in the visitors' area were recorded. No biggie, since he was already as good as convicted—the print on the murder weapon matching the handprint on our library's glass door.

A few days had passed since the auction, and things had calmed down regarding the senator and Peggy Sue and myself, the senator's poll ratings actually benefiting from all the media atten-

tion, the public (in general) loving the reuniting
of two parents and their child—hip hip hooray for
family units, family values, and the family way.

I was outside playing with Sushi and Rocky—or
rather, I was watching them play in the piles of
leaves I had raked—when my cell phone rang in
my jacket pocket.

Delighted to see my niece Ashley's I.D. on the
screen, I chirped, "Hey, girl! What's up?"

All I heard in response was sobbing.

"Honey, what's wrong?"

I waited for Ashley to compose herself.

"Brandy, how can you be so *happy?*"

Confused, I asked, "Why wouldn't I be happy?"

You would be, too, if your Prozac had kicked
back in.

She went on. "I mean, after what Mom and that
. . . that *senator* did to you? Not to mention *me!* I
had to find out on TV that you were really my *sister!* Couldn't you have *told* me?"

Oh, for blankety-blank sake. Peggy Sue hadn't
told her.

"Half sister," I corrected.

"Like that makes a difference! Do you know
what this means? My whole life has been a lie! I am
never going to speak to Mom again. Never."

"Ashley, I know how you feel, believe me . . . but
don't you think that's a little harsh? Your mother
was barely out of high school. She did what she
thought was best at the time."

"How can you *defend* her?"

Yes, how could I? Only a few months ago I had
been as angry and disillusioned as Ashley.

Who was saying, "I'm *especially* mad about what they did to you."

"Look," I said evenly, "I can fight my own battles and handle my own neuroses. I have come to grips with my parentage, and I suggest that you—"

"I don't mean *that!* The photo!"

"What about it?"

"Don't tell me you don't know? *They* leaked it! It was *them!* Mom told me one of Senator Clark's aides took it, on his cell phone. Sneaked it of you two at the hospital. The whole thing was *planned* to get him ahead in the polls. You were *used* to get him reelected."

I was unable to speak, as if I'd been kicked in the stomach.

Ashley continued: "Anyway, I just called to say I'm dropping out of school. You can tell Mom because I have no intention of doing so."

Finally locating my voice, I pleaded, "Don't fly off the handle, honey—college is too important."

"Already quit. I'm leaving for New York tomorrow."

"But New York . . ." She was just a kid! "What will you do there?"

She laughed humorlessly. "Oh, I don't know. Maybe I'll join an escort service—let *them* explain *that* to the media."

"Stop it. If you do something rash, you'll only end up hurting yourself."

Which, from experience, I knew for a fact.

But my niece/half sister wasn't listening. "I'll send you my new e-mail, Brandy, and cell number. But don't you *dare* give it out."

Her only good-bye was the click in my ear.

I don't remember walking around the side of the house to the front porch, to sit in the old rocker; but I must have, because half an hour later I was still there, rocking listlessly, weighing what I could, or should, do to help Ashley, when a huge silver Hummer pulled into the drive.

I wondered what kind of moron would drive such a gas-guzzling monster these days. My question was answered by the driver who jumped out.

My ex-husband, Roger.

What was he doing here, showing up unannounced, coming all the way from Chicago?

Wearing a navy jacket over a pale yellow shirt, and tan slacks, he hurried toward me, locks of his brown hair flying out of place, his normally pleasant features clenched grimly.

Immediately my adrenaline began to rush.

I flew down the porch steps to meet him.

"Is it Jake?" I asked.

"Brandy, is he here?"

"No! Why . . . what . . . ?"

His sigh quavered. "I was afraid of that."

"Roger! Stop scaring me. What's going on?"

"Jake's run away."

Stay tuned for more exciting adventures of Brandy Borne.

Vivian: *Excuse me? Shouldn't that be "More Exciting Adventures of Vivian and Brandy Borne"?*

Editor: *How about "Brandy and Vivian Borne"?*
Vivian: *Agreed! I may not have gotten the entire last chapter, but for once I got the last word.*

A Trash 'n' Treasures Tip

If your conscience bothers you about taking other people's possessions, turn over personal items such as photos to the storage unit owner— most are far more trustworthy than Big Jim Bob. And by the way, since (for better or worse) I, Brandy Borne, write these tips . . . ? Mother did *not* get the last word.

About the Authors

BARBARA ALLAN

is a joint pseudonym of husband-and-wife mystery writers Barbara and Max Allan Collins.

BARBARA COLLINS is a highly respected short story writer in the mystery field, with appearances in over a dozen top anthologies, including *Murder Most Delicious, Women on the Edge, Deadly Housewives,* and the bestselling *Cat Crimes* series. She was the co-editor of (and a contributor to) the bestselling anthology *Lethal Ladies,* and her stories were selected for inclusion in the first three volumes of *The Year's 25 Finest Crime and Mystery Stories.*

Two acclaimed hardcover collections of her work have been published—*Too Many Tomcats* and (with her husband) *Murder—His and Hers.* The Collins's first novel together, the Baby Boomer thriller *Regeneration,* was a paperback bestseller; their second collaborative novel, *Bombshell*—in which Marilyn Monroe saves the world from World War III—was published in hardcover to excellent reviews.

Barbara has been the production manager and/or line producer on various independent film projects emanating from the production company she and her husband jointly run.

MAX ALLAN COLLINS has been hailed as "the Renaissance man of mystery fiction." He has earned an unprecedented sixteen Private Eye Writers of America "Shamus" nominations for his Nathan Heller historical thrillers, *True Detective* (1983) and *Stolen Away* (1991). The first Heller novel in ten years, *Bye Bye, Baby,* was published in 2011. His other credits include film criticism, short fiction, songwriting, trading-card sets, and movie/TV tie-in novels, including the *New York Times* bestsellers *Saving Private Ryan* and the Scribe Award-winning *American Gangster.*

His graphic novel *Road to Perdition,* considered a classic of the form, is the basis of the Academy Award-winning film. Max's other comics credits include the "Dick Tracy" syndicated strip; his own "Ms. Tree"; "Batman"; and "CSI: Crime Scene Investigation," based on the hit TV series, for which he has also written six video games and ten bestselling novels.

An acclaimed, award-winning filmmaker in the Midwest, he wrote and directed the Lifetime movie *Mommy* (1996) and three other features; his produced screenplays include the 1995 HBO World Premiere *The Expert* and *The Last Lullaby* (2008). His documentary *Mike Hammer's Mickey Spillane* (1998/updated 2011) appears on the Criterion Collection discs of acclaimed film noir, *Kiss Me Deadly.*

Max's most recent novels include *No One Will Hear You* (written with Matthew V. Clemens) and *Lady, Go Die!* (completing an unfinished Mike Hammer novel from the late Mickey Spillane's files).

"BARBARA ALLAN" live(s) in Muscatine, Iowa, their Serenity-esque hometown. Son Nathan graduated with honors in Japanese and computer science at the University of Iowa and works as a translator of Japanese to English, with credits ranging from video games to novels.

Murder and mayhem abound in
the next Trash 'n' Treasures mystery
ANTIQUES CHOP,
Coming from Kensington in May 2013.
Keep reading to enjoy a preview . . .

Chapter One

Chop Meet

Previously, in *Antiques Knock-off* . . .

I don't remember walking from the backyard, where I'd been working, to the front porch, to sit in the old rocker . . . but I must have, because half an hour later I was still there, rocking listlessly, letting the cool fall breeze rustle my shoulder-length bleached-blond hair, when a huge silver Hummer pulled into the drive.

I wondered what kind of moron would own such a gas-guzzling monster *these* days, when my question was answered by the driver who jumped out.

My ex-husband, Roger.

What was he doing here, showing up unannounced, coming all the way from Chicago?

Wearing a navy jacket over a pale yellow shirt and tan slacks, he hurried toward me, locks of his brown hair flying out of place, his normally placid features looking grim.

Immediately my adrenaline began to rush, and I flew down the porch steps to meet him, worried that something might have happened to our son.

"What is it?" I asked. "Jake?"

Out of breath, Roger asked, "Why haven't you answered your cell? I've called and called!"

Taken aback, I sputtered, "I . . . I've been in the yard all morning and didn't have it with me— what's going on?"

"Is Jake here?"

"No! Why?"

His words came in a quavering burst. "I was afraid of that."

"Roger! Stop scaring me."

A deep sigh rose from his toes. "I think he's run away."

As confused as I was concerned, I asked, "Why would he do that? He seemed fine yesterday when I talked to him."

Then I frowned, recalling what our conversation had been about. "Only, uh . . ."

Roger gripped my arm. "Brandy, if you *know* something that might have motivated Jake taking off like this, you need to tell me *now.*"

Removing his hand gently, I said, "Roger, you better come sit down. Of *course,* I'll tell you what I know. . . ."

And turning, I led him toward the porch.

As we sat in matching rockers—like the married couple we'd be if I hadn't ruined everything—I told Roger of my recent discovery of my true parentage: that thirty years ago, my older sister

Peggy Sue had conceived me with then-state repre-
sentative Edward Clark, while she had been a summer intern on his campaign. And that the
grandmother I still called "Mother" had raised me
as her own.

Roger's shock morphed into irritation, his eyebrows trying to climb to his hairline. "And you
thought this information should be shared in a
phone call with an impressionable thirteen-year-old
boy?"

I spread my hands. "There was no other way—
with the senator's reelection campaign all over the
news, my soap-opera parentage was going to be
everywhere. I'm surprised you didn't hear about it."

He frowned, but his irritation had faded. "I've
been away on business, pretty much constantly in
meetings. When I got back, Jake was gone."

"Have you notified the police?"

Roger shook his head. "Hasn't been twenty-four
hours yet. What a damn dumb rule! Don't they say
that the more time that goes by, the colder the
trail gets?"

I stiffened. "You don't think Jake has been *kidnapped?* Is *that* what you're saying?"

Roger certainly had the kind of money to war-
rant our son being that kind of target.

My ex leaned forward, rubbing his forehead.
"No . . . no . . . I don't think there's much chance
it's anything like that. There's been no phone call
or note or any such thing."

"Then . . . what *do* you think this is about?"

Roger took another deep breath. "Jake's been,
well, a lot more of a handful than usual. Acting out
at school and at home. All because lately he's been

unhappy. He doesn't say so, but it's clear that's the problem. That's why I thought he might have come here. He's always been able to talk to you."

"What's he unhappy about, Roger?"

He shook his head. "Who knows what a boy of his age is thinking? School, friends, girls, he keeps it all inside. His grades are okay but his teachers complain about his attitude."

Suddenly I thought of someone who *might* know. "I'm going to ask Mother when she last heard from Jake," I said, already on my feet. "You think he talks to me? He and his grandmother are thick as thieves, texting each other fast and furious."

Which she'd just mastered, after having a cell for five years.

He nodded his okay and I left my dejected ex on the porch while I headed inside.

Just under one minute later, I returned. "You should come in," I said, crooking a finger.

Roger followed me back in the house, and I led him into the dining room where Mother sat drinking a cup of coffee at the Duncan Phyfe table. She was wearing her favorite emerald-green pantsuit, her silver-gray hair neatly pinned in a bun, her magnified eyes behind the large glasses turned our way.

Next to her sat Jake.

He had on jeans and a gray sweatshirt with Chicago Bears logo, and held a can of Coke in one hand, while the other draped down, scratching the head of Rocky, the mixed-breed mutt (complete with black circle around one eye) that we had recently taken in.

Sushi—my blind, diabetic, brown-and-white shih

tzu, the "child" *I'd* retained custody of after the divorce—sat a few feet away, her little mouth in a pout, apparently due to the attention Jake was giving the new-dog-on-the block.

"Oh, hi, Dad," Jake said, layering on a matter-of-fact attitude that didn't fully mask his sheepishness.

For a moment Roger's anger trumped his relief, but only for a moment. Father ran to son, throwing his arms around the boy's shoulders, hugging him.

Roger quite naturally scolded Jake for disappearing; Jake just as naturally apologized to his father for scaring him; Mother came to the defense of her grandson; Rocky—a former police dog—growled at my ex for his threatening tone of voice; and Sushi started yapping, not to be left out. For a while, I was glad just to be an interested spectator.

But finally, to stop the commotion, I raised my voice. "Jake, how did you get here, anyway? And if you hitchhiked, please lie to me and say you took a bus."

The boy looked my way. "I really did take the bus. Then walked from downtown."

Mother said to me, "You were out back, dear, when he arrived, about forty minutes ago. You seemed to have a lot on your mind, and I didn't want to disturb you."

Before I could decide whether to shake her till her bridgework rattled or just kick her in the keister, Roger exploded, "Forty minutes!"

"Well, of course, that's an approximation. . . ."

"And it didn't occur to you, Viv, to *call* me? You didn't think I'd be worried half to death?"

Mother lifted her eyebrows above the big glasses. "I *would* have gotten around to it, Roger dearest, but my immediate concern was that Jake was all right. Besides, talking to the boy, he indicates you've been away on business for several days, and called him only once."

"That isn't fair."

"Leaving him alone in that big house. Why, he might have had one of those wild rock 'n' roll parties you see in the movies! Dancing in his underpants and with nubile young things doing the boogaloo in bikinis around the backyard pool!"

"I wish," Jake said.

Roger's mouth was open, but words weren't coming out.

Leaning against the doorjamb, arms folded, I said quietly, "Let's not make a federal case out of it, Roger. Mother was dealing with things in her own inimitable fashion. Our son has been found, and he's fine."

Or was he?

Suddenly impatient, Roger tapped Jake's shoulder. "Get your things, buddy boy."

Uh-oh—"buddy boy" was never a good sign . . . .

Roger was saying, "We're going home *right* now."

But Jake stuck his chin out. "I just got here," he said stubbornly. "Why can't I stay a few days?"

And before Roger could protest, Mother said, "I understand that the boy has all of this week off. A rare benefit of being in one of those year-round schools."

Roger trained hard eyes on her. "And *you* want *me* to *reward* him for what he did?"

"No, dear," Mother said patiently. "Jake staying here for a few days wouldn't be a reward exactly . . . more an opportunity for him to see that . . . despite this distressing news about our, well, family tree . . . nothing has *really* changed in our lives. Same-o same-o!"

"Even *I* can see that," Roger muttered, rolling his eyes. "Doesn't seem to really matter which branch of the family tree *you* swung in on, Vivian."

Did I mention that my ex never had gotten along with Mother?

Suddenly Jake's eyes became moist. "Does this mean I have t'call *Aunt Peg* 'Grandma'?"

"Certainly not, sweetheart," I interjected. "We're not at this late date changing the lineup on the team. Peggy Sue is still 'Sis' to me . . . . Just because she screwed up as a kid, that doesn't mean anything has changed."

Roger gave me an arched-eyebrow look that said: *Screwed up? Really?*

And I gave him a pained look that said: *Double entendre* not *intended.*

Mother leaned closer to Jake, peering into his face. "And so *what* if I'm technically your great-grandmother? Can you imagine a greater grandmother than *moi?*"

That made Jake smile. "You *are* great, Grandma." He met his father's eyes. "Can't I stay, Dad? Please. I realize I was out of line, just taking off like that. Cut me a break, and I'll clean up my act back home. I promise."

Roger thought about it.

"Just for the week, Dad—I promise I'll behave."

Roger, with a half smirk, glancing Mother's way (and mine), said, "It's not *your* behavior that worries me, son."

"Oh, *we'll* behave," Mother responded, smiling a little too broadly. Sort of like the Cheshire Cat in Disney's *Alice in Wonderland* (cartoon version), right before he disappeared. "Won't we, Brandy, dear?"

"Sure. You're in luck, Roger. We're not involved in a murder investigation at the moment."

Roger shot me a reproachful glance. "I don't really find that funny, Brandy."

Wasn't meant to be. It was *Mother's* propensity for getting involved in such investigations that got us into trouble—not mine!

Jake jumped to his feet, threw his arms around his dad, gazed up with angelic innocence—it was over-the-top acting worthy of his grandmother. "Can I please stay?"

I already knew what my ex was going to say; I'd fallen prey to my offspring's baby blues many times.

"All right," Roger said, then waggled a finger. His next move on the parental/child chessboard was predictable and even kind of pitiful. "But when you get back, I want that room of yours cleaned."

Oh, so very little has changed in the negotiations between kid and parent. Well, some things have changed—you used to get sent to your room for punishment. Now every kid's room is a technological Briar Patch.

And before Mother could say something that would give Roger a change of heart, I offered to walk with him out to his Hummer, so we could finalize plans. Roger and I did get along, and we made a point of not using Jake to get back at each other.

As we descended the porch steps, I asked, "You'll be back on Sunday, then?"

Roger, digging in a pants pocket for keys, responded, "Late afternoon. That way we can be home in time for Jake to clean his room."

Did he *really* think that was going to happen?

"I could meet you halfway on the interstate," I offered.

Roger nodded toward the beast parked in front of his Hummer. "Not if you're still driving that broken-down Buick."

He had a point; last week a windshield wiper flew off while I was driving in pouring rain—luckily, on the passenger side.

We were by his Hummer now.

"Why don't you get a newer car?" he asked. "I'll buy it for you, if that's the problem. . . ."

I looked at him sideways. Yes, we were on increasingly better terms, as the divorce faded into history; but things hadn't gotten *that* much better.

Then my astonished ears heard myself saying, "No, thanks. The Buick keeps me from having to take Mother very far on her escapades."

Wait, what? I could *use* a new car!

He grunted. "Speaking of escapades—do you think you can manage to keep that woman out of trouble for an entire week?"

"I'm sure."

"You are?"

"Pretty sure."

"Nothing homicidal in the works?"

"Really, Roger. Get serious. It's incredibly unlikely that Mother manages to get herself involved in these, well, mysteries as often as she has. This is a small town. If there's one more homicide, the police will start looking at us as the real perpetrators behind all this carnage."

He laughed. "You're right. Statistically speaking, you're safe. Another murder in sleepy little Serenity? Not going to happen."

"Right."

His eyes narrowed at me. "And there's no other trouble she could get herself into?"

"I'm sure not."

Pretty sure. Almost sure. Not sure at all.

He read my expression and asked, "She *is* current on her meds, isn't she?"

I nodded; Mother was bipolar, which was why I was also current on my meds. Prozac.

"And you'll keep a *really* close eye on Jake?" Roger was saying. "And call me if *anything* seems wrong?"

"Roger . . . what aren't you sharing with me?" Adding, without contention, "I *am* his mother."

He looked down at his feet for a moment. "I said earlier that Jake's been unhappy. But I wasn't, uh, as frank as I should have been."

"Then you *do* know why he's unhappy."

He nodded. "It's that private school. He hates it."

"Is he being bullied?" I couldn't imagine anyone picking on him, or him letting them do it. But bullying was so common these days . . . .

Roger shook his head. "Claims the other kids are snobs, and into drugs."

I didn't like the sound of either of those.

Shielding my eyes against the sun, I asked, "Why don't you just move him to a public school?"

Roger laughed once, humorlessly. "A public school might be fine in Serenity, but not in Chicago."

I touched his arm. "Look, Roger . . . don't worry about our son. Jake is one tough kid. We'll figure this out."

My ex cocked his head. "He misses you, you know."

"And I miss him."

"Brandy?"

"Hmm?"

"I . . . I shouldn't have punished you by taking sole custody of our son. I was angry after . . ."

"After what I did?" *Went to my ten-year class reunion without him, and slept with an old boyfriend?*

Oh, did I mention? I'm not perfect, but I am trying. Some of you have probably already found me "trying," at that.

Roger winced. "Yeah. After what you did, I was . . . you know how bent out of shape I was."

Actually, I didn't. He'd taken it stoically. I would have preferred screaming and kicking and crying and . . . and anything that would have indicated there was still something emotional going on between us.

"If it's any consolation," I said, "I hear my 'mistake' is on his third wife, totally broke, has gained fifty pounds, and has a terrible case of adult acne."

"That's supposed to make me feel better?"

"Doesn't it?"

He smiled. "A little."

I smiled back.

Roger said, "Look, uh . . . getting back to Jake? I think maybe it would be better for us to have joint custody." He put both hands on my shoulders. "Better for us. Better for Jake. A boy needs his mother, too."

My Prozac protective emotional wall was crumbling. I felt tears trying to make a break for it from my eyes.

Roger, suddenly a tad uncomfortable, said rigidly, "We'll talk about it when I come back on Sunday."

"Okay," I sniffed, dabbing away tears with my fingers.

I stepped back as he climbed into the Hummer with a sad little smile and a sad little wave. Then I watched until the vehicle disappeared down the street.

Returning to the house, I found Mother and Jake still at the table, having what looked disturbingly like a conspiratorial confab, and suspiciously like shenanigans.

How was I going to keep my promise to Roger with those two in cahoots? And what kind of mind in the twenty-first century comes up with words like *confab, shenanigans* and *cahoots,* anyway?

Jake said, "Hey, Mom, Grandma wants to take us to lunch at a nice new restaurant." He looked at her. "What's it called again?"

"The Cottage Inn, dear. Everything is made from scratch, and is simply delicious."

Well, nothing disturbing or suspicious about that stilted, over-rehearsed exchange, right? On the other hand, I'd been wanting to try the new eatery, which also specialized in desserts to die for, so if they had a hidden agenda, I did too.

"I'm game," I said.

Mother was studying me. "Brandy . . . perhaps you'd like to put on something . . . more . . . *presentable.*"

I looked down at myself. What was wrong with jeans and a rugby? The Cottage Inn wasn't a fancy restaurant.

"Yeah," Jake said. "Maybe a dress? And you're a little smeary." He pointed to his eyes and crossed them—nice touch.

So my mascara could use some attention. What was it to Jake?

"*Fine,*" I sighed. "I wouldn't want either of you to be ashamed of me."

This was where Mother and Jake were supposed to assure me that they weren't at all ashamed . . . but didn't.

Dutifully I trudged upstairs, thinking, *You want presentable, I'll show you presentable.* I changed into a Ralph Lauren denim shirtdress I'd gotten 75 percent off because somebody stole its leather belt (not me!). I slipped on short brown Lucky Brand cowboy boots—legs left bare showing off the last of my summer tan—and picked out (from the tangle of purses on my closet floor) a small cross-body green parachute-material bag by Nicole Miller.

(Regarding big heavy leather designer purses: I get crabby just toting my airport bag from one gate to another—why would I want to lug a monster purse around *all day*?)

At my round-mirror Art Deco dressing table, I

reapplied make-up, then—convinced any further spackling would be counterproductive—headed downstairs.

Sashaying into the dining room, I smirked at the nonbelievers. "Now, is this presentable or is this presentable?"

Jake was grinning. "I knew you could do it, Mom."

Mother nodded. "Indeed, dear. You will make a *splendid* impression."

For what? On whom? The restaurant owner? The other diners? Somehow I couldn't imagine my fashion sense being a topic of discussion.

"Can we go?" I asked. "I worked up an appetite, looking this good."

Suddenly, Sushi began dancing excitedly in front of us.

"What's up with her?" Jake asked.

Mother sighed. "Your mother said a *no-no.*"

Jake frowned. "All she said was, 'Can we go?'"

Sushi's excitement escalated, stopping just short of jigging on her hind legs and doing a back flip.

"The no-no word is *G-O,*" I explained, "because she wants to *G-O* with us."

Now Sushi began twirling in a circle, as if chasing the tail she couldn't see.

"I hate to break it to you," Jake said, smirking, "but that dog can *spell.* Anyway, she can spell *go.*"

And Sushi began to punctuate her canine choreography with barks.

"Oh, dear," Mother sighed. "Now we have to appease the little rascal, and we'll be late to lunch."

I frowned. "We have a reservation?"

"Oh, yes. This bistro is very hard to get into because it only opened recently."

Which was typical of a small town with limited cuisine . . . although I doubted any restaurant in Serenity could ever be worthy of the designation "bistro," much less "cuisine."

I was shaking my head. "We're out of turkey, and I can't think of anything else on hand that Sushi really likes."

"I brought some beef jerky along," Jake offered, "in case I got hungry on the bus."

"Probably not the best thing for her," I said, "but it'll have to do."

He dug into the duffel bag by his chair, then handed Sushi a stick of the stuff. Rocky, stretched out contentedly in a stream of sunlight, smelled the treat, and gave a low ruff, and Jake tossed him a piece, to keep the peace.

Mother, standing, emitted a Nero Wolfe–like "Satisfactory," but *I* knew we wouldn't be sure if the bribe had taken until completing a full inspection of the house upon our return for tooth marks and/or piddle. (Sometimes I didn't find Sushi's latest little "gotcha" for days.)

We hurried out to the battered Buick and climbed in, Mother riding shotgun, Jake in back. I had a little trouble coaxing the car to life, but after a symphony of sound effects worthy of Golden Age radio—a rattle, a clank, and a couple of backfires—we were backing out of the drive.

I took Mulberry Avenue, so Mother could view the still-grand homes set back from the street, porches decorated with pots of colorful fall mums, towering trees in full autumn glory, some beginning to drop their leaves on the grass in paintlike splashes of red, orange, gold.

Jake said, "I've read some of your books."

Mother twisted her neck. "*Have* you, dear? How do you like them?"

"Oh, they're pretty cool for something by old people—'specially the one I was in—*Antiques Maul?* Only—"

"You wish *I* had written more of the chapters?" Mother prompted, rotating her head Linda Blair–style.

"No, Grandma. I was going to say that *sometimes* you *seem* to not be telling the, uh, whole truth . . . exactly."

A diplomatic way of calling her a liar.

"Goes for you, too, Mom."

Us liars.

With a cracking swivel, Mother returned her head to its forward position, then blew out a *pshaw.* "Jake, dear, sometimes a writer must embellish the truth just the teeny-weensiest bit."

"Why?"

"Well, in order to make a book more interesting or advance the plot, we take what's called 'artistic license.' "

"Didn't you have your license revoked?"

She frowned at Jake in the mirror (I was smiling). "That was my *automobile* license, dear."

"I mean," Jake said, "take that part at the Old Mill when—"

"Honey," I interrupted. "Some people haven't read that book yet . . . you don't want to spoil it."

"Oh. Yeah. Sorry."

"Anyway, the unreliable narrator is a well-accepted literary device."

"Well, then," Jake said with a shrug, "I guess you and Grandma are doing great."

We had arrived in the quaint downtown—snugged on the bank of the mighty Mississippi—four blocks long, three wide, consisting of everything a little burg such as ours might need, modern buildings blending well with structures of the past in a sort of aesthetic stalemate.

The Cottage Inn, neither a cottage nor an inn, was located on Main Street on the first floor of a recently regentrified Victorian building.

Main Street had free curbside parking, and I kept circling the block to find an open space—if I took a metered side street, Mother would start digging in her purse for slugs instead of coins to feed the meter. And I was pretty sure city hall was on to her.

Jake leaned forward from the back seat. "Mom, you better call on that magical feather of yours."

He was referring to my Indian spirit guide, Red Feather, who was great at getting me parking places. (I was working on winning on the lottery, but so far, no dice. Perhaps I needed to actually buy a lottery ticket for that to work out.)

"Red Feather," I murmured, as we again approached the Cottage Inn, "parking place please. . . ."

Suddenly a middle-aged man in an unzipped navy windbreaker, sides flapping like wings, came running out of the restaurant, jumped in his car, and took off, leaving me a space right in front.

Mother said, "I bet the poor soul doesn't even know where he's headed."

"Probably just got the sudden urge to leave," I said, "in the middle of his meal."

"Spooky," Jake said.

I claimed the spot, we exited the car, and entered the eatery through an antique etched-glass-and-wood door. The restaurant had retained its original wood floor and tin ceiling, but had added a German/Swiss theme of stenciled walls, blue-and-white checked tablecloths, and mismatched secondhand-shop wooden dining sets.

The entry area—where we stood waiting to be seated—was a bakery with a glass display case filled with homemade pies and cakes and cookies, sweet enough to give your diet amnesia.

A young woman greeted us, menus in hand. She had a heart-shaped face, dark hair neatly pulled back, and was wearing a red gingham full-skirt jumper over a white dotted-Swiss blouse. Thanks to our reservation, we were ushered swiftly away from those tempting treats.

The dining room was packed with patrons—mostly women, but a few families, farmers, and businessmen, talking and laughing between bites of delicious-looking homemade meals, their voices drowning out the polka-style background music, which was muted already, thankfully.

Since the restaurant was full, I couldn't see where the waitress was going to put us; the only chairs left were at a table for four, where a male patron was already seated, busy texting on his cell.

When it became clear we were going to have to eat with a stranger, I almost protested . . . but he *was* good-looking. Or maybe *he'd* protest at the intrusion . . . .

But Mother shushed me, saying, "Dear, I'd like you to meet Bruce Spring."

Good Lord! Was Mother playing matchmaker again? Was *that* what this luncheon was about? She knew I had just started dating Brian Lawson, the current chief of police. But *I* knew she didn't entirely approve of Brian . . . .

The man stood, smiling. Perhaps mid-thirties (judging by his line-free face) with prematurely white hair (judging by the black eyebrows), alert sky-blue eyes, prominent nose, and sensual mouth, he was wearing an expensive black tailored suit jacket over a shirt the color of his eyes, and designer blue jeans. He had a great tan. As he extended a hand toward me, a diamond ring winked on one finger while a gold Rolex watch glimmered on his wrist.

"I'm very pleased to meet you, Miss Borne."

"If this was my mother's idea," I said, "I do apologize. Mother . . . shall we go?"

Mother was struck temporarily (and atypically) mute, but Jake blurted, "Mom . . . that's *Bruce Spring,*" as if I should have known. Then, responding to my blank stare, he added, "You know! Host of *Extreme Hobbies?* And *Witch Wives of Winnipeg?*"

"Oh," I said, nodding. "Reality TV. I'm afraid I don't watch it." I had enough reality in my life as it was.

In case you're wondering, I knew I was being boorish; but I'd been bamboozled by not only Mother (which was to be expected), but my own son!

Still, that was no reason to take it out on a stranger.

Extending my hand, I said, "Nice to meet you, Mr. Spring."

His grasp was firm. "I apologize, Miss Borne . . ."

"Brandy."

" . . . Brandy. I thought you knew all about this meeting."

"Now, children," Mother said, including Bruce Spring in her collective brood, "that was just my silly, eccentric sense of humor. I thought Brandy would get a charge out of running into a celebrity at one of our little local eateries."

If Bruce Spring was a celebrity, I was Lady Gaga.

"And I must admit," Mother rambled, "that in retrospect it would have been wiser to discuss our potential business with Brandy on the way here in the car. But we got talking about other things and—"

"And besides," Jake said to Bruce Spring, "we didn't think Mom would come if we told her."

Bruce's eyes were fastened on me in an intense but friendly manner, as we stood there by the table, awkwardly frozen on our feet. "Whatever the case, Miss Borne . . . Brandy . . . I hope you'll stick around. I'll buy you lunch and make you a God-father offer."

"One I can't refuse, huh?" I shrugged. "Well, I *am* hungry." I pulled out the chair across from him, and plopped down.

"Fine," he said with a white smile against the Hollywood tan. He waited until Mother had settled next to him on the right, and Jake on the left, before returning to his chair.

While I studied a menu, Mother made small talk.

"Bruce, dear," she said, looking coyly over the top of her menu, "'Spring' seems an unusual last name. Whatever is its origin?"

The TV star, uninterested in his menu, said, "It's really Springstein. For obvious reasons, I thought it wise to shorten it."

Mother's eyes widened behind the thick lenses; in that green pantsuit, she looked like a surprised bullfrog. "Wise indeed! One mustn't get on the wrong side of the Boss!"

The waitress returned for our order.

Since "Bruce, dear," was paying, I began with a cup of homemade spinach and cheese soup, followed by turkey and mashed potatoes with chives, topped off by French apple pie with cinnamon ice cream. I'd actually gotten a little too thin of late and could indulge. Mother ordered just the soup (bowl), and Jake, a cheeseburger (rare) with American fries, plus chocolate layered cake. Our host wimped out with a small garden salad, sans dressing.

After the waitress left, Bruce got down to business.

"I've just stepped down from hosting shows on Discovery to act as both on-air talent and a producer for the new Extreme Interests channel. My current mission is to find fresh talent to feature in reality shows. Extreme won't have a single focus, but will look at various hobbies, sports, and professions . . . but 'extreme' examples."

"We write books," I said, "and have a booth at a local antiques mall. That doesn't strike me as very extreme."

He raised a forefinger, politely indicating I should wait. "I happened to catch Vivian on CNN a few weeks ago, and thought she handled herself very well."

A barrage of reporters and camera crews had

shown up on our doorstep to cover the startling news that Senator Clark had fathered a love child (me) in the early days of his political career. Mother, thinking they'd come to cover us about the string of murders we had solved in Serenity over the past year or two, had babbled on incoherently until realizing her mistake.

Mother took a dainty sip from her water glass, pinkie extended as if dining with royalty. "Unlike some theatrically trained performers, I have no difficulty appearing before the camera. One simply dials it back a shade, as it were."

Gag me with a spoon. And my soup spoon was handy . . . .

"You're a natural, all right," Bruce said, with a straight face. Was he an escapee from an asylum, I wondered? A very cute one with a great tan? "You are very much at ease in front of a camera—which is important."

Relieved that I was out of the mix, I said to the producer, "Hey, if you want my blessing for Mother to appear on one of your existing shows, I think that's just peachy."

Reaching for my water glass, I managed not to add, "We could use the money." Or that it would also keep Mother busy and out of trouble.

Bruce gave me the kind of smile a runaway gets from a guy she just met outside the bus depot. "Not an existing show, Brandy, but a *new* one. And not just Vivian, but *you.*"

Mouth full of water, I nearly did a spit take. I was doing show biz shtick already!

I managed to swallow and say, "You can't be serious. I have the stage presence of a potted plant."

Mother, eyebrows hiked above her thick eyeglass frames, said, "Why not? I have a lifetime of stage experience, and can carry a potted plant around with me, if I so choose."

Really? She had trouble lifting Sushi.

"Be that as it may," I countered, "what kind of show could possibly interest an audience in us? I'm not into eating worms, or jumping off a cliff. And if a bachelor handed me a rose, I guarantee I'd bleed to death from the thorns."

Okay, maybe I *had* watched a *little* reality TV . . . .

Jake piped up. "Mom, just listen to the pitch, will ya?"

The pitch? So Jake was show biz now, too?

I sighed and sat back, arms folded. "Okay. Why not? As long as it doesn't involve Donald Trump, I'm listening."

Bruce, elbows on the table, hands folded as if in prayer, said, "The reality show I have in mind will be about antiques—similar to *Pawn Stars, American Pickers,* and *Auction Hunters*—but with a heartland twist . . ."

He made us wait for it.

" . . . murder."

Mother clapped her hands, like a little girl getting a pony for Christmas. "I love it already!"

Bruce continued. "It will be called *Antique Sleuths,* and—"

Mother, her giddy grin turning to a frown, interrupted, "Could you call it *Antiques Sleuths?* 'Antique' makes it sound as if Brandy and *I* are antiques, and that hardly applies to either of us."

"Fine. *Antiques Sleuths* it is." Bruce, having lost his momentum, asked, "Where was I? Oh, yes. *An-*

tiques Sleuths, starring Vivian and Brandy Borne, who run an antiques store, and—"

"We don't *have* a store," I interrupted.

"We'll get you one," Bruce said, with just the teeniest bit of irritation.

"Rent or buy?" Mother asked.

"We'll lease a building, with an option to buy, if the pilot is picked up. You'll have a budget, to be determined, to fill that store with items to supplant what you already have in your booth."

"But what's the format?" I asked. "If it's reality TV, we can't solve murders. There may not be any more in Serenity, and anyway, the police are unlikely to cooperate."

"And," Mother said, "a few of my investigatory techniques might not be anything I'd want recorded by a camera crew."

Not a few—most.

"We understand that," Bruce said. "We'll do periodic little minidocumentaries on the murders you've already solved . . . which will increase your book sales, I might add. The format of the show will be about 'sleuths' in the sense that people come in with antiques that you evaluate. On-the-spot evaluations, or you can research those pieces that are outside your existing areas of expertise."

I said, "We just sit around and wait for customers to bring stuff in?"

Bruce grinned. "When we announce this show, people will be lining up to haul in their latest finds. It's basically the *Antiques Roadshow/Pawn Stars* format. If it goes, we'll only be shooting thirteen weeks a year . . . and the rest of the year, you'll just be two very famous TV personalities with an antiques shop that customers will flock to. Just selling T-shirts alone will make you girls very, very flush."

Mother banged the table with open palms, startling the silverware. "Then it's settled . . . . I'm in. Bruce, I assume you have a standard contract? Naturally, our legal representation will want to see it. I'll give you the contact information. In other words, have your people talk to my people."

Mildly amused, the producer turned to me. "Vivian's given her answer—what about you, Brandy?"

"Oh, I'm in," I said with a smile.

Not just because doing the pilot would keep Mother happily occupied, but because *not* doing the pilot would make her unbearable to live with. Besides, I'd take perverse pleasure in subjecting millions of viewers to her antics.

And I certainly wasn't bothered by playing second fiddle. My participation would be relegated to playing Ethel Mertz to her Lucy Ricardo.

Our food arrived, and the conversation thereafter consisted of Jake asking Bruce questions about his other reality shows, and Mother giving advice on how they could be improved. By the time desert was finished, the producer looked thoroughly exhausted, and I wondered if he was having second thoughts.

Bruce informed us that tomorrow we'd be meeting with our new show's line producer, Phil Dean, who was also the director of photography.

With that, we parted company, Bruce staying behind to settle up with the bill.

Climbing into our car at the curb, Jake said, "Know what? We should do some, uh, what do they call it? Location scouting. You know, for the antiques shop?"

Mother, fastening her seat belt, said. "No need, dear. I already know just the perfect place."

"Where, Grandma?"

"Why, the murder house, of course."

A Trash 'n' Treasures Tip

Location, location, location! When starting an antiques business, your store should be in a high-traffic area, easily accessible, with good parking. A notorious murder having once occurred there is optional.

GREAT BOOKS, GREAT SAVINGS!

When You Visit Our Website:
www.kensingtonbooks.com

You Can Save Money Off The Retail Price
Of Any Book You Purchase!

- **All Your Favorite Kensington Authors**
- **New Releases & Timeless Classics**
- **Overnight Shipping Available**
- **eBooks Available For Many Titles**
- **All Major Credit Cards Accepted**

Visit Us Today To Start Saving!
www.kensingtonbooks.com

All Orders Are Subject To Availability.
Shipping and Handling Charges Apply.
Offers and Prices Subject To Change Without Notice.